GIVE MURDER A HAND

LIZZIE ~ BOOK 2

THE WESTPORT ROMANTIC MYSTERIES

BETH PRENTICE

BOOKS BY BETH PRENTICE

The Westport Romantic Mysteries

Lizzie
A Sinister Sign ~ The Prequel
Dangerous Deeds
Give Murder A Hand
Deathly Desire
The Christmas Gift – A Mini Lizzie Mystery
Molly
Wicked Little Lies
Gracie
The Ivory Veil – a novella
Chloe
Killer Unleashed
Deadly Tails
Alexandra
Invitation to Murder

The Aloha Lagoon Samantha Reynolds Mysteries
Deadly Wipeout
Lethal Tide
Fatal Break
Tidal Wave

The Dandelion Ponds Mysteries
In High Spirits
The Hollyday Spirit - novella
That's the Spirit

The Dun Roamin' Romantic Mysteries

Tilly ~ Before Dun Roamin'
Matilda's Wish

Author: Beth Prentice

Website: www.bethprentice.com

Copyright 2015 Beth Prentice

First Published in March 2015

The moral rights of the author have been assured.

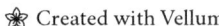 Created with Vellum

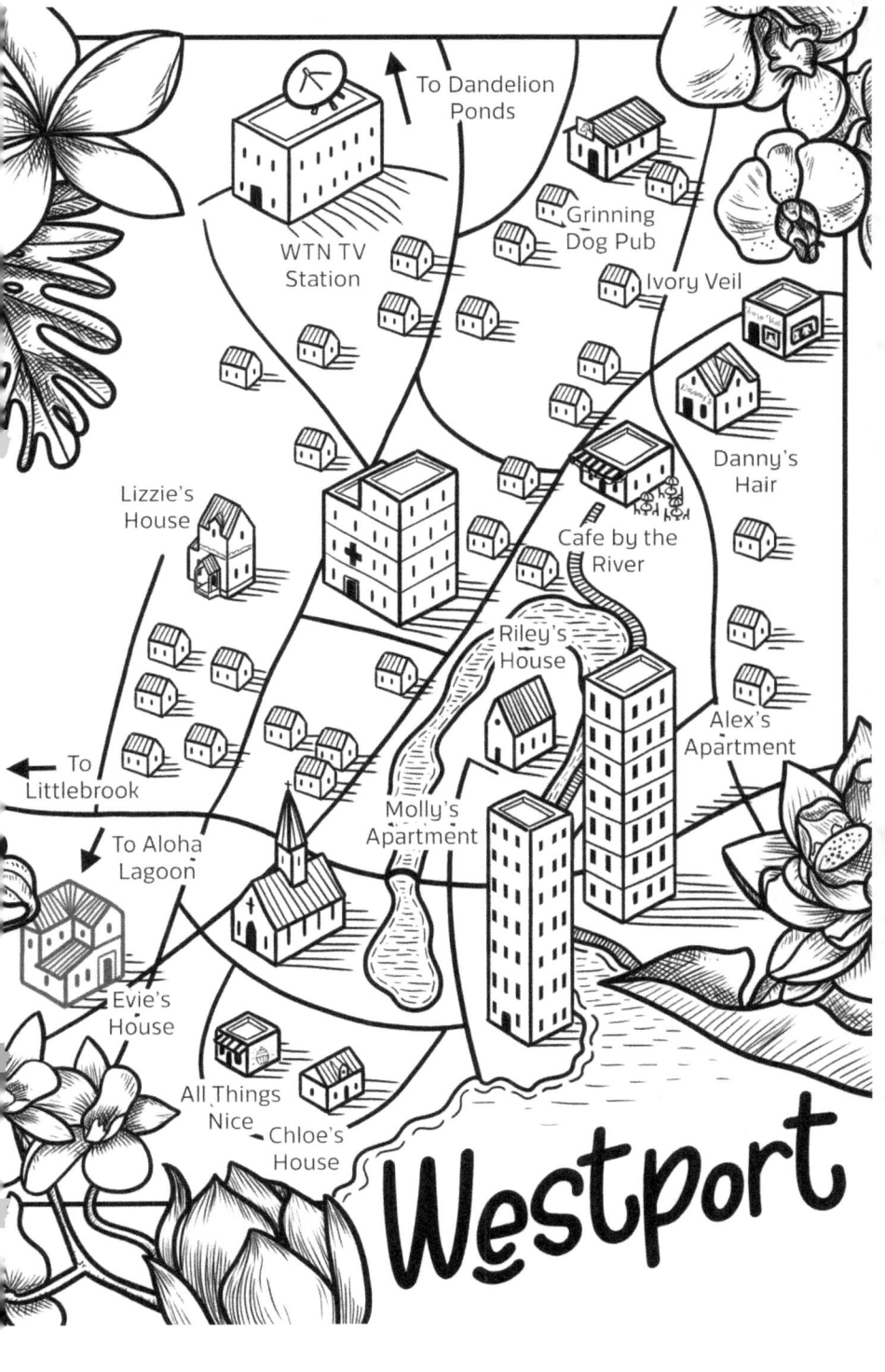

CHAPTER 1

I sat on my rotting back deck, looking at Molly as she checked the time on her new watch. Her watch matched the rest of her. Perfect. It was a designer brand and matched her designer dress, which was a bit too short, a bit too tight, and cut low enough to show everyone who cared just how ample her bosom really was.

I looked down at my T-shirt dress and wished—not for the first time—that I could just be a little more like her.

Maybe if I had her budget I'd be able to dress like that. I sighed. The truth was, even with her budget, I still couldn't pull that outfit together so effortlessly. Molly is my sister and she's beautiful. We've been told that we look very much alike, but honestly, I am a watered-down version of her.

My name is Lizzie Fuller, and I'm the tallest female member of my family, measuring in at five foot two inches. Barefoot, Molly is shorter by half an inch, but that half an inch is very important to me. Our brother Danny towers over both of us at five foot eight, but both Molly and I have a much more impressive D-sized cleavage. I am however, the only sibling to have inherited two dimples. Where from? Who knows? Grandma

Mabel was a bit of a wild card, so we have no idea what's hidden in the family gene pool.

The day had turned into a bit of a scorcher which, as it was summer, I guess should be expected. My deck was old and rotten, but it was safe if you sat on the end nearest to my neighbors, Hazel and Allen. Of course that had the disadvantage of Hazel, the quintessential busybody, being able to hear everything I said. But as long as I didn't talk about her, it wasn't really a problem.

I sighed contentedly, and pretended to listen as Molly dreamily told me about a new man she was interested in. Honestly, my attention was on her dog, a little Maltese Terrier named Harper. Every time Molly came over for a visit, Harper went out to the garden, and frantically dug in the same spot. I usually went out and shooed him away, but next visit, there he was again. I'd decided to let him go for it. I wanted to plant some trees anyway so he was saving me the trouble of digging the hole. Plus, I always looked at him with his bright eyes and his tongue hanging out, and thought how enjoyable his life was. Seriously, when it's my time to be reincarnated, I want to come back as a dog.

I turned to look at Molly, still dreaming about the new man, her eyes bright and her tongue almost hanging out, and right there and then I believed people really did look like their dogs.

Lucky for me, I owned a cat, and that rule didn't apply to cats. Did it? I was about to ask Molly when she shouted at Harper.

"Harper! Get out of there!"

I looked, wondering where he was as I couldn't see him anymore, when I realized he was in the hole he'd dug.

"Come here, boy," she called. He stuck his head up out of the hole and barked. *Woof.*

"Don't bark at me," she scolded. "Just come here."

Eventually he came, but he didn't come clean. Harper was usually white and fluffy but right then, he was brown from his shoulders down, and had dirt stuck to his snout. He also brought something from the dirt to give to Molly. I noticed her eyes bulging as the realization dawned that she had to put him back into her beautiful shiny SUV. I stifled a giggle.

"Oh, Harper! Look how *dirty* you are," she chastised as she stood and walked towards him. "And what is that?"

"Don't yell at him," I said. "He looks happy." And he did. His eyes shone brightly as he trotted up the three steps onto my wooden deck, and dropped the gift at Molly's Jimmy Choo-clad feet.

"Eww, that's disgusting!" She squirmed, moving her toes to push it back down the stairs.

I knew she was squeamish about things like that, but as she turned towards me, her complexion paled, she swayed, and then fainted...right on top of Harper's gift. Shit. *Shit.*

Running over to help her, I looked at Harper. "Good one, Harper. *Now* what am I supposed to do?"

I wasn't good in stressful situations, especially medical ones. My heart rate increased, as my heart pounded against my ribs, leaving me short of breath. Calling an ambulance would probably be a good idea, but my phone was inside the house. Years ago, I'd completed a first aid course, and a memory stirred about how to put a patient in the recovery position. I knelt down next to Molly, grabbed her shoulder and shook her. Not exactly the recovery position, but it felt like the right thing to do. She moaned. That was a good sign, right?

"Molly!" I yelled, shaking her a little more. "What the hell are you doing?"

She moaned again. At least I knew she wasn't dead.

I grabbed her shoulder and rolled her onto her back.

"You're going to be in big trouble when she wakes up," I said to Harper, my heart rate decreasing slightly as Molly's eyelids fluttered.

"Urgh," she gurgled, stirring.

"Molly!" I shook her shoulder once more. "Molly, wake up."

She opened her eyes wide and stared at me, her gaze unfocused.

"Molly, can you hear me? Molly!"

My yelling must have worked—well, either that or the shaking I gave her—because she groaned and sat up.

"Stop yelling at me," she whispered, her eyes rapidly moving about, as she tried to figure out what happened.

As she moved, a bone rolled out from under her. Harper saw his chance, grabbed it and ran straight into the house, towards my couch—my white couch.

"Harper!" I yelled. I didn't care how happy he was. I did not need a big muddy stain on my favorite chair. Leaving Molly to get herself up, I ran through the kitchen door after Harper, but he was quicker than me. I wasn't sure how though, as that bone was almost the same size as him. Before I could catch him, he'd run through the kitchen, across the hallway, and straight into the lounge room. He was settling into place as I ran through the door.

"You naughty boy!" I chastised, stepping up to him. "That couch is nearly new and I happen to like it!" As I spoke, I looked down at the bone.

As Harper nuzzled it into position, it overbalanced, rolled off the chair, onto the floor, only stopping once it was under my timber coffee table. I gave a disgusted sigh and knelt down to retrieve it, wondering what poor family pet it would once have belonged to.

Feeling around the dirty carpet, I shuddered as my hand made contact with it and I felt the cold, damp soil lodge under my fingernails. As I dug my fingers in and pulled the bone out, I looked down at my hands, nausea rolling in my stomach. A clod of dirt fell onto the mat. The world swayed slightly as I saw looking back at me...a skull. But it wasn't the skull that freaked me out, it was that I was pretty sure this one didn't belong to a dog...or a cat.

In fact, I was pretty sure this one was human.

❧

STOMACH CLENCHING, my vision blackened, and sweat broke out on my forehead. As the sickening feeling consumed me, I dropped the skull, sank to the floor and sucked in some air. My body shook as I pulled my knees up and put my head between them. I vaguely heard Molly enter the room.

"Lizzie?" she called. "Lizzie, are you okay?"

I waited for the dizziness to stop before responding. "What do you think?" I croaked. "Your dog just dug a *skull* up from my garden!" Panic seemed the appropriate emotion for the occasion.

"Well, it's not exactly my fault," she said, falling onto the couch.

"Whose fault is it then?" I asked, my voice getting louder with every syllable.

"You bought this stupid house. I told you not to, but did you listen to me? No! Of course you bloody didn't!"

"Well, I'm sorry!" I yelled as Harper slunk off the chair and moved behind the couch, sensing that maybe some of the blame would fall on him.

"And you bought the dog. Did I ask you too?" Molly, too, seemed led by panic. Thankfully my front door opened and in walked Riley.

Riley's my boyfriend. He's six foot three, same age as me (thirty-two and I promise I'm okay with that—honestly, I am), he has blond hair and the most amazing blue eyes I have ever seen, but it was his eyelashes that undid me. They aren't overly long, but they are black and thick. To sum him up, he's sex walking.

"Is everything okay?" he asked, his deep voice having an instant calming effect on me.

"Not exactly," snapped Molly.

My eyes filled with tears, realizing that a responsible adult

5

could now take control of the situation. Riley took one look at me, moved into the room and dropped to his knees in front of me. I put my head on his shoulder as his arms pulled me in close.

"What happened?" he asked, his voice filled with concern. Reluctantly I pulled away from him and pointed to the skull that had once again rolled under the coffee table. He moved and retrieved it, his brow creasing.

"Is it what I think it is?" I asked, my voice slightly wobbly.

"Where did it come from?"

"Harper dug it from the back garden," explained Molly, her voice barely above a whisper as she looked at the skull in Riley's hands.

I thought about those hands and how I might make him acid wash them before he ever touched me again. Then I looked into his eyes and thought, bugger it, he could touch away.

Riley placed the skull on the coffee table, stood and moved towards the kitchen. Molly and I stood and followed him, gratefully leaving the skull behind. Harper, realizing the danger had passed, stepped out of his hiding place. He stopped to sniff at the bone.

"Harper!" yelled Molly. A second later he trotted past us, his tail between his legs.

Once in the kitchen, we passed through the back door and continued to follow Riley down the steps and to the garden bed where Harper had been digging. At this point, Harper overtook us all and immediately jumped back into the hole. I heard Molly suck in her breath as he came out, another bone clenched in his jaw. For a dog with one tooth, he certainly excelled himself today.

Riley took the bone off him and moved into the dirt himself. I grabbed Molly's arm as I held my breath.

"I think we should call the police," said Riley.

"How many are there?" I asked incredulously.

"I'm not sure but there's a lot more than this."

I felt the nausea swirl as Molly sat her designer dress down on the grass before she fainted again.

ॐ

IT ONLY FELT like a few minutes between Riley dialing his phone and the police and the television cameras pulling up, but in reality it had been closer to twenty. Riley took this time to move Molly and myself back into the kitchen, and gave us both a hot cup of coffee.

Even though the outside temperature still hovered in the high thirties, the hot coffee calmed the shaking that took hold of my body. It had been a good few months since I had shaken like this.

You see, at the time I bought the house, the purchase contract had omitted a few extras I apparently got for free. Like the cat, the hidden engagement ring, and the stalker. The stalker was the cause of most of my anxiety and shaking. And of course, the nightmares that followed the day he had caught up with me, but…that's a whole other story.

Right now, I sat curled in the crook of Riley's arms and held my coffee close, feeling the heat from both seep into me. Molly had settled for cuddling Harper. Not a bad second choice, I thought.

The television cameras were set up in my garden and followed every movement of the police from a distance. I was unsure how they had gotten here so quickly, but maybe they listened to police scanners…or maybe my neighbor Hazel had alerted them. I had noticed her peering through her window as Riley stood in the hole that Harper had dug, her ears flapping with every sound.

She'd since moved closer, suddenly needing to do some late afternoon gardening, right next to the fence we shared. Honestly, we didn't need the six o'clock news. Once she had hold of the story the whole town would know about it.

I heard voices coming from the back deck and Riley went to investigate.

"Oh, hi. Are you the owner of the house?" asked a male voice.

"Kind of," answered Riley. "Can I help you?"

"Oh, um...well...um, I was hoping to speak to the owner of the house. I'm Matt. Matt Wilson. I'm a reporter with WTN news..."

"Sorry, we don't have a comment at this time," replied Riley, closing the door in Matt's face. Molly sat up straight in her chair, her eyes a bit brighter than a few seconds before. She placed Harper on the floor and smoothed her dress.

"Who was that?" she asked.

"Just a reporter."

"I might get some fresh air," she said, standing and running her fingers through her long curls in an attempt to straighten them.

I caught my reflection in the window and knew I needed more than my fingers to straighten my mess. The humidity had had its affect, and all I had was a mass of frizz.

I watched as she ran her fingertips under her lashes, removing the imaginary excess mascara. Like I said, Molly was perfect, even her make-up didn't dare run. I watched her move to the back door and step into the chaos.

Walking to the window, I looked out at Molly talking to the reporter. It didn't take long for her to start flicking her hair, a habit Molly had when she was flirting.

"Oh my God! She's chatting up that reporter!" I said to Riley.

Riley seemed uninterested in what Molly was doing but he joined me at the window. We stood together and watched as the police taped off part of my yard, making a lot of notes as they went. My neighbors had given up the pretense of gardening and were all peering over their fences, obviously wondering what the crazy woman next door was up to this time. It was only when the police knocked on the door that Riley and I moved away.

"Hello, I'm Constable Davidson," said a young officer. "I was hoping to take possession of the skull your little dog found."

Bugger. In all that had happened this afternoon, I'd forgotten it was still on my coffee table.

Riley led the way and I stood back and watched as the officer placed the skull in a bag, and stepped out the front door. I thought of that table and knew, even though it was the least of my worries, it had to go. It was bad enough I had a skeleton in the back garden. I didn't need the house contaminated with it too.

I moved to the coffee table, grabbed the opposite end of it and dragged it after the constable, stopping when it was out on the footpath. Then I moved back into the house, up the two flights of stairs to my office and got a sheet of paper. I wrote *It's yours if you want it* in big letters with a marker pen, ran back outside and taped it to the front of the table.

I turned to see Riley smiling at me. The world swayed once again, but for a whole different reason this time. Even after months of Riley and I being together, his smile still made my world stand still.

He pulled me in close and kissed the top of my head. "There's not a disinfectant in the world that can kill skeleton cooties," I explained. Luckily for me, Riley understood my hang up with germs, especially after the horrors I'd been through.

Thirty minutes later, the collection of official vehicles in my driveway had lessened, and Molly finally stepped back into the house.

"Lizzie," she called. "Would you mind coming here for a moment, please?" Geez, why was she so formal all of a sudden? I followed her voice and found her standing just inside the back door with the reporter I recognized from the six o'clock news. I noticed the dazed look in his deep brown eyes as he gazed at Molly.

"Umm…this is Matt." She smiled. Matt looked around our age with short sandy blonde hair that curled at his collar. He was a little shorter than Riley and, as far as I could tell, had no muffin top hanging over his waistband. The biggest surprise for me was the dazed look in Molly's eyes as she smiled up at him. "He would like to ask you a few questions," she explained.

"Oh, really?" I stuttered as a cameraman walked closer and pointed his equipment at me. Yes, get your mind out of the gutter —it was his camera. Even though he looked sexy—so maybe I wouldn't mind his other equipment pointing at me—I shook my head, remembering Riley and how he had all the equipment I'd ever need.

"Yes, if that's okay?" Matt extended his hand for me to shake.

My mind stuttered as the camera came closer.

"Um…this is Sam, my cameraman. You don't mind, do you," he asked uncertainly.

I looked at Molly as she mouthed 'please'. "I…I guess not," I answered quietly.

Matt dropped his hand and tried to pull his phone out of his pocket. His fingers caught on the seam of his jeans and he dropped his phone onto the timber deck. He swore quietly as he bent to retrieve it but misjudged how close he was to Molly.

As he stood, his head caught her elbow and caused her to slop her now cold coffee all over her white designer dress. Geez, her dry cleaner would be busy. She gasped and I waited for her to yell at him. Instead, she simply smiled.

"I'm…I'm so, so sorry," he stammered, using the sleeve of his shirt to wipe at her bodice. Only when he realized he was actually rubbing her ample chest, did he stop. I looked at Sam and saw his smile from behind the viewfinder. He'd caught the whole thing on camera.

Molly took Matt's hand and gently moved it away, smiling as she did so. "It's okay. No biggie. It needed dry cleaning anyway."

It was this reaction that made me realize Matt was the man Molly was telling me about earlier, the new man she had her eye on. Well, judging by the color of his cheeks, I thought he would fit in with our family very well. Maybe he could even contribute to my book, *101 Ways to Embarrass Yourself.*

"Why are you so interested in this?" asked Riley, stepping up behind me and putting a protective hand on my lower back.

"Oh...well...um, news is a bit slow in Westport today," explained Matt. "Plus not everybody digs up a whole skeleton in their back garden."

"A whole skeleton?" I asked. That was the first I'd heard exactly what the police had found.

"Yes, they think so. I don't think they have it all yet, but the unusual thing about this skeleton is...it has three hands."

CHAPTER 2

$\mathcal{I}$ closed the door behind Molly, leaned against it and sighed. Cat sauntered out. Who knows where he'd been hiding, but he seemed to know exactly when Harper had left. I inherited the cat with the house, and even though my pet owning history was bad, Cat seemed not to care. As long as his bowl was full of food and he could stretch out on my comfy bed, all was good in his world. We also both shared a dislike for my neighbor, Hazel. Though, he could poop in her garden bed.

Riley walked down the stairs towards me carrying my pillow.

"Are you ready?" he asked. You guessed it…tonight we were sleeping at his house. Riley owned a small converted church that backs on to the river. It looks, smells and feels like Riley. I loved it. Since he was renovating my house, we'd divided our sleeping arrangements between the two homes. This seemed to work well, but personally I loved the nights at his house the most.

"Sure, just let me get Cat's travel box and put him in it."

"He'll be okay here for the night, won't he?"

"Maybe, but I don't like the thought that whoever that body belonged to may not have crossed to the other side. I've watched

Ghost Hunters and I know exactly what dead people are capable of."

Riley sighed. "Lizzie, I don't know much about dead bodies, but I know enough to know that the one they dug up in your garden has been there a very long time. He's had plenty of time to walk to the light."

"How do you know it's a he?" I asked.

"I don't. I guessed and I've got a fifty percent chance of being right." Riley flashed a smile.

"Fair enough, but if you're wrong, I'll make you pay for it later." I laughed, using Riley's catch phrase on him. Making me 'pay for things later' was a favorite saying of his. And when he says 'pay' he doesn't mean with money. Personally, I try to find things that I will need to 'pay for' later.

Riley laughed. "It's a bet."

"I could always pay in advance—you know, just in case you're right and I'm wrong. I wouldn't want to have a debt like that hanging over my head."

Riley moved toward me and pulled me in close. His lips touched mine and I felt the sizzle all the way to my toes. After a moment of skin-melting body contact, I pulled up for air and tried to regain my senses. Truth is, Riley has the ability to fry my brain. I have a secret fear that I'll be totally brain dead by the time I'm thirty-three, but damn it'll be worth it. I averted my gaze and refused to look into his eyes. If I did, I'd be a goner.

"Not here," I breathed.

"What?" asked Riley, his lips moving down my neck.

"Not here. We have to wait until we get to your house."

"Why?"

"In case the ghost is watching us. That would be creepy, don't you think?"

"Lizzie, there is no ghost," explained Riley patiently, lifting the collar of my dress and kissing my shoulder. "And besides, we've done it here loads of times. If there is a ghost, he's seen it all before."

"But what if the ghost wasn't here before? What if it's been watching and has seen its body uncovered and now it's pissed off."

Riley sighed and lifted his head. "You're serious, aren't you?"

"Yes," I said, happy my voice sounded a lot more resolute than I felt. Looking into Riley's brilliant blue eyes made me have second thoughts. I heard him sigh once again, but thankfully he stepped away from me.

"Okay, here's the plan. You get Cat and I'll get his travel box. I'll meet you back here in one minute. If I speed and take the short cut, I can be at my house in ten minutes. Then you're all mine."

AFTER I DROPPED my pillow and Cat at Riley's—and paid him my debt of course—we headed over to Mum's for dinner. It was a tradition that every Friday night I would get together with my siblings. Tonight however, Mum had moved Sunday dinner forward as Dad was taking her out on Sunday for their anniversary. Honestly, this made me a bit restless, as Dad wasn't known to ever even have remembered their anniversary, let alone take her to a nice restaurant, but who was I to question the sudden change of heart?

In a previous life, Mum's dining room was the bedroom Molly and I shared growing up. Now, both the room and the table weren't quite big enough as our family grew, but somehow we all squeezed in. It's just 'elbows in', everyone. This worked well as long as you didn't get the seat next to Grandma.

Today however, I had that privilege. I guess I couldn't complain. The only reason we were last to arrive was because of paying my debt to Riley and that was more than worth it.

I looked around. There were eight of us in total. Mum and Dad sat at the opposite heads of the table, I had Grandma Mabel to my right and Riley to my left. Opposite me was my brother Danny, who had Molly to his right and his partner Andrew to his left.

In her younger days, Grandma Mabel had been beautiful with long black curly hair and deep brown eyes. Danny, Molly and I all inherited her dark curly hair and brown eyes, but only Danny truly got her free spirit. Thankfully he has Andrew to keep him grounded.

I looked at Andrew. He was about seventeen years older than Danny, graying at the temples and had started work on a very small muffin top. I knew he worked hard to keep the weight off, as Danny resembled a walking skeleton, but I guess age catches up with us all at some point.

Next to Danny, he was very conservative. Danny and Andrew were not only life partners; they were also business partners, owning their own hairdressing salon on River Road. Personally, I thought Andrew must actually be some sort of saint.

"Hey Molly, Sexpo's in town. I was wondering if you wanted to go?" asked Danny looking hopefully at Molly, his eyebrows raised.

"Why don't you go with Andrew?" she responded.

"He won't go with me," said Danny, sulkily. "He says I'm too embarrassing."

"You are too embarrassing." commented Andrew.

"Well, excuse me if I just happen to show my enthusiasm!" snapped Danny, turning his back on Andrew and giving his full attention to Molly. I knew what Molly was thinking. She thought Danny was embarrassing too.

"Umm, I'm not really sure. I'm pretty busy with work at the moment."

"I'll go!" piped up Grandma Mabel. "It'll be great. I might learn a few new things." I felt Riley smile next to me. He loved Mable. He thought she was a hoot.

I could see Danny mentally calculating how he could retract his statement about going. "Oh...well...umm..."

"Mum! Really!" chastised my mother, horrified.

"What?" asked Grandma.

"What would the ladies at Seniors' group think?"

"They'd think it was great. In fact, I might see if I can get a group of us to go. We could get all sorts of new toys. And maybe the men may learn a thing or two," she said, swishing her bottom teeth around.

I smiled as Danny eyes widened and he looked for the exits.

"Daniel, if you take your Grandmother to Sexpo I will stop making you chocolate cake," continued Mum. That was a threat we all took seriously. "And you," she said, turning towards Grandma, "you need to start acting your age!"

"Humph," said Grandma, forking her potatoes. "Sounds like you should be the one going. It might loosen you up a bit."

We all held our breath as we heard Mum suck in hers. Mum may be small, but when she's upset, it's time to get out of her way and hide. I snuck a look at Mum and saw her death-stare Grandma, deciding whether or not it was worth the fight. After a few minutes of silence, she must have decided it wasn't.

"Lizzie, I need you to take your Grandmother to the doctor's on Monday," she said, looking at me.

"I'd love to, Mum," I replied, noting the forced calmness of her voice. "But my car is in for a service. I won't have any transport. Sorry. Maybe Molly can take her?"

"Sure. Why not?" said Molly. "I can move work around to do that for you, Mum. But Lizzie, you really should join us." She looked at me, her smile tight. "It'll be nice spending time together."

Spending time together, my ass. She just didn't want to take Grandma on her own. As I mentioned, Grandma is a bit of a wild card and I emphasize 'wild'. Grandma now lived with my mum and dad after she accidentally set the oven on fire. She'd had only ever been married once in her life, and as far as we knew had had a long, faithful marriage. However, since Grandpa had relocated to somewhere beyond the Pearly Gates, Grandma seemed to be making up for lost time.

"Great!" said Grandma, coming in on the end of our conversation. "You can pick me up early and we can go shopping. I need a new dress."

"Good. That's sorted then," said Mum, standing up and clearing the plates as she went. Silently, we all helped her, too afraid to say anything that may upset the peace. Only when dessert was served—sticky date pudding with custard—yum!—did the tension in the room lift.

"What's happening with your dead body?" asked Danny, looking at me.

"It's not my dead body," I responded, shivering.

"Possession is nine-tenths of the law..." said Danny. "...or something like that anyway."

"Tomorrow, the police are bringing in a team of experts to dig up the rest of the yard, looking for whatever's left of it," explained Riley. "They believe it's a whole skeleton, but the officer I spoke to this afternoon, is hoping there's only one."

"Only one what?" I asked.

"Skeleton."

"What? There could be *more* than one?" Okay, that thought maybe made me a little anxious.

"It's okay, Lizzie. They're only checking. I'm sure one is all you have." Riley put his hand on my thigh and gently rubbed it up and down. I know it was supposed to calm me, but honestly it was much more distracting for another reason. I swatted it away.

Riley smiled his very wicked smile. He knew the effect he had on me.

❧

SATURDAY DAWNED BRIGHT AND SUNNY, which was in complete opposition to my mood. I'd had another restless night. Since my run-in with my stalker and his attempt to murder me, I'd had a lot of restless nights. Only last night instead of dreaming about stalkers, I'd dreamt about dead bodies and ghosts. Hence, this morning, I felt slow and sluggish.

Riley and I had completed the morning routine of teeth-cleaning etc. and then made our way back to my house in May Street, where we found the police vans already in place. I will admit to being a bit overwhelmed by the amount of people it took to dig up my garden. At first I thought at least they were saving me the job of digging the soil for the new garden beds, but when I saw the bobcat moving the piles of discarded soil, I thought again. No garden bed needed to be that deep.

I tried to distract myself and not think about what they were finding, but it all became a bit difficult when the news cameras returned and hundreds of people stood at my front fence, hoping to get a glimpse of what was happening.

Riley did tell me there weren't actually hundreds of people—more like twenty—but it felt like hundreds. I only hoped that when the *For Sale* sign went up, my house would be just as popular.

It was early afternoon when the police officer knocked on my door. I let Riley open it, unsure as to whether or not I actually wanted to hear what he had to say. It was only when Riley called my name that I reluctantly walked into the kitchen.

He handed me a cup of coffee and pulled out the chair for me to sit on. "Officer Helms would like to have a chat." I looked at Officer Helms and recognized him immediately. Not too many men were six foot tall and head-to-toe gorgeous mocha skin. He was the policeman who had helped me when Joe Woods—aka my stalker—had declared his love for me. At least this time my life wasn't in danger.

"Hi, Lizzie. It's nice to see you again." He smiled. I noticed how white his teeth looked against his skin. I smiled back at him.

"Thank you, it's nice to see you too."

"We've finished digging your garden and you'll be pleased to know that we only found one skeleton." There was that smile again.

"Umm...I guess I'd be happier if you actually found no skeletons," I replied.

I instantly felt bad when his smile faltered. "Well...yes, of course...sorry."

"Is it true you found three hands?" asked Riley.

"Yes, we did. At this stage we're unsure as to why but we'll certainly be looking into it. I just wanted to inform you that you need to stay out of the garden for the time being. No digging. In fact, we'll be leaving the tape up until we are sure that we have all the evidence we need."

"You don't need to worry about me," I said. "I don't think I'll ever be digging in that soil now."

"That's understandable." Officer Helms nodded. "I can recommend a good gardener if you ever need one." He smiled warmly, his eyes full of compassion.

"Do you know much about the skeleton?" asked Riley, ignoring the look Officer Helms gave me.

"Not really. I've been informed that it's male and has been there approximately sixty years, but until the Coroner does his thing we don't know much more than that."

"Will we be kept informed about the findings?" I asked. As much as I didn't like the idea of a body in the backyard, I did like the idea of knowing why it was there.

"I'd be more than happy to keep you up to date. I'll give you my private phone number. Call if you need anything."

I thought his offer was very kind, but I felt Riley tense next to me. Maybe he thought the offer was a little too kind.

"Thank you, Officer Helms," I said.

"No worries...and please, call me Ed."

About an hour later Danny wandered in the front door. "Geez Louise. Who would have thought you'd be this popular?" he commented, looking at me.

I huffed. "Nice to see you too," I said. My bad mood had not lightened as the day continued. In fact, if anything it had gotten slightly worse.

"I had to park *way* down the street. Don't those gawkers know family has priority parking around here?" Danny walked past me, gave me a peck on the cheek, and put a backpack on the ground. "Oh, I've made you an appointment for Tuesday to get your hair done," he said.

"You only did my hair about a week ago."

Danny responded by smirking at me. "Yeah, I know. See what you have to say when I show you last night's news. I found it on the internet." He smiled, walking into the lounge room and towards the TV. I followed him.

"Why? And more importantly, why are you showing me?" I asked, standing in the doorway watching as he turned my TV on, pressed a few buttons on the remote, and then pulled up the search engine.

"Because you're on it," he said, moving to sit on the couch. I sighed and sat beside him. I thought back to yesterday afternoon when Matt had interviewed me. I'd actually forgotten all about it last night and never once thought to switch the news on.

"That probably explains the hundreds of people standing outside my fence," I commented.

"Lizzie, you're a bookkeeper. Surely you can count past twenty," said Danny.

"Of course I can count past twenty. And that's how I know there are far more people than that standing out there," I huffed.

"Whatever. Here, watch this," said Danny, pressing play once he found the video he was looking for.

I instantly regretted owning a forty-eight inch TV. Seeing my face blown up to that scale was awful. I never realized that when I'm nervous I bite my bottom lip and it makes me look ridiculous. Plus I'm starting a new diet tomorrow. I can only hope the rumor that the camera adds ten pounds is true and correct.

"You're right. I definitely need that appointment. And I think I should join the gym."

This certainly had not helped my mood.

§.

AFTER DANNY HAD his fun at my expense—lucky I love him, that's all I'll say—he got ready to leave.

"I have to head off. Andrew's parents are in town and we're going out to dinner with them." Danny sighed.

"Ahh, I wondered why you were here alone on a Saturday afternoon," I said, referring to the comment about the in-laws. Danny glared at me.

"Lizzie, I live with Andrew, I work with Andrew, and I sleep with Andrew. I need my time without him thank you very much."

I smiled. I figured Andrew needed his time without Danny just as much.

"Just you wait until the honeymoon period is over with you and Riley. Sure now it's all sex and smoochy, lovey-dovey stuff, but it wears off you know."

Just then Riley stuck his head in the doorway, pulling a clean shirt over his head. Both Danny and I were rewarded with a glorious view of his naked abdomen.

"Hey Lizzie, I'm just running down to the hardware store. I'll be back in about half an hour. Will you be okay?"

"Sure will." I smiled and looked at Danny. I noticed the glazed look in his eyes as he smiled at Riley. Once he was out of earshot, Danny looked at me.

"Okay, I retract my last statement."

"Of course you do," I commented, laughing. "If it's up to me, the honeymoon period will never end."

Danny sighed. "How do you ever get any work done?" he asked, seriously.

I laughed. "Yeah, some days it's really difficult to concentrate when I know he's downstairs doing manly stuff." We sat silently for a moment, thinking our own private thoughts about Riley. Only when Danny's phone beeped, signaling a text message, did he give a final sigh and stood.

"I have to go. Andrew's warned me not to be late."

"Okay well, have fun," I said, following Danny to the door. Opening it, I looked out at the crowd of people mingling around my fence.

"What do they think they are going to see?" I asked.

"News is obviously quiet in Westport. Either that or they are really bored."

LATER THAT NIGHT the nightmares began again.

It was a cold clear night and I stood in the backyard, looking into the open grave as Joe Woods looked back at me. I felt relieved he was finally dead. Only just as I smiled, he floated out of the grave and moved towards me, his shiny blade glistening in the moonlight. I screamed and turned to run, but before I got too far I found myself back in my bed with him standing over me.

The now familiar fear ran through my veins, as I pushed past him and ran for the door, my only hope for survival. I could feel his breath on my neck. Slamming me into the back of the door, his fingers dug into my arm as he attempted to pull me close.

Grabbing at the handle, I wrenched the door open and ran for the stairs.

I heard my blood-curdling scream. Tripping on the top stair, I fell to my knees and I slid to the bottom, my stalker right behind me. Pain shot through my knee as I dragged myself to my feet and moved to the front door, praying I could open it and run to freedom. It was locked.

My heart pounded loudly in my ears as desperation and fear consumed me.

It was my screams that woke me, and I found myself standing on my doormat, face to face with a terrified looking Riley.

"Lizzie. It's okay," he said, shaking. "You were just dreaming." I looked at him and fell to my knees as the sobbing started. He sat next to me and pulled me in close, the heat from his body surrounding me as I moved into his arms, the fear from the dream still lingering.

"It's okay," he whispered, his voice shaky. "It was just a dream."

I held on tight, unable to speak. Riley allowed me to stay there until the sobbing stopped. Only then did he tilt my head back, moved my hair from my face and kissed my forehead. As he wiped my tears, the dream lifted and a feeling of safety took its place.

The room was only lit from the streetlight outside, but it gave enough light that I could see the torture on his face. My heart squeezed.

"You really need to talk to someone about it," he said.

"I'm…I'm sure the dreams will stop," I whispered.

"It's been eight months, Lizzie. You can't go on like this forever. Please."

"I'll be okay," I said, snuggling closer. If I could just get a little bit closer to him, I'm sure I could push the memory of the dream to the back of my mind. True, the *To Be Sorted* bin back there was probably overflowing, hence the nightmares, but I really didn't want to open that box.

"He can't hurt you anymore, so what are you afraid of?" he asked, placing his hand under my chin and tilting it to face him.

I thought about his question. What I was afraid of was, once I opened that box, I may never be able to close it again. "I'll think about it," I said.

"Promise me you will."

"I promise I'll think about it."

"No. You have to promise to get some help. I hate that you have these nightmares."

"I'm sorry. I don't mean to upset you," I said quietly.

"I don't care about that. I just hate that it scares you." He gently kissed my forehead, and squeezed me tight. I let out a breath I'd been holding and thought about what he had said.

"Will you come with me?" I asked.

"Sure." I felt him smile in the darkness as the relief washed over him.

He helped me to my feet, ready to go back to bed. As we turned, he flipped the hallway light on and we both stopped dead, neither of us daring to move…because in front of us, in droplets sprayed across the wall, was blood.

I felt fear grab at me and held on tight to Riley. I heard the clock ticking off the seconds, as I held my breath and looked around wildly.

Riley stepped in front of me protectively and moved to it.

He picked up a hammer he'd left lying on the floor and handed it to me. "Stay here," he commanded. "I'm going to look around."

I took the hammer and looked back at him, the fear from the dream returning.

"No way, I'm not staying here on my own."

Riley sighed. He knew better than to argue with me. "Fine, but stay close."

No need to tell me twice. I grabbed the back of his boxers and stayed on his heels. We systematically checked every door and window in the house, only to find they were all securely locked.

Returning to the hall, Riley let out the breath he'd held, and moved closer to the blood.

I shuddered. "How the hell did it get there?" I asked, my voice barely above a whisper. I was having a really bad week. I already had nightmares to deal with, but now I had a dead body found in my backyard, and blood dripping down my walls.

"I don't know," said Riley, his shoulders dropping.

"I don't want to be here anymore," I said, a lone tear escaping and sliding down my cheek. "Can we sleep at your house for the rest of the night?" Riley looked at the clock on the wall. It read two thirty.

"Please?" I gave Riley puppy dog eyes, secretly praying he would say yes.

"Sure," he said, sighing.

Once we were back in bed at his house, I snuggled my face into his chest and after a few minutes the gentle rise and fall of his chest lulled me back to sleep, all thoughts of the blood pushed to the back of my mind. There's nothing nicer than snuggling someone you love after a bad night.

CHAPTER 3

I leaned against Molly's shiny black SUV and looked at her.

Today had turned into another scorcher, but even though I had sweat running down my neck and between my breasts, Molly's skin just had a slight sheen to it. I tugged at the hem of my T-shirt in an attempt to stop it sticking to me.

"Molly, can we wait in the car with the air conditioning on, please?"

"No. I'm saving money and I don't want to waste fuel," she explained. I looked at her, my eyebrows raised. Molly had never been known to save money. I was just about to ask her if she actually had heatstroke when the door to the doctors' surgery opened and out walked Grandma Mabel, pushing her red walker, her purple patent handbag precisely placed on the seat in front of her.

"Oh, thank God," muttered Molly, moving away from the car door and towards Grandma.

"Not so fast, girlie," snapped Grandma. "I'm not done yet." I watched as she swished her false teeth around, contemplating her next move. "I have to have a blood test done."

"Oh okay," I said, standing next to her. "You can get that done next door," I said indicating towards the doorway very conveniently located next to the doctors. Molly took the relevant paperwork off Grandma and stepped towards it.

"Hang on a minute," said Grandma. "I need to fix my hair."

"There's nothing wrong with your hair," said Molly. I looked at Grandma's neat rows of purple tinted curls and agreed with Molly.

"You look fine, Grandma," I said, nodding.

"Yeah well, I need better than fine. I just saw Barry Crosby go in there and he's a cutie. I need to look my best if I want to turn his head."

"First of all, you are eighty-two, when are you going to stop looking at men?" asked Molly. "And second, Barry Crosby is married. I remember Mum going on about it at dinner once."

"Well," answered Grandma, "I'll stop looking when I'm dead. Which is exactly what his wife is. I read her obituary in the paper yesterday."

"If his wife just died he's hardly going to be looking for another one so soon," I said, rolling my eyes.

"You don't know that. And anyways, he may just file me in his memory bank for a later date. A good looking man like him won't stay single for too long, and when you're my age you got to stay on top of things like that. The number of eligible men is dwindling fast. Women live longer than men, you know. Competition's fierce," said Grandma with a wistful sigh, looking at Barry through the glass window of the pathologist. I followed her gaze. Barry Crosby stood with a hunched back, his nose hair visible even from this distance and his pants tied somewhere around his armpits.

"Well, I guess you've got to do what you've got to do, Grandma," said Molly, her nose crinkling. She mouthed 'yuck' as she turned to me and giggled.

"Yep, wish me luck. Not that I need it of course," said

Grandma, smoothing her blue polyester dress, taking the paper-work from Molly and pushing her walker towards the pathologist.

"That's going to be us one day," I said to Molly, thinking that loss of eye sight with age was probably a good thing.

"Puh-lease...I would never wear polyester."

We watched in awe as Grandma chatted to Mr. Crosby and then made her way to where she had to give blood.

"Actually Molly, do you mind if I just pop into the doctor's. I need to make an appointment."

"You've been standing here all this time and now you remember?"

"Yeah, sorry about that." I'd realized Riley was right and the memory of the night my stalker caught up with me wouldn't stay buried amongst all the other crap I had buried at the back of my mind. Go figure.

"Well don't be long," said Molly as her phone beeped, signaling a message. She pulled it from her bag, read the screen and looked around the carpark, her face suddenly animated with excitement. Obviously her message was a good one. She looked back at me. "Well, what are you waiting for?"

"Nothing," I replied. "Just thinking I might stay here and check out the scenery instead. I can always phone through an appointment."

Her sigh could be heard a mile away. I grinned.

"Lizzie, you're such a pain," she muttered as she turned her back and crossed the carpark. I giggled and moved into the doctor's surgery, looking back out at her whilst I waited my turn. She walked between two cars and stopped, talking to someone in a white sedan. I could tell by her smile that whoever it was, he was male. And obviously cute, because I had never seen Molly flick her hair as much as she did at that moment. I stood on my tippy toes trying to get a better look, but as he was sitting in the car, I couldn't see anything. I wondered if it was Matt.

My attention was one hundred percent on Molly and her attention was one hundred percent on the occupant of that car, so neither of us noticed Grandma Mabel exit the pathologist.

"Ahh, Lizzie," said the receptionist, "I think you should go and see if Mabel's okay."

"What?" I asked, turning my attention to her.

"Your grandma," she said, pointing outside the glass. "I think something's wrong." I followed her finger and saw Grandma arguing with a woman, who in all honesty looked perplexed. I quickly opened the door and went to see what was going on.

"Call the police!" yelled Grandma, to anyone that was listening. "This woman is trying to steal my granddaughter's car!"

The woman in question turned to me as I pushed through the surgery door, her face bright red. "I'm not. Honestly, this is my car," she said, pointing to the black SUV Grandma was trying to get into. I looked at Grandma struggling to get into the back seat.

"Women like you should be locked up," yelled Grandma, as a small crowd gathered to see what was going on. "My granddaughter is hard working and pays for things and you shouldn't go around stealing it. Anyway, I know your mother—God rest her soul—and she'd be disgusted to know this is what you're up to." Grandma crossed her arms over her chest in a 'don't mess with me' stance as Barry Crosby walked past.

"Everything all right, Mabel?" he asked, stopping to help. I quickly moved towards them.

"I'm so sorry," I said to the accused woman. As I looked into her red face I realized it was Sharon Williams, a girl I had gone to school with.

"Lizzie, you really need to keep your grandmother under control," she huffed, her embarrassment now turning to anger she directed at me.

"Oh, as if I have any chance of doing that," I replied on a sigh.

"No, everything is not alright, Barry," said Grandma, turning her watery eyes to Barry. "I've had a very traumatic few minutes."

Her hand shook as she put it to her heart. "But I did manage to stop a thief. I just don't know what the world is coming to these days when an old, frail woman has to become a crime fighter."

"Now, now Mabel. You're not old. And frail is not a word I would use to describe you. I would say you are fearless." He smiled, his false teeth shining brightly, his oral hygiene impeccable.

"Oh Barry," giggled Grandma, all signs of her ordeal now gone.

"Umm, sorry to interrupt, Grandma, but you need to get out of the car," I said, stopping this interaction before I had any chance of overhearing something I could never un-hear.

"I'm alright now, love," she said. "Maybe we could go home though so that I can rest a bit."

"Yeah sure, Grandma, but we need to go in Molly's car."

"This is Molly's car," she stated.

"No. It's not. Molly's is over there," I said pointing to the black SUV parked right next to us.

Grandma looked through the windows to the car parked next to the one she was presently sitting in.

"Well, I'll be buggered," she said. "Fancy that."

৯৯

MOLLY SIGHED ALL the way back to Mum's. By the time we got there, I thought she might be slightly light-headed from all the oxygen she forced out between her gritted teeth.

"What's wrong with you?" I asked quietly. Grandma's gentle snores drifted my way, alerting me to the fact that she had nodded off and I didn't want to wake her.

"Nothing," she snapped. Clearly it was something. I looked at her, my eyebrows raised. She sighed again. "It's just that whenever I meet a really nice guy, this family has to come along and spoil it."

Now I should be offended as I was a part of this family, but I got her point.

"The right man won't be bothered by your family," I said philosophically. "Look at Riley. He's stuck with me looking my absolute worst, he's the main witness to me embarrassing myself 101 ways, he's been railroaded by Mum whenever Auntie M's around, and he's still here," I explained.

"Yeah. I'm still wondering if that man is actually human," mused Molly, indicating and turning the car into Mum's street. Grandma's internal GPS stirred her awake.

"Who is he anyway?" she asked.

"Riley. We're talking about Riley," answered Molly, pulling the car into Mum's driveway and parking behind her silver Mazda.

"No you weren't. I may be old but I'm not stupid." I too was curious to know the answer to Grandma's question.

"It's nobody."

"I bet it was that guy you were talking to at the doctor's. The one with the nice head of hair."

I looked at Molly and noticed her ears had gone a light shade of pink. Grandma was sharper than any of us gave her credit for.

"So…was it Matt?" I asked, smiling.

"It was no one you need to worry about," she snapped.

"It's all right, Molly. He gave me a wink as I got into the car," explained Grandma. "He'll fit right in with us lot."

"If he ever calls me again," sulked Molly.

"You should ask him out and wear that black dress you bought last week. It shows a lot of leg, that dress."

"I don't think so, Grandma but thanks for the advice."

"Well can I borrow it then? I think Barry Crosby is going to ask me out and I'll need something to give me the edge over Vera Cartwright. She's got big boobies and Barry likes big boobies."

"How do you know that?" I asked.

"Because his poor dead wife had massive ones. She had a hump on her back because of the weight of 'em," she explained.

"So, can I borrow it then?" she asked Molly, her watery eyes sparkling with enthusiasm.

Thankfully, Mum opened Grandma's car door before Molly had to reply.

᠀

AFTER WE DROPPED Grandma home and made sure she was tucked safely under Mum's wing, we both let out a sigh of relief. Honestly, I loved my grandma—in fact, there were times when I wished I was just a little bit more like her—but most of the time she exhausted me. It appeared Molly shared this sentiment. I opened my bag and retrieved a pack of chewing gum. "Want some?" I asked Molly, offering her the packet.

"No thanks."

"Suit yourself," I replied, popping a piece in my mouth

"Did you book your doctor's appointment?" asked Molly, her brow furrowing.

"Yeah, I got an appointment for Thursday."

"Are you okay?"

"Yep. She just booked me an appointment to speak to a counselor. Some memories don't want to stay buried." I shrugged my shoulders in an attempt at nonchalance.

"Is this about what happened with Joe Woods?"

I shivered at the mention of his name. "Aha. Riley thinks I need professional help."

"Are you sure he was referring to a counselor?" asked Molly, grinning.

"Ha ha, you're a real comedian." I smiled sarcastically and Molly giggled. "So when are you inviting this new man of yours to our family dinner?"

Her giggling stopped immediately. She glanced sideways at me as she turned her car into my street. "Not for a very long time."

"Are you going to tell me about him or do I have to pry the information out of you?"

She sighed. "Okay, but please don't tell Danny, Mum or Grandma. They'll just want to meet him and once that happens he'll run for his life."

"Our family's not that bad," I said. Molly death-stared me. "Okay. They have their moments but for some reason we love them anyway." Molly pulled her car up outside my house. "Are you coming in?" I asked, my hand on the door latch.

"No. I need to get going and get back to work. I have a favor to repay the head of the newsroom at WTN. He's down a cameraman and needs some still photos for a story they're running tonight." You've probably already guessed it, but in case you haven't, Molly's a photographer and a very good one at that. "How about afterwards, I go home, get Harper and come back for afternoon tea?"

"Sounds good…you can fill me in on the details then." I smiled, leaning over and giving her a kiss on the cheek.

After Molly left, I had a quick tidy up and then ducked to the shops to buy a cake for afternoon tea. I didn't exactly inherit Mum's cooking abilities so I thought buying one was best. I locked Cat in my bedroom and waited patiently for Molly to arrive. I knew she was here when I heard Harper scratching at the door to get in. As I opened the door, he immediately ran to the kitchen looking for a treat, his tongue hanging out the side of his mouth and his eyes bright with joy. Harper was a rescue dog and a present Danny and I had given Molly for her birthday. He no longer resembled the skinny, dirt-stained dog we had purchased, but was now brilliant white, fluffy and bordering obese.

"Hello, beautiful boy," I said, bending down to scratch behind his ears. "Do you want a treat?"

"No!" shouted Molly. I stopped and looked up at her.

"What?"

"Please don't give him any treats. He's on a diet. Mike the Vet got quite cranky at me last week when I put him on the scales."

"Surely one little treat won't hurt?"

"According to Mike, one treat is equivalent to a Big Mac, so he's now on a special diet of dried biscuits."

"Oh you poor boy," I said, bending down to pick him up. Snuggling him under my arm, I thought that Mike was right. Harper was a little heavy. Molly closed the door behind her and we wandered out to the back deck.

"Do you want a coffee or a cold drink?" I asked Molly, placing Harper on the ground. He immediately trotted off into the backyard.

"I'll have something fizzy, if you have it."

"Oh, you'd better get Harper back. We're supposed to stay this side of the Police tape."

Harper had trotted to the hole that started this mess. I left them alone and wandered into the kitchen to put the cake on a fancy plate. Getting a cake knife, plates and forks and pouring two cold drinks, I placed everything on a wooden tray, along with a stray flower I'd picked from the front garden. Am I domesticated or what?

Walking back outside, I looked at Molly. She was reading another message and it looked to be a good one at that. "So are you going to give me the details on Matt?" I asked, handing her a glass. Her cheeks turned a slight shade of pink, as she put her phone down on the table.

"There's really nothing to tell. We met through work and we hit it off," she shrugged.

"Have you gone out with him yet?"

"No, he hasn't asked."

"Molly! What's that saying...*take my advice, I'm not using it.* Don't you remember the advice you gave me about Riley? You said if I wanted him then I was to go and get him," I reminded her.

"Yes, I know," she grinned. "I'm just giving Matt some time to realize how great I am."

"Judging by the glassy look in his eye the other day, I think he already does." Molly giggled. "Don't wait too long. He's pretty cute and he's on TV so he'll probably already have a fan club."

"Hmm…I never thought of that. Maybe I should Google him? See what I can find." Just then her phone beeped again and she picked it up, her attention now solely on it. Judging by the grin on her face, I'd say it was the man himself on the other end of the conversation.

Waiting whilst she texted her response, my attention strayed to a man who had wandered into my backyard. He looked about twenty, wearing official-looking black trousers, white button-up shirt and matching jacket and he led a pack of approximately ten people.

"And here we are," he pronounced in a loud voice, his back to me, facing his audience. This was followed by a lot of *ahhs* from the crowd. Two women who looked to be in their seventies, huddled forward to the police tape.

"Umm…can I help you?" I asked, standing and moving to the steps. The man leading the group ignored me as he too stepped up to the tape.

"Now this is the location where the bones were exhumed a couple of days ago," he explained excitedly, as the two women pulled cameras from their pockets and clicked away. I looked over at Molly, perplexed.

"Hello," I called again, moving onto the grass. "Can I help anyone?"

"Oh don't mind us," said another lady. "We're just here on the tour."

"The tour?" I replied.

"Yes. The tour of Westport."

"What tour of Westport?" I asked. Honestly I had never heard of a tour of Westport and I'd lived here my whole life.

"Bradley," she said, pointing to the official looking man, "runs a tour of the historic sites of Westport. It leaves the Wharf every Monday," she explained.

"Oh, okay." I looked towards Bradley, realizing how young he really was, and then I looked around his group. I was sure every one of them was a member of Grandma's seniors group.

"Lizzie?" called Molly, leaning against the railing of my deck. "What's going on?"

"Umm...I honestly have no idea, but Bradley runs tours. Who knew Westport had tours?" I said, looking at her and shrugging my shoulders, intrigued by this new information but actually annoyed by the invasion.

"Who's Bradley?" she asked.

The lady next to me turned and looked at Molly. "He's such a lovely man. My friend Maud told me about these tours, and when I saw the news the other night I knew I had to go on it," she explained.

Meanwhile, Bradley continued his announcement. "As I explained, this grave is approximately sixty years old and the very strange thing is that they uncovered three hands. Now, I am privy to some information that others aren't, and I found out that the hand does not belong to the body." He smiled, smugly, obviously very proud of himself.

Well, it didn't take a detective to work that out.

I made a mental note to call Officer Helms later and see what information he had, and maybe ask his advice on how to keep unwanted visitors out of my garden.

Molly moved to stand next to me. "But why is Bradley in your backyard?" she asked.

I looked at the woman next to me.

"I told you," she said. "It's a tour!"

I sighed. "Bradley!" I yelled. Bradley stopped talking and turned to look at us.

"I'll be taking questions in a moment," he said and continued speaking to the crowd.

I didn't really want to wait a moment though, so I pushed my way through the small crowd, and stepped up in front of him.

"No, I'm sorry. I won't wait a moment. What exactly are you doing here?" I had no problem confronting Bradley. He didn't look threatening, and I had Molly as back-up.

Bradley looked at me, obviously deciding his tactic.

"This gravesite could be of historic value to the town of Westport," he said. "People want to know what's happening." His fingers fiddled with the hem on his jacket and I could see the sweat bead on his lip. I got the impression he wasn't as confident as he tried to portray.

"Well, this is private property, so could I see your permit to conduct this tour, please?"

Bradley's ears turned a slight shade of pink. "Well, I haven't had time to get the approval just yet. But my application is in," he beamed.

"In with who?" asked Riley, who up until now had been inside the house.

"W...well," stuttered Bradley. "The Council?" It was more of a question than an answer.

"I think it's time you leave," suggested Riley, pulling himself to his full height. Now, I'm not sure how tall Bradley was, but six foot three was a lot taller. Bradley quickly assessed the situation.

"Of course," he said, clearing his throat. "We're pretty much finished here anyway." He gathered his crowd and ushered them all to the front, the disappointed sounds of ten senior citizens following him.

CHAPTER 4

The gossip grapevine had gone into frenzy since my fifteen minutes of fame, and word of the Westport Tour had spread. Believe me; the residents of Westport made the most of it. Every day dozens of people filled my backyard, all standing around the police tape, looking into the hole in the dirt. Not much happens in town, so I guess I shouldn't be surprised.

I had phoned Officer Helms and he'd informed me that I could get the police to forcibly remove everyone, but in all honesty it felt like a waste of police resources. And so long as they all stayed this side of the police tape, then I guess no harm was being done. I was also pretty proud of myself with the way that I was learning to trust strangers again. It's funny how brave I am when Riley's not far away.

Today, I'd had errands to run for work, and when I got home I struggled to get my Mini into my driveway. Walking around to the back of the house, I did a quick estimation and guessed there to be about thirty people, all standing around with their hands in their pockets or scratching their heads. I walked over to them and looked down into the dirt. Maybe there was something in there that was of great interest, but I couldn't see it.

After a few minutes of looking, I concurred that my initial thoughts of everyone having gone a little bit crazy were correct.

Bradley stood back and beamed at me. He was an annoyance but his excited grin was pretty cute. He raised his hand and waved. I reluctantly waved back, thinking how he reminded me of Harper—all bright eyed and happy. Turning away from him and walking back towards the house, I noticed an old man looking at my garage. My garage *is* a bit of an eyesore. It's single storey with a mezzanine floor made of the same timber the house is made of. I worry every time we have a strong wind because I think it could fall down. I've only looked in there once and that was when I first bought the place. I've been too afraid to go back in there since.

I looked back at the man and noticed he seemed lost in another world, completely unaware that Bradley was now calling for the group to return to the bus.

I was about to walk over to him and ask if he was okay when he turned to look at me. I figured him to be in his eighties and he dressed very much like some of Grandma's suitors. I thought he looked quite sweet as he stood, one hand in his pocket and the other holding his walking stick.

He noticed me staring at him and smiled, his nicotine-stained teeth bared. He lifted his walking stick in a wave and limped after the crowd now moving down my driveway.

It didn't take Grandma long before she heard about the tours, so by Wednesday, I cleared my diary and invited her and her friend, Eunice over to see the crime scene. Today had the advantage that it was raining, which meant her visit would have to be taken from the safety of the back deck. This was a Godsend really as I was a bit concerned about her being that close to a gaping big hole in the ground. Yes, I know we're not supposed to cross the police tape, but I really couldn't trust Grandma all that much. I truly love her, but seriously, even I find myself rolling my eyes when she's around.

Mum, Grandma and Eunice all arrived around morning tea time. I heard the car pull into the driveway and opened the front door ready to help them all into the house. I watched as Mum got two walkers out of the trunk and pushed them round to her passengers. I stepped over the threshold and moved towards them.

"Hi everyone," I called.

Mum answered me with a sigh, as both Grandma and Eunice smiled and pushed their walkers up the path, but not before they fought for first place. Grandma won of course. I stepped aside so that she could pass, kissing her cheek as I did so.

"Do you need any help?"

Grandma wore her new dress and once again, had her purple handbag hanging on her arm.

"Well, I could do with Riley helping me into the house," said Grandma. "My arthritis is playing up today."

"Your arthritis is in your hand," called Mum, rolling her eyes as she spoke.

"Humph," said Grandma.

"He's not here, sorry Grandma."

"Humph."

"Let me take your bag," I said, lifting her bag from her walker. I felt my shoulder pull.

"What the hell is in this purse?" I asked, shocked at how heavy it was.

"Grandpa…he's put on a bit of weight."

"Grandpa died years ago," I replied, confused.

"I know, but I take his ashes wherever I go."

"Did you not want to put him in a lighter container?" Allowing them all to go ahead of me, I closed the door behind us.

"Where are you going?" I asked as she shuffled her way through my kitchen.

"What do you mean?"

"Well, you're all dressed up. I wondered where you were off to after this." She stopped and smoothed her dress. "Nowhere…just thought I should respect the dead."

Can't argue with that, I guess. Mum followed everyone through the house and out to the back deck, where they had a much better view of what was going on. Mum sat down heavily on a chair and sighed.

"Are you okay?" I asked.

"What do you think?" She really didn't want to know what I thought. "I'm worried sick about you." She did actually look a bit tired.

"Nell," said Grandma. "I told you in the car, dead people don't ever hurt anybody."

"I know that, but someone made that body dead and then buried it in the garden. I mean, who does such a thing?" Mum's voice sounded awfully like Minnie Mouse's.

"Have you taken your tablets today?" asked Grandma, looking at Mum.

Mum responded by giving Grandma the evil eye. "I do not need medicating," she said.

I gave Mum a closer look and noticed her short curly hair was a lot straighter today. At first I had thought it was because of the rain, but now I wasn't so sure.

"Everything's okay, Mum," I said, reassuringly. "No one is going to hurt me. And anyway, I've got Riley to protect me now."

"Yes, and thank the good Lord for that, but I would still feel better if you sold this house."

Yeah, so would I. "Also, I'm pretty sure that body has been there a long time." I didn't want to admit that I was still pretty freaked out about it. That would only add to Mum's anxiety.

"Yes, but what if whoever buried it is still around?"

"Well they have no reason to come looking here. The body has gone and so has the evidence." I hoped I sounded a lot more convincing than I felt.

Mum huffed and folded her arms across her chest, obviously no more reassured than before. Luckily I hadn't told her about the blood.

"Lizzie, I'm leaving them here with you for a little while. I have some errands to run and it'll be easier on my own," Mum said in a tone that suggested this wasn't negotiable.

"Sure. No worries." For the first time since she'd pulled up, Mum's shoulders relaxed and a smile played on her lips.

"Thank you, Lizzie. I'll make sure I bake a chocolate cake with dinner this Sunday." I gave Mum a hug and waved as she walked back into the house, closing the door behind her.

"I bought some biscuits," said Eunice, opening the seat of her walker and retrieving a plastic container. Taking it from her, I opened the lid and smiled at the smell of home-baked cookies floating my way.

"You didn't have to do that," I said, secretly happy she had.

"I'm never one to turn up empty-handed." She smiled as she looked at the group of people starting to wander around my garden.

Bradley, moved to stand near the steps, grinned and waved. I wasn't exactly sure how I felt about his tours, but I had to give him points for his enterprising spirit...and points for the fact he hadn't let Riley scare him off.

Grandma shuffled over next to me.

"Do you want a biscuit?" she called to Bradley.

Bradley's grin got bigger and he moved towards us.

"Oh yes, please. I missed breakfast today and I'm starving. I didn't know how I was going to make it to lunch."

"You've got a bus load of senior citizens there. Surely one of 'em will have a packet of biscuits," said Grandma. "Eunice here never goes anywhere without hers."

"Always prepared!" trilled Eunice.

An elderly man who'd been standing just behind Bradley looked up. "That's what I used to say when I was a boy scout. Long time ago that was though, but it was a lesson I never forgot." He gave us a toothy grin and moved closer to Grandma. I looked down on him from my position on the deck and a memory stirred. Now I'm not very good with names, in fact I'm pretty crap at it, but I never forgot a face. And this man had a very familiar face.

"My, my…you were at the front of the queue when good looks were handed out, weren't you?" he said, extending his hand up to Grandma. "I'm George…George Burnett."

George looked to be in his mid-eighties, his hairline had receded so much it was now pretty much non-existent. His skin sagged, his jowls sagged, in fact everything sagged, and he pretty much looked like Droopy Dog.

He over balanced slightly as he propped his walking stick against his body and took Grandma's hand.

"Well, aren't you a charmer," she said. Her smile told me she was sucked into every syllable he said though. "I'm Mabel Phillips," she answered, removing her hand and smoothing down her dress as she spoke.

I think Bradley had heard enough. He took his biscuit, grimaced at George behind his back and moved away, but not before giving me a wicked smile. I gave up on being annoyed at him and grinned back. After all, he wasn't here to hurt anybody.

"It's a pleasure to meet you, Mabel. And is this your lovely home?" he asked, gesturing to the house and garden.

"No. It's my granddaughter's. She was on the news, you know?" said Grandma, looking at me smugly.

"Ah yes…I *do* remember that news report, now that you mention it. How are you, Lizzie?"

He knew my name? My heart missed a beat and suspicion creeped in. I didn't like strangers knowing who I was. I bit my lip as anxiety stirred. How did he know my name? I was positive the news report hadn't named me. I'd specifically asked Matt to leave it out. Maybe Bradley told his passengers who I was. I took a deep calming breath and reminded myself not to overreact.

"I'm fine, thank you." It was then I remembered why he looked familiar. I'd seen him here on another day. "You've been here before."

"No, no I think you're mistaken." He bared his nicotine-stained teeth and moved his attention back to Grandma. I was about to question him on it when I heard Riley call. I moved inside wondering why George would have lied about it.

Riley had returned from the hardware store and continued on his mission to remove the overhead kitchen cupboards.

"Sorry, I didn't hear you return," I said.

"That's okay. Can you pass me the pry bar please?"

Pry bar? "Um...sure." I looked around the kitchen, hoping I'd recognize it when I saw it.

"It's in my toolbox in the hallway."

"Oh, okay. I wondered why I couldn't see it."

I moved into the hallway and looked into Riley's toolbox. It was filled with a lot of different tools, only some of which I recognized. I picked up the hammer and then instantly discarded it. Unless a pry bar was a type of hammer. Was it? Who knows?

I put it down and continued to look through his tools. I found a couple of screw drivers (I knew what they were), a tape measure, a funny looking knife, some safety glasses (I'd have to ask Riley why he wasn't wearing those) a packet of chewing gum (spearmint—my favorite), some metal grippy-looking things, an old dirt bike maga-zine, and an even older paper bag advertising Bartley's Bakery. I wasn't opening that one. Who knew how long it had been there?

I quickly realized you could learn a lot about a man by looking in his toolbox, but I was still none the wiser as to what the hell a pry bar looked like.

"Lizzie, can you hurry up please?" called Riley.

I picked up two metal bars about as long as a school ruler. Were these pry bars? I sighed and decided to take both bars back to him. I held them up for inspection.

"The one on the right," he said. He seemed to be supporting the weight of the cupboard with his left hand and as he reached out to take the bar from me, I saw that his shirt had ridden up which gave me a good view of his hard abdominal muscles glistening with sweat. If only Grandma Mabel could see him now.

"Thanks," he said.

"My pleasure," I said and genuinely meant it. Grandma's laugh carried in on the breeze. "Do you need anything else?" I asked, torn between wanting to watch him work a little bit longer and needing to get back to Grandma. It wasn't a good idea to leave her on her own for too long, even if she did have a friend with her.

"Not at the moment, but I'll call you when I do."

Walking back outside I saw Grandma giving George a little finger wave as he walked back towards the crowd.

"What did I miss?" I asked, taking a seat opposite Eunice.

"What a lovely man," said Grandma watching George's retreating back. "I gave him my phone number."

"*What?* Is it a good idea to give out your number?" I asked, thinking about how he had lied to me. Mum was going to have a fit. She left me in charge for an hour and already Grandma had given out her number to a strange man.

"I had to give it to him. How else would we arrange our date for next Thursday night?"

I put my head in my hands and groaned. Mum was going to kill me.

Grandma stood and moved to the edge of the deck. I watched her swish her teeth backwards and forwards and then open her bag. It took her a minute, but finally she emerged with her

45

mobile phone in her hand, a Christmas gift from all of us last year.

At the time we didn't really know whether it was a good idea or not, but she insisted that all the ladies at Seniors Club had one so she should too. We upgraded and bought her a smartphone. We figured that was pretty easy to use and mostly she just wanted it so she fitted in with the crowd. The added advantage to a smart phone was the *Find My Phone* app. After the last time she went missing, we thought this idea was ingenious. I was actually quite surprised at how well she could use the phone though.

Eunice stepped up next to her and pulled out the same phone. Obviously she'd been showing Grandma how to use it. Not wanting to disappoint the ladies at Seniors Club, they proceeded to take photo after photo of my backyard, complete with police tape and very large hole. When Grandma turned her back to the garden, put her phone up in front of her and smiled, I realized she was taking a selfie. As the flash went off causing me to blink I realized she hadn't quite perfected it yet.

"Grandma, you have to turn the camera around," I explained.

"Oh, that's right. I forgot that bit." With this, she turned the phone around and smiled again. "But I can't see what I'm looking at now." It was my turn to smile as I moved to take the phone off of her.

"I'll take it for you," I offered.

"Thanks. And make it a good one. This one's going on my Facebook page."

"You have Facebook?" I asked.

"Yep, and I got Twitter too. I'm following Tom Jones. And now that I've got the right Tom Jones, it's even interesting. I saw a picture of his new Wellie boots yesterday."

"Nice. Now smile," I said and took the photo.

"Good. Now I want one with you. Eunice, take this picture will you?" she said.

"Why do you want a photo with me?" I asked.

"Tomorrow's show and tell at Seniors Group and some of the girls have taken the tour of your garden, but only I get a photo with my famous granddaughter."

"I'm not famous, Grandma."

"You've been on the news. Close enough."

I smiled as Eunice took the photo.

"Now I want one with Riley. Where is he?"

"He's busy. Why do you want a photo with Riley?"

"Cause he's good to look at," replied Grandma, looking at me like I was crazy.

Can't argue with that logic I guess.

CHAPTER 5

*T*hursday dawned bright and sunny once again. I got up and dressed in one of Molly's hand-me-down dresses. The advantage of having a sister addicted to fashion was that I got all her cast-offs. This dress in particular was one of my favorites. It was yellow, about mid-thigh in length and fell loose from my bust, which was especially good on days when you were going out for a big lunch, as no one could see how big my stomach looked.

I brushed my temporarily straight hair (compliments of Danny) and carefully applied my make-up. When I still felt inse-cure, I went back and added another layer of mascara and lip-gloss. Today I had my first appointment at the counselor. I'd never been to a counselor before and the thought that someone would be able to see the 'real me' scared me almost as much as my nightmares.

Riley had popped out to the corner shop to get some milk and the morning paper but he was coming with me for my first visit. I went downstairs and poured myself a coffee, using the last of the milk in the carton, hoping that a coffee would settle my nerves.

My appointment was booked for nine and, without looking at the clock, I knew I still had another forty-five minutes to get there. All I knew about the counselor I was going to was that her name was Allison Greene, she was about my age and highly recommended by my doctor. In fact, my doctor had been recommending her for the last few months, but I just hadn't been ready to take that step.

I sighed. I still wasn't ready. Maybe I could cancel. I'm sure I could get a grip on my nightmares without professional help. Yeah, maybe I should give myself another week. Running to my bag to find my phone to call off my appointment, I felt my nerves settle. Riley walked in the door as I was dialing.

"Who are you talking to?" he asked, kissing me on top of my head as he walked past.

"The counselor," I responded, listening to the ring through the phone. Riley's eyebrow rose. It was actually a really adorable trait he had. Only his left eyebrow rose when he was really curious. "I'm canceling my appointment. I've decided to give myself another week and then see how I feel," I explained.

Riley immediately took the phone from my hand and pressed the end button.

"Lizzie, you are not cancelling. You promised me you would go."

"Yes, and I will if I need to...next week."

Riley pulled me in close. "You need it now. I know you had another nightmare last night."

"Yes, but it wasn't as bad as the last one, so I'm obviously getting better."

"We're going to that appointment," he said, his tone suggesting no nonsense. "Now, grab your bag. I'm taking you out for a coffee. We'll go to your favorite café on the boardwalk."

Humph. He knew how to bribe me.

৪

RILEY LIVED at 12 Sunrise Drive, and the café in question wasn't that far from his house. Only about a five-minute drive, but it was on the other side of the river. Riley navigated traffic easily but once we got there, parking was a whole different story. I think every man and his dog had come for a coffee this morning.

"Hail Mary, Mother of Grace, please find us a parking space," I said, looking around, hoping a car would pull out of a park for us.

Riley laughed. "What did you just say?"

"I said a Hail Mary to the parking gods. I heard it on the radio once." Riley continued to smile. Obviously he was a skeptic. "Don't look at me like that. It works."

"Do you really think you should say a Hail Mary just to get a parking space?"

"Yeah, I have been a bit concerned about that, but I figure I'll worry about it when my time's up." I smiled because just at that moment the car in the nearest parking space put his reversing lights on and started to move out of the park. I looked at Riley and shrugged. "I told you it works."

I heard Riley's chuckle, low and sexy in his throat, as he pulled into the space.

Opening the car door and stepping out into the sunshine, I instantly felt the anxiety settle. I loved it here. Not only was the coffee exceptional and the staff friendly, but the view was spectacular. Whenever life got too hard, I put on my walking shoes, went for a walk and ended up at this coffee shop. Usually by then I had figured out whatever was on my mind, and if I hadn't, I'd buy a chocolate Frappuccino. Same difference.

It was a good start as Tom, my favorite Barista, was on duty. He not only made the best coffee he also had the friendliest smile.

"Good morning, Lizzie," he called as we entered the shop. "You're looking sunny this morning."

"Thanks, Tom. No classes today?" It was unusual for him to be here today as it was normally a busy day of lectures. What he was studying, I had never actually found out. Every time I asked, he gave me a really complicated response, which I didn't understand and I always felt too stupid to enquire any further.

"Nope, it's study week."

"Then why aren't you home studying?" I smiled.

"Because I'd miss you then, wouldn't I?" He laughed. See, that's why he's my favorite barista. "The usual?" he asked, looking between Riley and myself. We both nodded. "Take a seat then and I'll bring it out to you."

We wandered back outside and found a table under an umbrella that looked out over the river. The rain yesterday had stirred the water up so it wasn't the same aqua blue it usually was, but it was still gorgeous just the same. I looked at Riley as he pulled his sunglasses down over his eyes. Today he'd chosen to wear his usual jeans, but he'd accompanied it with a button down shirt that he'd left open at the collar. The sleeves were rolled to his elbows and accentuated his perfectly toned arms, his skin tanned against the white of his shirt. His hair was slightly longer than normal and curled sexily at his collar. The realization that he was all mine brought a smile to my face.

He caught me staring and smiled his mega-watt smile. I pulled my own sunglasses down, dazzled by it. Sure, I should be immune to it by now, but it still caused my heart to flutter. He reached out and took my hand.

"Are you okay?" he asked, his voice deep and sexy.

"Yep, I will be." I smiled, squeezing his hand. "Thanks for being there for me today."

"Lizzie, I'll always be there for you," he said, leaning forward and gently kissing my lips. I felt the happiness surge the second his skin touched mine.

"Get a room, you two," laughed Tom, putting our coffee on the table.

"You're just jealous because my boyfriend is totally gorgeous," I laughed.

"I bet I make better coffee than him though." That was true, but Riley had other skills that a girl only dreamed about. Tom looked at my grin, shook his head and walked away.

IT TURNED out that my counselor was actually a psychiatrist. Humph.

I looked around the room as I sat nervously waiting for my turn. The waiting room was small with only two chairs for patients to wait. Thankfully it appeared that Riley and I were the only people here. The reception desk was tall and made of bleached pine. It had a computer, a phone and a bunch of sunny flowers on it. I suppose their purpose was to make us happy and maybe it did.

The sign on the desk announced that Allison was presently with a patient and to please take a seat. I'd done as asked. Riley appeared much more relaxed as he flicked his way through a fishing magazine from the side table between us. My leg jiggled as I waited.

After what felt like an eternity, the door finally slid open and out stepped Allison, a male patient following her. As he wiped at his tears, anxiety gripped my stomach. Allison however, seemed relaxed and in control.

Recognition flashed. I just couldn't pinpoint where I'd seen her before. She looked younger than me even though I knew she was about my age, with straight blonde hair cut in a bob that fell just below her ears, showing off her sparkling diamond stud earrings perfectly. Her make-up was subtle yet immaculate, and accentuated her massive grey eyes. She dressed in designer pants, a fitted button-up shirt and her shoes were genuine Jimmy Choo's. I only knew that because Molly had the exact same pair. The smell of Victor Rolf's Flowerbomb floated towards me. I felt my earlier insecurity kick up a notch. When she finished showing the man to the door, she turned her attention to us, and her smile widened.

"Oh my gosh," she said, her white teeth flashing against the black of her shirt. "Riley Thomas!"

I looked at Riley and noticed him blush as he stood.

"Allison," he said, moving towards her. "I wasn't expecting to see you." He smiled as she reached up and hugged him. "I thought we were seeing Allison Greene," he added.

"I've changed my name since I saw you last."

"Married?" he asked.

"No. Well, yes I was. I'm divorced now though. He was threatened by my success apparently." She laughed. "Gosh, I haven't seen you since you left for the army. I don't think my heart ever recovered from you leaving," she trilled, giggling.

"Ha. It looks like you've done really well for yourself."

Allison looked around her and shook her head. "What are you doing here anyway?" she asked.

"I'm here with Lizzie," he responded, turning his attention to me.

Maybe it was because my anxiety was already high but something felt off here. Allison turned to me. I noticed the very subtle up and down look as she took me in, her smile frozen in place as recognition flashed in her eyes. I stood and smoothed down my dress, wishing I was anywhere but here.

"Hi," I smiled and gave a little wave.

"Oh, yes of course. I do remember Lizzie being booked in today. It's lovely to meet you," she said, extending her hand for me to shake. I felt her cool skin against mine and my anxiety reached a whole new level. I got the distinct impression she *really* wasn't happy to meet me at all.

"Well, why don't you go through, Lizzie. Make yourself comfortable and I'll be in shortly," she said, indicating to the door that she had just come through. She turned her attention back to

Riley. "Wow. I can't believe you're here. You look great, by the way," she gushed, touching his arm as she spoke.

To be honest I was used to girls flirting with Riley but this felt completely different. It didn't take a genius to figure out they had a history. But so what? I knew Riley had partners before me. True, we hadn't really spoken too much about them. Every time I thought about Riley with another woman, I felt sick in my stomach, but I knew they existed.

"Go through, Lizzie," she repeated.

I looked at Riley, hoping he would stay with me. Even though —watching Allison flirt with him—it might be better if he waited outside.

Riley looked at me and smiled. "If it's okay, Allison, I'm going to stay with Lizzie for this visit."

"Of course it's alright. I'd love to have you."

I bet she would.

Walking ahead of them both, I entered the little room and sat down on the chair provided, and looked around me. I'm not sure exactly what I expected but this wasn't really it. The room was painted a very subtle latte color with a plush chocolate-colored carpet. The chairs were white, high-backed and comfortable, with a small glass table between myself and where Allison would sit. The white shelving on the wall behind her held an assortment of books, flowers and a burning candle that filled the room with the overwhelming smell of gardenia.

Now I usually liked the smell of gardenia but as there was not a single window in the room, I could feel my eyes sting and a headache start. But then, the headache could be from my unusually high blood pressure at the moment. Riley sat in the chair next to me and I watched as Allison sat and crossed one long leg over the other, her peep-toed Jimmy Choo showing her pedicure to perfection.

"Now Lizzie, what brings you here today?"

"Umm…I'm…umm…having some nightmares," I said, my

voice croaky. I cleared my throat, hoping I sounded a lot more confident than I felt.

"Really? Well, why don't we start with some basic information about yourself. What's your family situation, where you live, that kind of thing?"

I spent the next ten minutes telling her my life story including what happened with my stalker. "To be honest with you, until I bought the house, I'd never had nightmares before."

"Okay. What we are going to do is..." she responded, opening a folder on her lap "...I'm going to give you this questionnaire. I want you to fill it out for me, and then I'll get a better indication of how you're really feeling." she explained, passing me some paperwork. I flicked through it and noted the forty-two questions.

"I want you to answer them and circle the statement that applied to you most in the past week. And there's no right or wrong answers. Just be completely honest."

I picked up the pen from the table and started to read the questions. Allison turned her attention to Riley and lowered her voice.

"So Riley, did you ever marry?" she whispered.

I noted Riley shake his head.

"I tried it once," she continued. "Didn't go for it much really. He just wasn't the right man. I think the right man got away from me years ago."

What? I looked up from the paperwork I was meant to be filling out. Allison ran her fingers through her hair and I watched as it fell back into place perfectly, her white smile locked onto Riley.

"Oh sorry, Lizzie. Please keep writing," she said. "Maybe we should step outside Riley and let Lizzie concentrate. That questionnaire is very important to her treatment."

Riley looked at me, worried.

"Sure." He stood and took my hand. "I'll be right outside. Yell out if you need me, okay?"

"No, you don't have to go. I can concentrate just fine," I said, holding his hand tightly.

"Really, Lizzie," interrupted Allison. "You shouldn't have any distractions." With that, Riley squeezed my hand and she ushered him out the door, closing it behind her.

Damn. I'd already decided I didn't like Allison and that I probably didn't want to tell her my darkest fears, so what was the point of filling out this stupid questionnaire? I stood and opened the door. Allison had her back to me, standing right between Riley and myself.

"Are you okay?" asked Riley, realizing I was staring at them.

"Yes, but I just remembered I was supposed to do that thing for Mum. Maybe I could rebook this appointment and come back another day?" I had every intention of cancelling the rebooking.

"What thing?" asked Riley.

"Oh, you know...I told you about it last night."

Shit. Why did men have to be so slow on the uptake some days? Surely Riley could tell I was trying my hardest to make something up just to get out of here. He looked at me, his eyes soft. He knew.

Allison moved towards me. "Lizzie, it's really important you put your health before anything else. I'm sure your mum won't mind waiting a little longer for you to do whatever it is that needs doing." She moved to close the door again. "The quicker you answer those questions, the quicker it will be finished and you can go and do whatever you need to." She walked close to me, forcing me backwards into the room. When I was in far enough, she smiled and closed the door.

I sighed and sat back down. Maybe I should send Riley a text message asking him to help me out of here. Quickly pulling out my phone I sent a text to Riley. Get me out of here, I typed and pressed send. I jiggled my leg as I waited for the door to open. Instead my phone vibrated, indicating I'd received a message. I swiped it open.

No xoxo.

Bloody hell. Now what? I sighed again and looked at the paper still in my hands. As much as I hated to admit it, maybe Allison was right—the sooner I completed it, the sooner I could go home.

All right...here goes. It had a rating scale, zero meaning it didn't apply to me at all and three meaning that it applied to me very much. Okay, this didn't seem too hard. I started to read the questions but I could hear Allison's voice from outside the room.

I tried to shake off the jealousy and concentrate, my breathing getting shallow and rapid.

She laughed, the sound resembling a tinkling bell. My heart missed a beat.

Concentrate Lizzie.

Okay. Question one—I find myself getting upset by trivial things. That's definitely a zero. Not me at all.

Riley's laugh echoed through the walls. The palpitation caused my breath to hitch.

This questionnaire was really stupid. No I didn't have a dry mouth. I reached for my glass of water. Well, not usually anyway. I circled a few more zeros.

The outer room had gone silent and I wondered what they were doing. It was so obvious they had a history, and I imagined Allison's long legs wrapped around Riley as the thought of her kissing him made my stomach flutter.

I stood, moved to the door and pressed my ear against it. I could hear Riley's voice, low and sexy and my imagination went into over-drive. I knew what it felt like to have that voice whisper in my ear, I knew how it felt for him to look at me with that inti-mate smile he has. Yes, his mega-watt smile was enough to stop me in my tracks, but the small intimate smile stops the world turning. Had he ever given her that smile?

My heart was palpitating at an alarming rate as my breathing became ragged. Stop Lizzie, and concentrate on the questions.

I sat back down and looked at the paper. Okay. Question six— I tended to over react to situations...zero.

I hurriedly circled answers, not really caring about what I was doing.

Question twenty—I felt scared without any good reason. Nope.

Question twenty-eight—I felt I was close to panic. Never.

Question thirty-nine—I found myself getting agitated. Not until I came here! I circled the zero so hard I ripped the paper. Damn.

Question forty-one—I experienced trembling (e.g. in the hands). I noticed the pen shake as I circled zero and had a moment of thinking I really should go back and answer these questions again. But it didn't matter anyway. I wasn't ever coming back here. As far as I could tell, I felt a lot more stable before I walked in this door so obviously counseling wasn't for me.

Circling my last zero, I threw the pen on the table and stood. I pulled the door open in a hurry and braced myself for what I would see, my mind filled with images of Allison's blonde hair running through Riley's fingers as he looked at her intimately.

I stepped into the waiting room to find Allison quietly clicking on her keyboard and Riley to be noticeably absent. She looked up as I approached.

"Have you finished already?" she asked, her perfectly shaped eyebrows furrowing.

"Um...yes. Where's Riley?" I asked.

"He had to make some calls so he stepped outside. He said to meet him in the car when you're ready."

Oh, so I really had nothing to worry about? "Well, I answered all the questions," I said, handing her the paperwork.

"That's great. I'll make another appointment for you and we'll go over the results then. That gives me time to evaluate this and write a plan of how your treatment should go."

"Oh, don't hurry," I replied as she flicked through the questions, a confused expression on her face. "In fact, I'll call you and make the booking when I've consulted my diary," I said hurriedly, grabbing and turning the door handle. "It was lovely meeting you," I lied as I quickly opened the door and made a hasty retreat.

Sucking in the fresh air, I took a deep breath and instantly felt my heart rate decrease.

CHAPTER 6

*T*onight Danny, Andrew and Molly were all coming to my house for Friday night get-together. I had told them that Riley and I were sleeping at his house now, but Danny wanted to sit back and watch the groups of people gathering around my now famous hole in the ground.

We were all sitting on the back deck, a large pizza on the table between us. Thankfully the hordes seemed to have better things to do this particular Friday night.

"You know," said Danny, picking a piece of pepperoni off his pizza and feeding it to Harper, "I can't believe all the secrets held by this house. I thought you said the previous owner, Avis, was an old spinster."

"Yes, she was. I guess it doesn't mean she was boring," I replied.

"Danny, stop feeding Harper! He's on a diet," chastised Molly.

"He's fine. Leave the poor little thing alone," said Danny, giving Harper a pat.

"Have you ever found out any more about Avis?" asked Andrew.

"Not since we found who had given her the engagement ring."

"Maybe you should do some investigating. Find out some of her history," suggested Danny, sneaking Harper another piece of his pizza. "Maybe you'll find out why those bones were there. I figured she would have lived here at the time they were buried."

"Lizzie needs to leave it all alone," warned Riley, his body tensing next to me. "Let the Police do their job."

"Yeah, but aren't you curious?" asked Danny.

"I guess so," I replied thoughtfully. Riley looked at me, his brow creased.

"Please leave it alone," he said quietly. "It's history. It doesn't matter to us why they're there."

"It probably can't hurt," I said.

"You're still having nightmares about the last time this house uncovered a secret, remember?"

"Oh, that's right," said Molly. "How did the counseling session go?"

I looked at Riley. He still thought that Allison was going to call me to book another appointment.

"Oh, you know…fine," I replied, not looking him in the eye. "Does anyone want another drink?" I jumped up and moved towards the door, hoping to quickly change the subject.

"Yes please," answered Andrew. "But something non-alcoholic. I'm the designated driver tonight."

"Just bring the bottle out here," called Danny to my retreating back.

I closed the kitchen door behind me and moved to the refrigerator. I was about to open it and grab the bottle of wine when something caught my eye. I moved closer to the table and put my empty glass on it, and looked down at the floor. Sprayed over an area of about two square feet, was blood. Now I don't mean a couple of little droplets like someone had cut their finger, I mean it was sprayed from one wall to the next. Just like the night I'd had the nightmare.

I jumped away from it, looking around wildly, wondering where it had come from.

"Riley!" I screamed. "Riley, come here quick!" Thankfully Riley was fast on his feet and was next to me within seconds, followed by Danny, Andrew and Molly.

"What the...?" he asked.

"Is that blood?" asked Molly.

"It looks like blood," said Danny, his face screwing up as he spoke.

"But where did it come from?" asked Andrew.

"It's your mystery dead body," said Danny seriously. "It's not happy you dug it up."

"I didn't dig it up!" I yelled. "Harper did."

"Doesn't matter, it's not happy."

"It is not from the dead body," answered Andrew, exasperated.

"Well, how else would you explain it?" replied Danny.

Molly remained quiet, but she did pick Harper up and cradled him under her arm.

"I'm sure there is a reasonable explanation," said Andrew.

I really hoped so.

"Go ahead then, tell us what it is," challenged Danny, his hand on his hip.

Andrew was stumped. He honestly had no idea what it was from.

"It looks like someone has put it in an aerosol container and sprayed it," commented Riley, crouched down, looking at it closer.

"Well that's a stupid thing to say," said Danny. "Who would have done that?" He looked around our group, his eyes stopping on Molly.

"Don't look at me!" said Molly. "I didn't do it."

"Is it definitely blood?" I asked, hoping this was some sort of practical joke.

"I think so. I mean, I'm not positive, but I think it is," said Riley.

"I told you it's the ghost of the dead body," said Danny.

I stood and looked at him silently. Of course, I knew it wasn't a ghost that had done this, but that didn't stop the hair on my arms rising to the occasion.

LATER THAT NIGHT, tucked up next to Riley on his couch, I thought over the events of the last few days, and about all the secrets my house held.

"Lizzie, sit still please," said Riley, placing his hand on my knee to stop it jiggling.

"Sorry."

"What are you thinking about?" he asked, muting the ads on the television and turning to face me.

"Oh, you know, just how much I want to sell that house." I smiled weakly as Riley took my hand and squeezed it.

"It's nearly finished. I reckon another month and I'll have the kitchen out and the new cabinets in. Once we tidy up the garden, it'll be finished."

"But who'll want to buy it with a ream of police tape strung across the yard?"

"That won't be there forever."

"The fact that the body has now been removed, does that mean that it's no longer someone's grave?"

"It's no longer a grave," Riley reassured me.

"How long do you think it will take until they find out who it belonged to?"

Riley shrugged. "No idea, but it doesn't really matter does it?" he said, turning his attention back to the television and pressing the remote as Spiderman shot webs across the screen.

"Of course it matters," I said. "How can you think it doesn't matter?"

"The body's gone and as soon as the police have finished, the tape will be gone as well. Then we'll fill in the hole and plant some trees." This all seemed so easy for Riley.

"Riley, someone was buried in my back garden. Of course it's a big deal."

"Lizzie, it happened years before we were even born."

"Yes, I know that, but it matters. Whoever it was, they were still human and deserved to be buried appropriately."

Riley turned and looked at me, his eyes softening. He put his hand on my knee and squeezed. "I'm sure the police will find out who it belonged to and contact any family that may be around today. They'll see to it that it's buried appropriately. If it makes you feel better we'll go to the funeral. Anyway, when's your next appointment with Allison? Maybe you could talk to her about it."

I shrugged and chewed on my thumb nail.

"Lizzie, you are going back aren't you?" Riley looked at me, his eyebrow raised.

"You know, you're really cute when you do that," I said, smiling.

"Don't change the subject."

Hmm, I needed another tactic. "I'm not. It's just that you look kinda sexy when you do that eyebrow thing." I moved closer and nibbled on his ear. If all else fails, you know what they say?

Thankfully, it worked a treat. Riley shivered and moved his mouth to mine. All thoughts of Allison forgotten.

It took until Monday, but Allison did start calling me. If only I'd known about her and Riley when I'd filled in my personal details, I would have given her someone else's number. Also I should have saved her number to my contact list, as when she rang all my caller ID showed was a phone number. So I stupidly answered the call.

"Hello?"

"Hi, Lizzie," said a voice I didn't recognize.

"Who's calling please?"

"It's Allison. Allison Greene."

"Oh, hi Allison." Shit. "What can I do for you?" I asked.

"Well, I've just checked my diary and you haven't rebooked your appointment yet. I have a cancellation tomorrow morning and I was hoping you'd be free to take it." She sounded really friendly, and I told myself to calm down and not over react. "Riley told me you're still having nightmares and I wanted to help you. I know that with a bit of time and the right techniques, we can make them stop."

"Oh really?" I thought of last night and how I really did want the nightmares to end. I just didn't want Allison to be the one to help me.

"The sooner we start the better," she continued. "So I'll put you into that spot tomorrow at 10.30. Try to arrive about five minutes early, that way you can relax before we start our session. See you then."

She ended the call before I even had a chance to say bye. But hang on a second...did she say Riley had told her? Why was she talking to Riley about me? And why didn't I just say no to the appointment? Damn she was good.

I threw the phone back into my handbag and sighed. I'd have to have a chat with Riley later and ask him why he was talking to Allison, and maybe get some more information as to how involved the two of them really were. That was not a conversation I was looking forward to. My stomach churned at the thought of it.

Riley had left early this morning and gone back to the house to get a head-start on the work that needed to be done today. I'd promised I'd help him as work-wise, I seemed to have a quiet week. I crossed my fingers and hoped my bookkeeping business wasn't suffering from all the publicity I'd been getting over the body in the backyard. Picking up my bag, I headed to my car, locking the front door behind me.

First thing I noticed as I pulled into my little driveway was the police car parked at the curb. I cut the engine and really hoped that Riley had the coffee on. I think I was going to need it.

"Hi," I called to Riley as I placed my bag on the couch in the lounge room.

"Hey," I heard him call back. "We're in the kitchen."

Walking into the kitchen, I saw Riley leaning against the counter and Officer Ed Helms sitting at the table, both with coffee in hand.

"Oh hello, Officer Helms." I smiled, stretching my neck to try to alleviate the tension that was already building there.

"Hi, Lizzie," he replied. "And please remember to call me Ed." He smiled a super-white smile, and extended his hand for me to shake. I accepted it and felt the heat of his skin as he held on for slightly longer than I thought was necessary.

"Sorry…Ed." I smiled back at him and removed my hand as Riley gave me a cup of coffee. "Thanks." I looked at Riley to see if he had noticed the handshake but it appeared he hadn't. Well, either that or he just didn't care enough to be jealous. Then again maybe there was nothing to be jealous of. "What's happening?" I asked.

"I've just removed the police tape we had out the back. It's okay for you to go back now."

"Great. Thanks," I said sarcastically. Ed's smile got a little bit bigger.

"It's okay, Lizzie. We removed all the cooties. There's nothing to be worried about anymore."

"Do you know anything about who it was yet?" I asked, cradling the coffee and allowing the heat to seep in me. Even though there was enough heat in the kitchen I couldn't understand why my hands were so cold.

"Not yet. But I promise I'll keep you up to date."

"Thanks."

"You're doing a really nice job restoring this old house," Ed said, still smiling at me.

"Thanks, but Riley is the one doing all the work."

"Yeah, but I'm sure you're the one with all the design ideas."

I felt the happiness surge as finally someone had given me some credit for the changes. I mean, I know Riley's the one doing all the hard stuff, but I'd put in my fair share too, designing and... stuff, like shopping. I mean shopping is a very important part of the process. Without it the house may not have a new kitchen waiting to go in. Or bench tops (even though I haven't quite made the decision on that one yet). Or that really lovely wallpaper Riley put on that one wall in the lounge.

"Lizzie has a lot of talents," said Riley, coming in on our conversation. "Decorating is only one of them." He gave me a very suggestive little smile and I had to check the floor to make sure my toes hadn't burnt a hole in it.

"I don't doubt it." Ed Helms understood exactly what Riley was suggesting. I felt the heat rise from my neck and spread its way across my face, only stopping once a sweat broke out on my forehead.

Thankfully, I was saved from any more embarrassment as the doorbell rang. Actually, I should say it screeched. I made a note to add *buy new doorbell* to the To Do list.

Opening the door, I looked out into the sunlight. Standing on my doorstep was Bradley. He looked younger than ever today wearing shorts instead of long pants. He still wore the white button-down shirt, and, I guess to make himself feel a little bit more business-like, he'd added a tie—a bright Mickey Mouse tie. He looked at me and smiled.

"Hey, Lizzie," he said, bouncing on the spot. "How's things?"

"Oh hey, Bradley. What's up?" As much as Bradley was becoming a garden ornament around here, it was rare that he rang my bell.

"I noticed the police car out the front."

"And?"

"I just wondered...you know...what's happening?" I looked at the enthusiasm in Bradley's eyes and couldn't help but smile.

"Nothing's happening, it's just Officer Helms. He removed the police tape."

"Oh! Is that all? I thought maybe they had some more news on what they'd found."

"Sorry, I guess we won't be seeing much of you from now on then."

I probably should be relieved at this, but in all honesty I didn't mind either way. Bradley had turned up every day with a different group of people and since he'd stopped parking in my driveway, we were getting along much better.

Bradley looked at me quizzically.

"You know, with the police tape gone, it just looks like I'm a messy gardener," I explained.

"Oh no, I'll be here." He smiled. "People are always interested in gossip."

"Did you buy a new bus?" I asked. Looking out to the curb, I saw an old rust bucket that I if I used my imagination, I'm sure could be called a bus. The white paintwork was faded and dull, but the eager faces looking out of it were anything but. Well, they were old. They just weren't dull.

"Yeah, isn't it great? My dad told me I couldn't borrow his anymore and these tours are getting really popular, so I thought why not invest in my future." Bradley shrugged and flashed a boyish grin. He could be annoying at times, but he was pretty cute. If you were into grown men who looked about twelve but dressed like fifty-year-old businessmen.

I was about to ask if his bus was up to the job when he turned and waved to the occupants. Twenty senior citizens jostled for first place to disembark, but unfortunately it was Norm Aldershott, Westport's' oldest resident, who managed to get the honor. God knows how. I'd seen snails move faster.

Bradley sighed. "I'd better go and help them. Otherwise you'll be inviting us in for supper." I smiled at Bradley as he skipped down the steps and hopped over the little garden bed I'd planted around my front porch. Credit where credit's due—he was far more patient than I was.

CHAPTER 7

*A*s the sun set on the day, I made a quick dash upstairs to grab a few extra things from my wardrobe. Even though Riley and I had never actually discussed our living arrangements, we both agreed on the fact that once the house was sold, I would move in with him—which was going to be good for more than one reason.

Yes, yes I know. What better reason could there be other than spending all that quality time with Riley? And of course that was at the top of my list. But other, more practical things were on that list too. Like having my clothes all in one place.

I'm not like Molly in that I don't need designer clothes, or even lots of expensive new clothes, but I do have a bit of an addiction to jumpers and cardigans. In fact, last time they were all together in one wardrobe, I counted twenty-six of them. You would think that because we live in a hot climate, I wouldn't need twenty-six of them, wouldn't you? And I would then ask you if anyone anywhere actually needed twenty-six jumpers.

But I liked them, and as I was usually a bit of a cold fish—especially when the air conditioning was on—I found myself always carrying one with me. Tonight, we were visiting Riley's parents for dinner and as his mum was going through menopause, the air conditioning was always on high, so I needed to grab a jumper that was a little warmer.

I walked into my bedroom and opened my wardrobe. It took me a few minutes but finally I chose my light grey cashmere cardigan. It was long enough to cover my bottom, button-up so it wouldn't be too warm, and the softness of it made me feel pretty giving me a little extra confidence.

Not that I needed it, of course. Riley's parents seemed to like me and made me feel welcome in their home. I'd only met them once before. They'd been on a world cruise when Riley and I first met and they only arrived home a month ago. They had invited us to dinner and I think that evening went well. I never actually embarrassed myself, which is really quite uncommon for me (I joke that I'm writing a book on 101 ways to embarrass myself, but in all honesty I think I should actually do it).

Well, that's not completely true. I was very embarrassed when I walked to the car and slipped on the wet grass, fell on my ass and showed everyone my knickers, but I don't think Riley's parents were looking at the particular moment, so it doesn't count, right? Anyway, I think tonight I should try a little harder, just in case they did saw.

I grabbed my new jeans, my floaty white singlet top and the only black heels I owned, and carefully put it all in a bag. Hearing the stairs creak I thought Riley must be ready to leave, so I quickly zipped up the bag and headed out to meet him. Only he wasn't there.

Oh well, I must be hearing things.

I walked down about four steps and stopped dead. Halfway down the staircase was a spray of bright red blood running down the wall. I strangled a scream and looked around to see if anyone was there, a creepy feeling running up my spine as if I was being watched.

"Riley!"

I stood completely still and waited for Riley to come running. It felt like an eternity and he never came. Shit. He must be outside. Alright, put your big girl pants on and have a closer look, I told myself.

Taking a deep shuddery breath, I moved down the stairs and stopped in front of the blood. It covered an area of about a foot round and once again looked like it had been sprayed on. Or maybe it was seeping out of the walls. I thought back to all the horror movies Danny had made me watch as a teenager and felt the fear grab at my throat.

"Riley!" I screamed again, this time much louder than the last. What if Danny was right about this house being haunted? I mean this never happened before Harper found those remains. My heart rate picked up even faster as anxiety gripped me. I scanned the hall for anything that may be scary but the only thing I came across was Cat who seemed to be having a bad hair day, his bed hair making him look like one side of his head was deformed.

Okay, think of this rationally. Ghosts are not real and blood does not seep out of walls.

But ghosts were real. I'd seen one before. Even though Mum had told me it was stress. Apparently stress can make you have hallucinations. And mums are always right, aren't they?

It had to be coming from somewhere. The adrenalin rush made my knees rubbery, so I sat on the step and tried to think calmly. As I was wondering how many people had died in this house and how many more secrets it could hold, Riley opened the front door and stopped.

"Working hard?" he asked. Then he saw my pale face and rushed up the stairs to me. "Lizzie, what's wrong?"

I nodded towards the wall where the blood was now trickling towards the skirting boards.

"There's more of it?" he asked, taking a closer look. He swiped his fingers through it, and then rubbed them together, smelling his fingers as he did so.

"Would you stop doing that?" I yelled. "Have you never heard of blood transmitted diseases? And besides that, it's *creepy!"*

He stopped, looked at me like I was crazy and then wiped his fingers on his jeans. I made a note to boil those jeans later.

"It smells wrong," he said.

"What do you mean?"

"I don't know. It just smells wrong."

"Riley, it's freaking me out! I really thought I heard you on the stairs before but instead this is what I found. Should we call Ed?"

"There has to be a sensible explanation," he said, looking around. "Blood does not appear from thin air." His gaze stopped on Cat. "It's not coming from Cat, is it?" he asked.

I hadn't actually thought of that. I stood and followed Riley down the stairs, stepping over Cat who was sleeping on the bottom stair.

Cat wasn't really one to like human contact. He only usually showed up when he was hungry or when he felt like sleeping somewhere warm and cozy. But if you tried to hold him for too long, he would squirm and claw until you let go.

He didn't give Riley the chance to try though. He sensed he was about to be held, sprang up from the step and hightailed it out of our sight.

"I guess we'll never know," sighed Riley.

"The noise I heard didn't sound like Cat."

"What did it sound like?"

"Like someone was walking up the stairs and stepped on that creaky board we have. If it was Cat, he should definitely go on a diet."

"I'll have a look around. Maybe some other animal has got some secret entrance that I've missed when I made sure the house was rodent-proof."

"Let's hope they do. It's creeping me out." Riley pulled me close and kissed the top of my head.

"Are you ready to go?" he asked.

"Yes. I'll just get my bag." I trudged back up the stairs and picked my bag up from the floor where I had dropped it, thinking I needed to add bleach to my shopping list, and knowing that the nightmares were about to kick up a notch.

꙼

RILEY'S PARENTS' home was very different to my parents' home. For starters, it was about triple the size and they hadn't converted Riley's old bedroom into their dining room. Their dining room held a table big enough for twelve, their furniture was mahogany and the crystal was Waterford. The wine was also something expensive, but I took their word for that. I wasn't much of a drinker and when I needed to be on my best behavior it was advisable for me to stay away from the stuff. Tonight I needed to be on my best behavior. Not only were Riley's parents, Anna and Mal going to be there, but his brother Jared was going to be there with his wife Shelly and their daughter Mia.

Mia is the cutest bundle of joy you've ever met. She's now eight months old, has her Uncle Riley's smile and resembles a baby Michelin man, with roll after roll of gorgeous baby fat. Last time I saw her she had learned to laugh. Apparently I was the funniest thing she'd ever seen.

We were at present all sitting around the large dining room table about to help ourselves to the meal Anna had prepared. It looked delicious—it really did. The only problem was it all seemed to be fish based. And fish was the one food I hated. I took a very large helping of salad and added a slice of the salmon quiche and handed the serving dish to Riley.

When everyone was served we all dug in. Not like dinner at Mum's house at all. There you started as soon as your plate was full, but I guess they had better manners here.

"How are the renovations going, Lizzie?" asked Riley's dad, Mal. Mal was in his mid-fifties and had obviously passed his good looks and genetics to Riley and Jared. Apart from the eyes, Riley was a carbon copy of him. Mal's eyes were a much paler blue and had a sharpness that reminded me why he was a successful property developer.

"They're going really well, thanks," I replied.

"We're not far from finishing the inside," added Riley. "We started to pull the old kitchen out today."

"Are the walls in reasonable condition? No water damage under the cabinets?"

"No...surprisingly. The house looks old and run down, but the structure is actually in good condition. Lizzie has a good eye for picking a house that's good to renovate." Riley looked at me and smiled.

"A house with good bones will always clean up well," added Anna.

"Speaking of bones, what's happening with the bones they dug up?" asked Jared.

"I was hoping you could tell me that," I said.

Jared was a detective, and I secretly hoped I could convince him to do some digging for me. I knew I could ask Officer Helms for help, but I kind of had a feeling that may cause a few complications of a different variety.

Riley stopped his fork half way to his mouth. "It doesn't matter what's happening with those bones. They're gone and so has our involvement with it." His tone suggested it was not negotiable.

"It's kind of intriguing though, isn't it?" said Shelly.

Shelly was my second favorite person at this table. She was much taller than I was, with big green eyes framed with extraordinary long eyelashes, long carrot colored hair, willowy arms and the grace of an angel. Don't be fooled...she may look elegant and full of class, but she had the laugh of an old sailor, which is actually the thing loved most about her. I looked at her and smiled.

"Yes, I think so, but Riley wants me to stay out of it."

"I'm just worried about you, that's all," he said quietly.

"What's to worry about?" asked Shelly. "Aren't those bones really old? Surely whoever put them there is no longer around?"

"Lizzie's still having nightmares about the last secret that house held. I just don't want it getting any worse."

"Lizzie, you really should get some counseling. It helps a lot. Or at least it helped me after Jared got shot," said Shelly, looking at me, her eyes huger than ever.

I felt a lump form in my throat. Shelly had told me that just after she found out she was pregnant with Mia, Jared was shot on duty. He was lucky the guy shooting at him had bad eyesight and had only got him in the leg, but Shelly had a hard time with it. It could easily have been so much worse.

I looked at Riley. What if it was him? I suddenly understood why he was worried about me.

"Lizzie is getting counseling," Riley said. "She's seeing Allison Greene." He took my hand and squeezed it.

"The same Allison Greene who was once your girlfriend Allison Abbott?" asked Jared, incredulously.

Riley nodded.

"And you went to see her?" Shelly asked, staring at me.

I nodded. "I didn't know who she was at the time," I said quietly.

"You aren't going back to her, are you?" asked Shelly, shocked.

"Why shouldn't Lizzie see her?" asked Anna. "She's a very good psychiatrist. Allison has done very well for herself you know."

"Yes, but that's like a conflict of interests or something, isn't it?" asked Shelly, her eyes wide with disbelief.

"Why would you say that?"

"Well, because Lizzie is Riley's girlfriend now. Don't you think that would be uncomfortable?"

"Lizzie has an appointment tomorrow," said Riley.

Hang on, how did he know that?

"Oh really? Well that's good," said Anna. "Did I mention Allison phoned me a few days ago? She wanted your number, Riley."

"And you gave it to her?" I asked, my voice getting slightly higher as I felt the agitation grow.

"Well, of course I did," laughed Anna as if I had just asked a stupid question.

I looked at Shelly, whose eyebrows had disappeared into her hairline. "Why did she want Riley's number?" she asked.

"Oh, she said that she'd run into him and that he'd mentioned how they should catch up some time, but he'd left before she'd got his number."

"Really?" I said, dropping my fork onto my plate. "You wanted to catch up with her?"

"Of course not, I was just being polite. You know, it's just a phrase like 'how are you?', 'what's happening?' I didn't really want to know."

"*How are you* is a lot different to asking someone to catch up sometime." The jealousy monster reared its ugly head.

"It's nothing to worry about, Lizzie," said Anna, defending her oldest son. "Riley didn't mean any harm."

"Well, I know I wouldn't be happy about it if Jared had said that to an old girlfriend," added Shelly, giving me some back up.

Jared shifted uncomfortably in his seat.

"You wouldn't actually say that to one of them, would you?" she asked, turning to him.

"I'm with Riley on this one," he said. Looks like the Thomas' stick together. "It's not like he's going to date her again or anything. I mean the only thing I ever really liked about Allison was her legs. She had the most amazing long legs." Jared flashed Riley a smile.

"You noticed that, did you?" asked Riley, smiling broadly. "You know it's not polite to check out your brother's girlfriend?"

"Yeah, I know, but you have to admit they were pretty magnificent legs." Shelly punched Jared in the arm.

Riley laughed.

I sat there watching the banter between brothers and felt invisible.

"How did you enjoy the salmon quiche, Lizzie?" asked Anna, smiling at her boys, and then changing the subject. "I'm happy to give you the recipe if you'd like it."

"Um...it was lovely, thank you," I lied. I'd actually passed it to Riley when nobody was looking. "It was...umm...very tasty. Delicious," I added, hoping she would forget that comment and never ever cook it for me again. I refused to meet Riley's eye, but I could feel his mega-watt smile from here.

"Have some more," she added. "There's a lot left. Riley, pass the plate to Lizzie will you?"

"Sure." Riley reached across the table and picked up the quiche dish. Putting it in front of me he asked, "How much would you like?"

I met his eye and felt my face flush. "Oh no, thank you. I'm full. Thanks anyway."

"You can't be full," he added. "You hardly had any." His smile was at full wattage. Bastard.

"No really. I've had plenty, thank you."

He put the plate down. "Okay. We'll ask for leftovers. Maybe you'd like it for lunch tomorrow?" I glared at him. He'd pay for that later and when I say pay for that later, I didn't mean the same thing he meant when he said it. In fact I meant the exact opposite. His smile faltered slightly. "On second thoughts, maybe Jared should have it. It's his favorite and I wouldn't want to deprive him."

§.

AFTER DINNER, Jared and I cleared the table as Mia was unsettled and only wanted her mum. Anna had offered to help, but Jared had insisted he'd do it. Mal and Riley were deep in conversation about a job Riley had put a tender in for, so Jared and I collected all the plates and moved to the kitchen. I placed my pile in the sink and turned the water on to rinse them.

"I'll let you pack the dishwasher," I said to Jared.

"Sure, I'm a pro at it anyway. Years of practice." Jared ran his fingers through his hair and moved awkwardly next to me at the sink, his mannerisms identical to Riley's.

I looked at their resemblance and smiled. Jared had the same blond hair and toned body Riley had, but he was slightly shorter and had slightly less vibrant eyes. He was still drop-dead gorgeous though. I sighed thinking how I really needed to take better care of myself. If I still wanted to be with Riley when I was old I needed to do something fast. I've seen my genetic heritage and let me tell you Grandma is so wrinkly she reminds me of a Shar Pei.

"Hey Lizzie, I just wanted to say sorry for my comments about Allison earlier. Shelly told me it was a bit insensitive." My stomach jumped at Allison's name.

"Don't worry about it. I'm not bothered," I lied. I could hardly tell Jared how insecure I felt next to Allison.

"She was never suited to Riley anyway. Not like you are."

I smiled at Jared's attempt to make me feel better. "Really it's okay. You don't need to say anything."

"But it's true. I've never known Riley to be so contented and happy as he is with you."

I stopped what I was doing and looked at Jared. "Do you mean that or are you just trying to be nice?" I asked. The truth was, earlier he had been insensitive but I really liked Jared.

"I mean it. If you believe in soul mates, I think you're his."

Okay, Jared was forgiven for this and every other thing he may do to me in his lifetime.

"Thanks," I said unable to hide my smile. We worked silently together for a few minutes.

"I was thinking also about that skeleton they pulled out of your garden. Do you want me to look into it for you?"

"I'd love you to, but Riley wants me to stay out of it."

"What do you want to do?"

"I want to know who it belonged to and why it was there. I know it happened years before I was born, but I'm still curious."

"I'll see what I can find out about it. Who was the local officer who did the initial investigation?"

"The only one that I know by name is Ed Helms. He seems really nice and helpful. He gave me his number in case I needed it. I can give it to you if you like?" I added.

"I'll just call the station."

"No worries, but if you need it, he gave me his personal number as well."

Jared stopped and looked down at me. "Wow, does Riley know this guy is interested in you?"

"What?"

"We only ever give out our personal numbers to people we find interesting. I'd say Officer Ed Helms has his eye on you."

"Don't be stupid, Jared. He knows I'm with Riley."

"Doesn't stop a man trying though, does it?"

I sighed. I certainly hoped it did. I did not need any more complications in my life.

THANKFULLY WE GOT out of there without me embarrassing myself. I came close when I went to kiss Mal on the cheek but didn't know what cheek to go for. He seemed undecided also, and I ended up planting a kiss smack bang on his lips. Nobody else seemed to notice so we both gave a small laugh and pretended it never happened.

I closed the door on Riley's truck and clicked my seatbelt into place. As he closed his door he looked at me and smiled.

"So are you always going to kiss my dad like that or was this a special occasion?"

Damn. I'd almost gotten away with it. "It was a special occasion," I replied.

"For future reference Dad always goes for the right cheek."

Riley laughed as he turned the truck around and headed for home. We sat in comfortable silence for most of the trip, my mind going over the earlier conversation about Allison and how Anna had given her Riley's number.

"How come you didn't tell me you were talking to Allison?" I asked eventually.

"She only phoned once. She was checking up on you, wanting to know when you were going to go back and see her. She's gone over your test and has the results."

"Oh." I looked out the side window at the streetlights flashing as we passed. Riley shifted in his seat.

"If you're not comfortable seeing her we can find someone else for you," he said.

I turned to face him, relief flooding through me.

"You wouldn't mind?"

"Of course I wouldn't mind, but I did check around and Mum's right, she's very good at what she does. I want you to see the best, Lizzie." Riley reached out and took my hand in his. I looked into his face and felt my heart squeeze. I knew he only wanted the best for me, but why did it have to be her?

CHAPTER 8

*T*he following morning dawned overcast and stormy but thankfully the rain held off as Riley and I made our way back to my house ready for another day of work.

I had my follow-up appointment with Allison today and I had put extra effort into my appearance. Molly had dropped a carefully selected dress from her wardrobe to me on her way to work. It was pale blue and fitted, skimming my knee and showing just enough cleavage to be classy. I paired it with my low strappy heels and added an extra layer of mascara. And with the miracle of a hair straightener, my hair fell in soft, silky layers around my face and down my back. The last thing I needed was for it to rain, whereby my beautiful swishy hair would swell and frizz, and once again become an unruly mess. I groaned as I opened my back door and stepped outside, looking up at the clouds that seemed to be getting darker by the minute.

I moved to the table, put my coffee down on it and sighed, dread sitting heavily in my stomach. Cat jumped up onto the deck and sat at my feet. I'd thought about leaving him at Riley's today, but I knew he preferred it here where he could roam outside safely and poop in my neighbor Hazel's flowerbeds. That was something I should somehow stop him doing, but seriously how do you stop a cat doing anything it wants...especially when the cat in question was old and slightly cantankerous.

I crouched down and stroked his back as he purred and rubbed himself against me. This lasted all of five seconds, when he suddenly turned, scratched my leg with his claws and took off across the garden towards the old garage. What the hell he did in there had me beat.

"Ow!" I cried, looking at the blood appearing on my leg. "What was that for?"

"Sorry, Lizzie. What did I do?" I looked up to see Bradley standing on the grass, frowning at me. I hadn't even heard him turn up.

"Oh, hi Bradley. Sorry I wasn't talking to you." He was followed by a group of what appeared to be Japanese tourists. "Not your usual group of senior citizens," I commented, nodding towards them.

Bradley grinned, his schoolboy like face lighting up. "Yeah, they all turned up this morning wanting to see your house. Apparently you're on the Internet. I haven't had time to check it out yet, but I will later today. I hadn't actually thought to advertise that way, but it's probably something I should look into."

"You're kidding, right?"

He looked perplexed. "No. Why would I kid about that?"

"How many stops do you actually have on this tour?" I asked.

"Ummm...a few."

"Maybe I should book Grandma Mabel on it."

"Oh, old George would love that. I think he has a crush on you, you know." Bradley grinned.

"You're sick."

"I'm serious!" said Bradley, laughing. "He's already been on this tour three times."

"Three times?" I asked incredulously. Bradley nodded. "I knew I'd seen George here before."

"He's booked again to come tomorrow. I'm not sure if he'll turn up now that he's got your grannie's phone number though. He can probably get closer to you through her." Bradley thought he was hilarious. Humph.

"You should really feed your tourists before you start your tour," I commented. We looked around at the group. The leader had a loaf of Turkish bread she was tearing apart and handing out to the group. Her helper walked behind her with a jar of peanut butter and a knife, allowing whoever wanted some to spread as much as they wanted onto their bread. A second helper was doing the same but she was offering strawberry jam.

"I guess they missed breakfast," shrugged Bradley.

I smiled and left Bradley to go back to his group, but instead of going inside the house, I sat quietly and listened to his spiel.

"Okay folks, gather round," he called.

The head of the group must also have been the translator as she immediately started to call to the group in Japanese. Seconds later they all gathered around Bradley.

He straightened his jacket and smiled. "Well, as you know this site is of great interest to the town of Westport after a sixty-five-year-old skeleton was dug up from this very spot. The reason why it was there is still unknown, but a source told me that it could belong to a missing person from 1949..."

Really? How come Bradley could get this kind of information? I made a note to ask him as soon as the tour was over.

"...and that's about all we know so far, but make sure to keep up to date with the investigations via my video diary I'll be starting today. I'll be checking in daily with all the latest information."

Applause broke out as Bradley beamed back at his group. I added *check Bradleys' video diary* to my To Do list.

"Feel free to wander around the site and take as many photos as you like. And for anyone who may be interested the owner of the house, Lizzie is with us today." Bradley waved in my direction.

Shit.

The group turned towards me and lifted their cameras. As the sound of nineteen digital SLR's clicked I had no choice but to smile and wave. Bloody Bradley.

"Would anyone like to ask Lizzie any questions?" he asked.

Immediately all nineteen group members shouted in Japanese. By the time all nineteen members had asked me their questions (seriously every single one of them pretty much asked the same thing—when will they see it dance? *What the...?)* and the leader of the group had translated the questions and the answers, I tried to signal Bradley that I wanted to ask *him* a question, but I had to wait. Everyone wanted a photo with me. I sighed. I was going to be very late for my appointment with Allison.

When my face started to hurt from all the smiling (actually it was quite fun) I grabbed Bradley by the arm.

"I want to talk to you," I hissed.

"I'm sorry, Lizzie. It just kind of popped out of my mouth."

"What did?"

"Telling the group that you were there and did they want to ask you a question." Bradley looked at me with his big eyes reminding me of a scared puppy.

"Oh, well that's something else I wanted to talk to you about," I said remembering to add that to the list. "First off, I want to know your source."

"My what?"

"Your source. You know, the person who gave you the info about the missing person?"

"Oh yeah, well sorry Lizzie, but I can't tell you. That's confidential information."

"Confidential, my ass. Tell me who it was, or I'll have Riley ban you from my property." I crossed my arms over my chest in a 'don't-mess-with-me' stance I'd learned from Grandma.

Bradley's Adam's apple bobbed up and down at the sound of Riley's name. Honestly, Riley wouldn't hurt a soul but Bradley didn't need to know that.

"Lizzie, I want to tell you, I really do. But if word gets around I've blabbed, who's going to tell me the gossip anymore?"

"The tourists won't like only being able to see this site from the road, will they?"

It was Bradley's turn to sigh.

"You're a hard woman, Lizzie Fuller."

I smiled. He was so easy to manipulate.

Bradley leaned in close and whispered in my ear. Seriously, what was this?

"It was an old man in the pub. He told me he remembered a person going missing in 1949 and he believed there was something fishy going on over here at the time. I worked it out and that's about the time that the bones were buried." Bradley stopped and looked at me.

"And?"

"And that's it."

"Who was this old man?"

"I think his name was Bob. Or something like that anyway."

"Bob?"

"Yep, Bob."

I sighed. "Bob who?"

"Just Bob."

"Which pub was he at?"

"Grinning Dog on Elm Street near the dance hall."

"What did Bob look like?"

"Old.

"Bradley!"

"Okay, okay, don't yell. The tourists are looking. He was old, sort of short, bald head, but he wore a turtleneck. I thought that was kind of odd. I mean the temperature's in the high thirties and there he is in a turtleneck. Poor guy must have been boiling. I asked him about it and he said he had some scarring and didn't like people to see it, so he kept it covered." Bradley shrugged. "That's it. That's all I know."

"Thanks."

"So you won't talk to Riley?"

"Not for the moment."

Bradley shook his head and turned back to his group, his shoulders sagging.

I looked at my watch and realized I was now *very* late for my appointment with Allison. Bugger. I ran to my Mini and hoped Riley didn't hear the motor and check the time, and if he did, I hoped he would have forgotten about it by the time I got back.

WHEN I REACHED Allison's office, I had missed my appointment altogether. She was just finishing up a phone call as I walked in. She looked up at me and waved for me to take a seat.

"Okay...no, it was fantastic talking to you...yes, I will..." She giggled, obviously flirting. I wondered who she was talking to.

I watched her as she spoke, casually tucking a stray hair behind her ear as she did so. Today she was wearing a dress in the same shade of blue as I was. It was very similar to the one I was wearing, but hers looked a hell of a lot more stylish on her than mine did on me. I ran my fingers through my hair and attempted to smooth the frizzies that popped up.

"You have an awesome afternoon won't you...okay, bye!" Allison finished the call, and put the phone back into place on the desk, her smile huge, showing her perfectly straight teeth. She turned to me.

"Lizzie, did you forget your appointment?" She laughed lightly.

"Umm, no I just got held up. Sorry."

"That's okay. I was just talking to Riley and told him that even though I couldn't fit you in for another appointment, I would take you out to lunch. We may not be able to get too personal, but at least we can get to know each other. On a friendly basis."

I felt the saliva in my mouth dry up. "You…you were speaking to Riley?"

"Yes, I was worried when you didn't turn up. I thought he would know where you were. You don't mind that I called him, do you?"

"No. Why would I mind?" I smiled. *Of course I bloody mind!*

"That's good. Some women might feel threatened by an ex-girlfriend, but I assure you that you have nothing to worry about. I can tell how much he loves you just by looking at him."

I felt myself relax slightly. Of course Riley loved me, and I had absolutely no reason to doubt that.

"Now, there's a little family-run cafe just down the road from here that makes the yummiest food. I thought we could go there for lunch. My treat," she continued.

Before I had the chance to respond, she picked up her handbag, walked to the door, and turned the sign to 'Closed'. She then opened it and waited for me to walk out first.

"We'll take my car. It's parked just over there."

I looked at where she pointed, and saw the sleek silver Mercedes parked in the shade under a tree. The car reminded me of the one my ex–boyfriend, Scott drove. It's funny, but Allison made me feel the exact same way Scott had—stupid and insignificant—even though I couldn't pinpoint why. She was nice enough to me. Maybe it was just my own insecurities and jealousy making me feel that way. I decided I should give her the benefit of the doubt and followed her to the car, her heels clicking on the cement as we went.

As she beeped the doors open, I got in the passenger side. "New car?" I asked, trying to be friendly.

"I've had it two months. It's nice isn't it?" she asked, without any pretention.

"It's gorgeous." I shuffled on the seat trying to get my skirt under me as the leather felt quite warm against my legs. *Broomph*.

Allison giggled.

I felt the heat flush my face. "Oh um...that was my leg on the seat," I explained.

"It's okay. You don't have to explain. It's just us girls, no one has to know."

"But I didn't—you know?" How did you say that to someone who you were insecure around? Do you say 'fart' or do you say 'pass wind'?

"Honestly, it's okay Lizzie," said Allison, winding her window down. I groaned and sank into my seat.

The café she selected was only a five-minute drive away but as it started to rain, I was grateful we were driving and not walking. As she pulled into a car park, I tried to judge how far away the door to the café was and thought if I ran, I'd be able to make it without getting my hair too wet. I waited for Allison to get out first and then made a run for it. She gracefully opened her umbrella and followed me across the road, dodging puddles as she went.

We went inside and I followed her to a table at the back of the room. The café was sweet really, decorated in French provincial style quite popular at the moment. The smells drifting out from the kitchen made my stomach rumble. I remembered I'd actually missed breakfast this morning as my stomach had been churned up at the thought of my meeting with Allison.

Sitting down, we picked up our menus and I took the moment to study her close up. It bothered me that I recognized her from somewhere but couldn't remember where.

"You know, Allison I'm sure I know you from somewhere," I said.

"Really? I wouldn't know where." She looked at me and smiled innocently.

I had a sneaking suspicion she did know where but didn't

want to say. "It'll come to me. It always does. Probably late at night when I'm trying to sleep, it'll just randomly pop into my head."

Allison smiled and busied herself with the menu. I looked at the menu in my hand and the chicken burger instantly appealed to me.

"What do you feel like, Lizzie?"

"Oh the burger sounds delicious," I replied, reading as I went. But then so did schnitzel. And the turkey wrap. I made a note to bring Riley here for lunch one day. He'd love the steak sandwich.

"Alright well, I'll go and order then," said Allison before I had a chance to change my mind.

"Oh, you don't have to pay for my lunch. Thanks anyway, but I can get it."

"No, really I insist. It's my treat." She stood and moved to the counter, her tiny ponytail bouncing as she walked.

"Oh Allison, can you just check the chef doesn't cook with peanut oil please? I'm allergic to it."

"Really? What sort of reaction do you have?"

"Oh, it's not pretty. My lips swell, my tongue swells and I get all blotchy and red."

"Well, that doesn't sound pleasant. Definitely no peanut oil then."

As she moved back up the queue, my memory stirred.

"I know!" I yelled.

"Pardon," she said, turning back to face me.

"I know where I know you from." I sat back in my chair and smiled. "You were at the auction when I bought my house. I remember because I was so impressed that you could get your hair into such a short ponytail."

"I think you must have me confused for someone else," she said, her smile tight.

"No, I'm positive that it was you."

"Really, Lizzie, I think you're mistaken. I wasn't at the auction. Why would I be?"

"But…" I petered out. I didn't know why she would be, or why she would lie about it. I shrugged.

Allison smiled and turned back to the queue, her posture rigid. Confused, I looked around the café and thought back to the day of the auction—the day I had bought my house.

I suppose I could be wrong about Allison. I mean that day was quite stressful and I was focusing on the auctioneer. There had only been one other registered bidder—an older gentleman who wanted it as a development site, but I remember the woman who I thought was Allison. She'd spent the whole time standing under the tree in the front yard, her agitation showing. The real estate agent selling the house had told me there was another interested party, but they hadn't got their finances together quickly enough. You couldn't bid at auction unless you had the money or finance approved up front.

"Lizzie," said Allison, calling to me from her place in the queue. I jumped as her voice pulled me back to the present. "I think I forgot to put money in the parking meter. Do you think you could check it for me while I order lunch?"

I looked across the road to the car and sighed. It was now pouring with rain. Could I just sit here and not go? Surely we could get away without paying for parking just once?

"Please?" she called. "I have another client in less than an hour and if I don't order our food now we won't get it in time."

"Sure." Well, there goes the straight hair.

I got up and moved to the door and stepped into the rain. By the time I had waited for the traffic, crossed the road, saw she *had* actually put the money in the meter, and had gotten back again, I was soaked. And freezing.

"Oh, you silly thing," said Allison sitting back in the seat opposite me, placing a glass of water on the table in front of me.

"You're soaking wet." She was observant if nothing else. "You should have taken my umbrella."

Yes, I should have.

"Didn't think of that, did I?" I smiled to cover my embarrassment caused by my own stupidity.

"Why? Why didn't you think of that, Lizzie?" Allison placed her elbows on the table, put her hands under her chin, and looked at me seriously. I felt discomfited.

"Ummm...because I'm an idiot?"

"Oh Lizzie, you're funny. I was just joking," she laughed, waving her hand in front of her. "But then...no. Just joking again."

She laughed like she was hilarious. I didn't find her funny at all.

"Now drink up and tell me what's happening with that old house of yours. Is it nearly finished?"

I spent the next five minutes sipping water, shivering against the cold of the air conditioning and telling Allison all about my renovations, grateful to be speaking about something I actually knew.

"I intend to sell it once it's finished," I said, finishing my monologue.

"Riley tells me you've done an excellent job choosing the décor and fittings."

He did, did he? "Riley's really kind. He's the one doing all the hard work and bringing the old house back to life."

"Riley *is* really kind," Allison said quietly. "He's probably the kindest, sweetest man I've ever had the pleasure of knowing."

My heart stuttered as she spoke, but I was saved from responding as our food arrived at the table. I looked at my burger, which was almost the size of the plate and was accompanied by a pile of delicious golden chips, and my stomach growled. I looked at Allison's Caesar salad and felt embarrassed...again.

"I hope you're hungry." She smiled, looking at my plate. "I

admire any woman who can eat like that. There's a week's worth of calories there." She laughed, but I felt the atmosphere shift and knew she was having a dig at me.

"I'm lucky like that I guess," I said, holding my head high. "I do of course watch my weight at times, but mostly I can eat whatever I want." That was a total lie. If I ate whatever I wanted, I would be about the size of my house.

"Well enjoy it. It looks delicious," she added.

I looked at my burger and debated which was the best way to eat it. I couldn't pick it up and take a bite as it would never fit in my mouth. I lifted the top off and opted to use a knife and fork. Sure it felt a bit weird eating a burger with a knife and fork, but if nothing else I looked a whole lot more lady like, and Molly's dress may make it home without beetroot dropped down the front of it.

"Riley loved it here," said Allison, pushing her salad onto her fork and taking a delicate bite.

The chicken stuck in my throat.

"We used to come here all the time. The steak sandwich was his favorite." She smiled at the memory.

I picked up my water glass and took a gulp, trying to push the food down my throat.

"Are you okay? You're not choking are you?" she asked, her concern evident on her face.

It probably wouldn't look good if one of her clients choked to death during a lunch date. I managed to get the chicken down, my eyes watering as I did so. "No," I choked. "I'm fine thanks. Just went down the wrong way."

"Well that's good. I'd hate to have to tell Riley that I'd killed you with your lunch."

Liar. You'd love it. "Yeah, he'd be a bit upset I imagine." I laughed unconvincingly.

"Riley would be upset, Lizzie. He's a very sensitive man. It's actually one of the things I loved the most about him." My heart stopped with her words.

"Are you still in love with him?' I asked, the words jumping out my mouth before I could stop them. I held my breath and waited for her reply.

She took her time to consider her response. "It doesn't really matter, does it? He loves you. That's what's important."

She placed her hand over mine in a friendly gesture. I felt the undertone. I wanted to question her more about it, but I honestly couldn't find the words. She was a threat and if she had the chance she would be back in Riley's life in every conceivable way.

My burger suddenly lost its appeal. I put my knife and fork down and nibbled on a few of the chips as we finished our lunch, my end of the conversation deliberately avoiding Riley. If only Allison had felt the same.

Instead I had to endure listening to her crunch on her salad, reminiscing about Riley. I looked at the door and wondered if I could actually be rude enough to leave, and how long it would take me to walk home.

CHAPTER 9

*I*t happened even before we'd finished lunch. I could feel my lips tingling and my tongue start to swell. I picked up my water and finished what was left in the glass. *Oh no.* The last time I felt like this, I found out I had an allergy to peanut oil.

Allison looked at me, her expression quizzical. "Are you alright?" she asked.

"Umm...not really," I replied. "I'm feeling a bit hot."

"Your face is covered in red blotches."

"You did ask them about the peanut oil, didn't you?"

"Of course I did. Do you think you are having an allergic reaction?"

I hoped not, but within minutes my lips had swollen to the point where they hurt, and I could no longer speak properly. Tears stung my eyes as I struggled to control my breathing and not panic.

"Oh," I heard Allison say. She grabbed at a passing waiter. "Excuse me, but this woman is having an allergic reaction. Can someone call for an ambulance, please?"

She said it all very calmly. Well, I guess that was because she wasn't the one swelling like a puffer fish.

The waiter gave me a horrified look and rushed towards a woman behind the counter, his arms waving towards me as he spoke. I saw her grab at the phone.

Within seconds, chaos erupted around me. I had waiters running about, the chef had appeared, and Allison was yelling at the top of her voice about how irresponsible they were serving a dish cooked in peanut oil when she had specifically told them I was allergic to it.

The waitress that had taken our order was in tears, shaking her head and saying she never heard her say that.

"Of course I said it!" yelled Allison. "This poor woman could die. I'm a doctor. Do you really think I would be that irresponsible?"

"If you're a doctor then help her!" said the chef.

Allison glared at him. "I'm not that kind of a doctor," she said calmly.

The last time I'd had a reaction to peanut oil, all I'd had was swollen lips and tongue. When I breathed through my nose, I had no difficulty whatsoever. This time I could feel my throat closing. It all happened so fast, I didn't even have time to panic. Seconds later, I felt weak and the room faded as confusion filled my mind. I heard a woman scream as I slipped off my chair and fell to the floor, the world momentarily going black.

When I opened my eyes, I was looking into the face of a paramedic. He was speaking to me in a calm voice, all the while jabbing me with a needle. I couldn't make out what he was saying, but I didn't care. An oxygen mask was put over my face as I was lifted onto a gurney and wheeled out to the waiting ambulance.

I HATED HOSPITALS. In fact, the very thought of having to go there made me break out in a sweat. Paramedic Jim asked me how I was feeling. Apparently anxiety wasn't helped by adrenalin, he told me.

Allison had followed me to the ER, and was waiting for Riley as a team of medical staff assessed my condition. It seemed that Paramedic Jim may have saved my life by administering said adrenalin just in time. They did also recommend that from now on I carry an auto-injector so that if this ever happened again, adrenalin could be given immediately and I'd survive without all the drama.

Sounded simple enough, but the doctor wasn't the one who had been struggling to breathe. The way I figured it, even with the adrenalin auto-injector, I'd still be freaked out enough to panic.

Thankfully, Riley arrived quickly. Just seeing his gorgeous face made the whole experience a lot more bearable, but feeling his strong arms hold me, the stress of the day took hold and the tears flowed.

"Thank God you're okay," he said, holding me tightly against his chest.

"I...was...s...so...scared," I sobbed.

"That makes two of us," said Allison, standing at the foot of my bed, her grey eyes huge.

"Thank you so much for your help, Allison. I'm scared to think what would have happened to Lizzie if you hadn't been there."

Really? I know things were a bit hazy and blurry at the time, but I didn't remember Allison doing very much to help, to be honest.

"Well, all's well that ends well. Isn't that what they say?" she replied.

"Yeah, thank goodness." Riley kissed the top of my head and released his hold on me.

I didn't want him too. Being held that tightly made me feel safe and secure, and I wanted to stay there

Just then my curtain was pulled back and a nurse entered our cubicle.

"Excuse me," said Riley, addressing her. "What happens now? Does Lizzie have to stay in for a while or can she go home?"

"She needs to stay for a few more hours just so we can keep an eye on her vital signs. If she responds the way we think she will, she'll be able to go home later this afternoon."

"Thanks." I heard the sigh of relief leave Riley, as he smiled.

I saw her swoon but she quickly regained her composure and checked a few machines I was hooked up to, wrote a few things down and left, leaving the curtain open as she went. I looked up to see Paramedic Jim smiling at me.

"You're looking much better," he said, moving closer to my bed.

"Thanks to you, apparently." I smiled. I didn't really know what to say to this man. The words *thank you* didn't feel adequate, but they were all I had.

"Thank you," I said, the tears welling once again.

"You, my lovely lady, are very welcome. You had me worried there for a minute, though. I thought we may not have got to you in time."

"Riley, this is the man who helped Lizzie at the café," said Allison, smiling brightly at Jim.

Riley instantly rushed to him, his hand outstretched.

"What can I say that will convey how grateful I am?"

"You don't need to say anything. I'm just happy this lovely lady is okay," said Jim, taking Riley's hand.

"Well, thank you." Riley, too, seemed at a loss for words.

"You stay away from peanut oil from now on, okay?" said Jim, smiling at me. "I don't want to see you in the back of my ambulance again anytime soon."

"I was staying away from it. Or at least I thought I was." I looked to Allison and wondered if she had actually passed the message to the waitress about my allergy. Of course she had. No one could be that mean.

Could they?

❧

THE REST of the week went past in a bit of a blur as I helped Riley gut the kitchen. By the time Friday came around, I was exhausted. Every muscle I had ached, including the muscles in my little toe. Actually, that had more to do with the hammer I dropped on it, but Riley told me it wasn't broken so I sucked up the pain and hobbled around silently. Well, my version of silent anyway.

I was just thinking about relaxing in a nice hot bath when my phone rang. It was my brother Danny.

"Hi Danny," I said.

"What's happening tonight?" he asked, getting straight to the point.

Friday night was the usual night I got together with my siblings. It was kind of a ritual. Sure, we saw each other every Sunday at Mum's for family dinner night, but Friday was the night we could all get together and discuss the subjects you couldn't talk about in front of Mum.

"Aren't we going to your house?"

"No. Andrew's mum's here and I need a night out. She's driving me crazy."

I laughed. "Well, what about Molly's? Can we go there?"

"I can't get hold of her. What about Riley's place? Can we meet there?"

"Yeah, okay. He won't be home until late because he's got a meeting with a client. Apparently tonight is the only night they could do it." I sighed. Friday nights were sacred to me. I hated it when he had to work.

"Oh, okay. Well, Andrew won't be there either so it's just the three of us. We'll have fun without them."

"Yeah, I'll text Molly and tell her where to be."

"See you soon."

After I hung up the phone and sent a message to Molly, I kissed Riley and headed to his house for a quick clean up before my visitors arrived.

I'd only just finished when there was a knock on the door. I ran down the stairs and opened the door to find Danny. Today he was dressed in his usual skinny jeans, which he'd accompanied with a bright yellow T-shirt and his hair was slicked back showing his diamond earring off to perfection. Ever stylish was Danny.

"Wow, you're bright today," I commented as he handed me a bottle of wine and pushed his way past me.

"I get sick and tired of wearing black at work so I have to make up for it on my time off. Besides that, Andrew's mother hates yellow and it annoyed the hell out of her." Danny smiled wickedly.

"I thought you liked Andrew's mother," I said, closing the door and moving to the kitchen to put the wine in the fridge.

"That was before she lived with us."

"How long is she staying for?"

"Too bloody long. It was only supposed to be for a week, but Andrew's concerned about her health as she's getting a bit older now. He's trying to talk me into letting her live with us." Danny followed me, sitting on a stool at the kitchen bench.

I looked at him shocked. "What about his dad? Where's he?"

"He went back home, quite happy to leave her with us for a while."

I looked closer at Danny and for the first time saw the strain around his eyes.

"Is she really that hard to live with?"

"You have no idea, Lizzie," said Danny, his eyes filling with tears. "She hates my cooking, says I can't clean for shit, and she even complained about the hairdo I gave her! I spent all bloody afternoon on that."

I sucked in my breath. You could complain to Danny about a lot of things and he would accept the criticism in the spirit it was given, but never, ever complain about his hairdressing abilities.

"Danny, you're an amazing hairdresser," I said, giving him a quick hug.

"I know! Look what I can do with your hair," he said, flicking his tears away.

Humph.

Before we got any further with our conversation, there was another knock on the door. This time it was Molly.

As I stepped back to let her in, I noticed she was a bit over-dressed for the occasion. She wore a very short dress, it looked like she'd been poured into and it barely covered her ass. Her abundant assets sat proud, ready to give any man a heart attack. Her hair was piled high on her head, ensuring the view of those assets was unobstructed, and her make-up was perfect, but very overdone for a night of pizza and wine with her siblings. She kicked off her spiked heels and barefooted it across the room towards the kitchen, placing a bottle of wine on the counter top.

Danny looked up from blowing his nose and frowned. "God girl, you look like a pole dancer."

"Geez, thanks Danny," she responded, glaring at him.

"You are a bit over-dressed, don't you think?" I added.

"I'm not staying. I'm heading into the city to that new club they've just opened."

"Are you the entertainment?" asked Danny, looking at her skirt as she pulled it a bit lower.

Molly sucked in her breath. I giggled. "No, I am *not* the entertainment!" she cried indignantly.

I had to admit, but Danny had a point. "Who's your date?"

She turned to me, and her scowl changed to a smile. "Matt."

"Where's Harper?" I asked. "Don't you want me to have him if you're staying in the city tonight?"

"Oh no, I'm not staying. It's only my first date with Matt, so I thought it would be best if I didn't drink too much and drove home later."

"Yeah, you don't want to give him the wrong idea," added Danny sarcastically, now looking at her chest.

Molly rolled her eyes and walked back to the door, stepping into her heels as she went.

"I only stopped by to leave the wine. I felt bad ditching you guys tonight."

DESPITE THE RADIANT smile she was wearing, I knew she genuinely felt bad for missing out on our get together.

"Well, have a good time," I said, kissing her on the cheek and getting a noseful of the new Roberto Cavalli perfume as I did so.

"I will," she replied, her eyes twinkling.

"And drive safe," I called after her as she almost skipped to her car.

Once she'd left, Danny and I ordered a pizza, filled our wine glasses from Molly's bottle of wine, and sat on the floor with my laptop, Googling her date Matt Wilson. We found he was a reporter with the Westport Television Network newsroom, he was thirty-four years old and had moved to Westport a year ago. Before that he'd been working overseas.

"Why would he have left New York to move to Westport and work for our crappy local newsroom?" asked Danny.

"I have no idea. I was actually wondering if I could get Molly to ask him to do some investigating in the news archives about the skeleton they dug up from my garden. Bradley gave me some interesting information the other day about a missing person he thinks was the original owner of the bones."

Danny turned to look at me, his eyebrows raised. "What kind of information?"

"Well he didn't have a lot to tell, only that an old man at the pub told him about a guy who went missing around the time that those bones were buried."

"What else did the old guy have to say?"

"I have no idea. That's all Bradley could tell me."

"Why don't you go to the pub and ask the old guy yourself?"

"Maybe...Riley wants me to stay out of it, though. He already hates my nightmares and he thinks this will only make them worse."

"The mystery of the skeleton in the garden would give me more nightmares."

"Is that what you're calling it is it?"

"Yep, it's like a *Famous Five* novel. *The Mystery of the Skeleton In The Garden,*" Danny added dramatically. "Do you remember those books Grandma gave you as a kid?"

I nodded. "They were my favorite."

Danny took a swig of his wine. "We could be the *Famous Five,*" he said excitedly. "We'd have to leave Riley out of it of course."

"*Famous Five?*" I questioned.

"Yeah...me, you, Andrew, Molly and Harper."

I shrugged. It sounded like a good idea, but then a lot of things sounded like a good idea after a glass of wine.

"Where do we start?" I asked.

Danny stood and put his glass on the coffee table. "We'll start at the pub. See if we can find this old guy and ask him what he knows. Come on, it'll be fun." He held out his hand for me to take. Pulling me to my feet, his excitement was contagious. "Which pub?" he asked.

"The Grinning Dog."

"Okay, you'll have to drive. I'm already on my third glass of wine."

"What about the pizza?"

"We'll drive past and pick it up."

"What about Riley?" I asked, biting my lip. "I don't want to upset him."

"We're only asking an eighty-year-old man to tell us a story. What harm can that cause? Besides, what he doesn't know won't hurt him."

"Okay, but if he gets angry you can say you're investigating and not me. I just tagged along for the ride."

"Sure. Whatever. Let's go."

❧

IT DIDN'T TAKE LONG to get to the pub, but it appeared that The Grinning Dog was a popular place on a Friday night. Now, I will confess to not being the most patient person in the world, so by the time I had followed a family to their car and waited while the dad carefully belted all the kids into their seats, then slowly got in himself and finally reversed out of the park, I was feeling quite agitated. Unlike Danny, I'd only had half a glass of wine and I was starting to worry about doing this behind Riley's back.

"I think you can do all the talking," I said to Danny, pulling the car into the spot and turning off the engine.

"Why? What's wrong with your voice?"

"Nothing, but you're Julian."

"What are you talking about?" Danny looked at me like I was crazy.

"*The Famous Five*. Remember? You can be Julian—the leader."

"Oh, but I don't want to be Julian. He was stuck up and boring. I want to be George. Or Dick. I liked Dick."

I looked at Danny and stifled a giggle. "Okay. You're a Dick," I said, opening my car door and stepping into the evening air. The evening had turned out quite humid and I welcomed getting back inside to the air conditioning. Danny quickly followed me as I walked towards the entrance doors and beeped the car locked.

"I heard that," he said. "And I am not *a* dick. I *am* Dick. He was the braver one, courageous and strong." Danny held his head high and walked ahead of me, opening the heavy glass door as I approached.

The Grinning Dog was more a family-friendly pub with a large restaurant at the front and the bar in the far corner. One side of the bar serviced the restaurant whilst the other side was the more traditional area with smaller tables and bar stools. A large Harley Davidson motorcycle sat in the center of the bar separating the two areas. I moved to a small round table in the furthest corner and pulled out a chair.

"So what does this guy look like?" asked Danny, moving to sit next to me.

"All Bradley could tell me was that he was in his eighties, bald-headed and wore a turtleneck."

"A turtleneck? It's like thirty degrees outside."

"Yeah, apparently he's got scarring or something and doesn't like people seeing it," I shrugged. Why he wore a turtleneck was really none of my business.

"Well go get me a drink and scope out the bar. I'll wait here and look around," said Danny, glancing around the room.

"Why do I have to buy the drinks?"

"Because this is your mystery."

I sighed. Fair enough. I stood and walked to the bar, scanning the crowd as I went. It didn't take long for me to spot the person we were looking for. He actually seemed to be the only person in here over the age of fifty. I ordered Danny a white wine and myself a coke, and moved back to the table.

"He's at the end of the bar, sitting alone," I said, handing Danny his drink.

"Yeah, I saw him. He's not alone though. He seems quite happy sitting next to that really ugly woman."

I smiled looking at the seven-foot tall statue of the dog

wearing a dress and lipstick, seductively sitting on the bar stool next to him. I guess that's why they call this the Grinning Dog.

"What do we do now?" asked Danny more seriously.

"You're Dick remember? You tell me." Danny picked up his drink and took a sip thoughtfully. We sat in silence for a few minutes, each lost in our own thoughts. "Maybe I should buy him a drink and ask to sit next to him?" I added.

"Sure. It's probably the closest he's come to getting lucky in a long time."

I whipped my head to look at Danny. "I'm not trying to pick him up!"

"Sounds like you are, but who am I to judge? If that's your thing then go for it. I reckon you'd be guaranteed to get the information you're after...providing he doesn't have a heart attack first."

Humph. "Well, what do you suggest?"

"I'd go the direct approach. Walk over there and ask him."

I looked at the man in question. He didn't look scary. In fact, he looked quite the opposite. He sat watching the football match showing on the big screen above the bar, his bald head reflecting the overhead lights. If anything, he looked lonely.

"If you talk to him then I won't actually be guilty of going behind Riley's back, will I?"

Danny looked at me and sighed. "If I do this for you, you'll owe me, okay?"

"Yep, no worries."

"You'll have to repay the favor in any way I see fit?"

"Sure...whatever you need, I'm your girl." That was a statement I knew I'd live to regret but right now, it seemed like the best choice.

"Alright, here goes."

Danny took the last swig of his drink and moved across the room to sit next to the old man. Now this is where I should mention that Danny's sexuality oozes out of him. There is no mistaking what his orientation is. The old man picked up on it immediately and shifted uncomfortably in his seat. I crossed my fingers and hoped he didn't think he was about to be chatted up.

Danny's skill at talking to people and making them feel at ease kicked in pretty quickly though, and within a minute the man relaxed and not surprisingly, he started to talk. I sat back and waited for Danny to return watching them closely for any clues. About ten minutes later, Danny returned smiling broadly.

"What did you find out?" I asked.

"I found out that Bert's wife died five years ago and that he's really lonely. His kids don't visit, even though I think they should. He had a heart attack a few months ago and they didn't even go to see him in the hospital. Spoilt brats...you work hard all your life to provide for them and that's what you get in return. Thank God I'm never having any." Danny sat and picked up his empty glass. "You didn't even buy me a drink?" he asked, incredulously.

"Danny, what useful information did you find out?"

"Lizzie, have some sensitivity. That old man is a person with feelings, you know!"

"Sorry, Danny. Would you like to invite him over for a drink with us?"

"I already did, but he's watching the game. I hate football so I left him to it."

"Did you ask about the missing person?"

"Of course I did, but he didn't tell me much more than you already know. Except I did find out that the house you are living in had a bit of scandal surrounding it in its day."

Now he had my interest. "Really? Like what?"

"There's rumors of an illegitimate child being born there."

"Really? How long ago?"

"About sixty five years." Danny's eye twinkled as he spoke. He loved gossip.

"That's about the same time the body was buried."

"Yeah, I know. It's also about the time of the missing person report."

"Did Bert say who the missing person was?"

"He said he couldn't remember the guy's name, but he did remember he worked for the local butcher and had a weird thing about stuffing things."

"Well that makes sense if he was a butcher. They stuff chickens all time." Personally I hated stuffing but Mum cooked with it all the bloody time.

"Yeah, but not that kind of stuffing. I mean, he stuffed animals like dogs and cats and put them on his mantle."

"Ooooh," I said, my lip curling. "Was his butchery very popular in the unusual meats section?"

Danny laughed. "Ha! Sometimes you can be quite funny, Lizzie."

I beamed. Danny never told me I was funny. Unfashionable—yes, unkempt—yes. He even complimented me once and told me I was pretty—but he had never told me I was funny.

"What do we do now?" I asked, sipping my drink.

"I think you should talk to that police officer who has the hots for you."

"Danny, he does not have the hots for me. And anyway, what happened to you doing the questioning so that Riley doesn't know I'm up to anything?"

"I'm pretty sure you'd get more out of the policeman than I would."

Yeah, but I bet if Danny had seen Officer Ed Helms, he wouldn't be arguing with me. "I'll think about it." I sighed and finished my drink, looking at the clock on the wall. "Anyway, I've got to go. Riley will be home soon."

"Yeah. I'd better get home to Andrew. Don't want him thinking I had too much fun without him."

We stood to leave and I followed Danny to the door. I looked around the restaurant as we passed and noticed the crowd had thinned out quite a bit. I guess as it was now just after nine pm, the mums and dads would have taken the kids home to bed. I smiled and was just about to walk through the door behind Danny when I stopped. My heart skipped a beat and I felt the air being sucked out of me as I looked into the far corner of the room and saw Riley. Sitting with a very beautiful looking Allison, her hand rubbing his forearm affectionately. He had his back to me so I couldn't see his face but it was definitely him. There was no mistaking it, especially when I heard his deep throaty laugh drift towards me across the room. Time stood still for a moment until I felt Danny grab my arm and drag me into the night air.

"Come on girl, hurry up. People are trying to get past you."

I snapped to and looked at Danny, my throat closing as I did. Riley had told me he had a meeting with a new client tonight, so what was he doing here with Allison?

"What's wrong?" asked Danny "You look sick. You're not going to throw up, are you?"

I shook my head, sat on the low wall running along the edge of the garden bed, and sunk my head between my knees. I sucked in air and tried to control the adrenalin rush that caused my hands to shake and my knees to wobble. Danny sat next to me.

"You look like you've seen a ghost," said Danny, placing his arm around my shoulders. He may seem abrupt and uncaring but Danny was actually one of the most caring men I knew.

"It was Riley. He was in there with Allison."

"His ex-girlfriend Allison?"

I nodded.

"Are you sure?"

I nodded again. Danny hugged me a little bit tighter and placed his head against mine.

"Maybe she's the new client he was seeing?" I hadn't thought of that.

"Do you think she could be?" I asked, lifting my head.

"I don't see why not. Riley's never lied to you before."

"But why didn't he tell me that's who he was meeting?" I asked quietly.

"Don't know. Maybe he was afraid of your response."

"Maybe."

"Do you want to go and talk to him?"

"No." From what I had seen they looked like the perfect happy couple. That was not something I wanted to see again. "I want to go home. I'll ask him about it later." Maybe.

"I can go in there and pretend to have run into him. Get a vibe on what's really happening," offered Danny.

I shook my head again. "I'm okay. It's probably nothing. I'm sure you're right anyway. She might be the new client."

"Alright, but I'm staying with you until he gets home."

"Thanks, I'd like that." At times Danny could be the best brother a girl could ever ask for.

CHAPTER 10

*I*t was late when Riley walked in the door. So late in fact that I had sent Danny home telling him I would be fine and I would call him if I needed him. I'd had a hot shower and put myself to bed. I'd closed my eyes and willed sleep to arrive and take away the picture of Riley and Allison together. My mind however, had other ideas.

Instead of sleep, it decided it was far better to play little scenes of the two of them together and what they could be up to. Like right now, I pictured Allison's long fingers running through his hair as she kissed him goodnight and I heard his blissful sigh as he snuggled into her neck, holding her tight. My mind wandered further down that path but I abruptly stopped it before it got too far. I already had to cope with the fact that Riley and Allison had actually been doing that at some point in history and that was torturous enough. I didn't need to actually see it in my own mind.

I gave up on sleep and wandered to the kitchen hoping a hot cup of cocoa would help relax me. I had just poured the milk into the cup when Riley unlocked the door and walked in. He looked happy and relaxed.

"Oh hey, I didn't expect you to still be awake," he said, moving to me and kissing me on the cheek. I discreetly sniffed at him, looking for the smell of perfume.

"Couldn't sleep." I smiled. "You're late," I commented, a knot forming in my stomach.

"Yeah, sorry, I caught up with some old friends of my dad's. They were chatty and I had a lot of trouble getting away."

"Oh, really? Is he the new client?" I looked up into Riley's face.

"No, I met the new client earlier. I was just leaving when I saw Richard and his wife, Debbie. They've been travelling a lot, and before I could stop him he'd pulled out his phone and was showing me all the photos he'd taken." Riley grinned.

"How did the meeting with the new client go?" I asked.

Riley turned his back to me and put his phone on the table along with his car keys. "It was okay. She wanted a quote for some renovations on a new house she's buying."

"Oh, are you going to do the job?"

"Maybe...I have to go and have a look at it tomorrow morning. She's just about to sign the purchase contract, but wanted an expert opinion before she did."

"Who was she?" I asked. He certainly didn't seem to be volunteering the information.

"No one important," he said, kissing my cheek. "How was your night? Did I miss anything fun?"

"No. It was just Danny and myself. Molly had a date with Matt."

"Where was Andrew?"

"At home, babysitting his mother."

"How was Danny though? What did you do?"

"We went out actually. We had a drink at the Grinning Dog." I watched Riley carefully to gauge his reaction.

"Really? I was at the Grinning Dog. I didn't see you there." Riley's answer threw me a little bit. If he'd been up to anything with Allison surely he wouldn't have said that? Should I tell him that I saw him? I felt my breath get shallow and come out in short sharp spurts as I debated what to do.

"Are you okay?" asked Riley. "You look a bit pale."

I stood and looked into his gorgeous blue eyes, the sound of his breathing calming me, and the delicious smell of Riley filling my senses, and before I could stop them, tears filled my lashes. Riley took my face in his hands.

"Lizzie, what's wrong? Did something happen?"

"I saw you," I whispered, the tears escaping and running down my cheeks. "I saw you with Allison." Riley sighed and pulled me in close. I could hear his heart beat through his shirt.

"There was nothing to see," he said, kissing the top of my head. "She's just a client."

"I know I'm being stupid, but I think she's still in love with you."

Riley stepped away from me, shocked. "Lizzie, she is not still in love with me. What I had with her was a long time ago, and I assure you there is nothing between us anymore."

"Then why has she asked you to do this job?"

"Because she wants the opinion of someone she trusts. Not someone who will tell her the house needs a million things it doesn't really need."

"Then recommend her to someone else." I wiped my tears with the back of my hand. A moment ago I was overwhelmed with fear, now I was pissed off.

"Lizzie, I don't say very much to you because I don't want you to worry, but I need the work. I've spent so much time working on your house lately I haven't been putting out any quotes. When your house is finished I won't have anything to go to."

"Well, let me pay you for what you've done." My voice was getting louder as my agitation grew.

"You're not paying me! We said we'd work out money once

the house is sold and we will, but I don't know how long that will be. It could take months for it to sell and in that time, I need income."

"I know that, but why does it have to be with her?"

"You have to trust me. There is nothing other than a working relationship between Allison and I."

Riley moved to me and put his arms around me. His warmth filled me and as he lowered his head and looked directly into my eyes. I was a goner. He'd won. And as he put his hands around the back of my head and pulled me close, he kissed me deeply proving to me I was the only woman he was thinking of, and I thought that right now, Allison didn't matter. Right now, he was mine.

THE NEXT MORNING Riley did however keep his appointment to meet her. I tried to calm my anxiety by cleaning his house, but an hour later I gave up. It wasn't dirty anyway. I found a magazine and flipped through it, looking for some gardening inspiration. I'm not much of a gardener, but I knew that once the kitchen in my house was finished, the garden would have to be done. I mean, I could hardly sell a house with a gaping big hole in the backyard. Then again, maybe I could. My house had far more attention since that hole had been there than ever before. I thought about Bradley's tours and remembered what he'd said about his video diary. I swapped the magazine for my laptop and did a quick Google search. I typed in *skeleton in May Street West-port* and hit enter. Within three quarters of a second, I had three point two million results. Thankfully not all of them were mine.

The first one I stopped at was the news report that Matt had filmed the day we found the bones. Next was Bradley's diary. I watched a few entries, but didn't find anything new. My mind wandered to why the Japanese tourists were interested. I switched on the internet and did the same search. I instantly found my answer. Some smart comedian had put up a video, complete with little jingle, of a dancing skeleton standing out the front of my house doing his thing. So far it had had just over two hundred and fifty thousand views. Actually watching it, it was quite funny. I almost wished I'd seen it being videoed.

I gave up on the internet search and put my laptop down. I knew what I had to do if I wanted to find out who the missing person in 1949 was. I had to phone Officer Ed Helms. I went looking for my phone and found his card in my handbag. Dialing his number, I held my breath.

"Hello," answered his deep voice.

"Oh hi. Is that Officer Helms?" I asked, uncertainly.

"Yes. Who's calling?"

"It's Lizzie. Lizzie Fuller. I'm not sure if you remember me, but you've been investigating the skeleton dug up in my garden in May Street," I added.

"Hi Lizzie, of course I remember you. How could I forget?" I heard the warmth and humor in his voice. "Is this a social call or is something wrong?"

"Oh um...neither really. I was hoping to ask you some questions about the bones though."

"Of course." I heard the disappointment in his voice and tried not to question it. "What do you need to know?"

"I've heard some rumors about a man who went missing around the time of the bones being buried and was hoping you could tell me something about it." I smiled hoping to get across through the sound that I was asking in a friendly tone.

"Yeah, I know what you're referring too. I've heard that rumor too. Maybe we should meet up and compare notes. I can fill you in on any details I can, and you can tell me what you've heard. How does that sound?"

I was hoping he could give me the information over the phone. "Okay. When and where?"

"Well, I'm not on duty but I am at the station. Maybe we could meet somewhere close by? How about the café on the river? In about ten minutes?"

"Sure, see you soon." I hung up the phone and had a mini panic attack, feeling guilty about doing this investigating behind Riley's back. But then I remembered who he was with right about now and thought, bugger him.

I checked my hair was behaving, smoothed my skirt and checked that Cat was sleeping nicely on Riley's bed. I grabbed my bag and my car keys, locked the door behind me, and made the five-minute journey to the Café on the River.

Ed Helms had made it there before me and sat at one of the tables under an umbrella overlooking the river. I had never seen him in anything but his uniform and I will say that if possible, he was even more gorgeous than before. I usually like a man in uniform, but in this case I liked the man even more out of it. His skin looked like melted chocolate against the white of his T-shirt, his sunglasses pulled down over his eyes, shading them against the glare of the sun on the water.

As I approached, he saw me and smiled, his teeth dazzling in contrast to his skin. He stood up, and I noticed his jeans slipped low on his hips and his toned biceps lifted his glasses to rest on the top of his head. I also noticed the women at the table next to him stare, their mouths hanging slightly open as they did.

He held out his hand to me as I approached.

"Lizzie! How are you?" he asked. At close to six foot three, he looked down on my five foot two. "Thanks for meeting me here."

"Oh no, thank you for meeting me so quickly," I said, accepting his hand. My hand was dwarfed by his as he held it and guided me to my seat. Waiting for me to sit first, he sat opposite me and smiled.

"You look beautiful. That color really suits you," he said. I looked down at my pale yellow dress that I'd chosen to cheer my mood this morning.

"Thank you," I said, blushing. "It's just something I threw on." God I sound like an idiot around good-looking men. Any minute now I'd be babbling, wishing someone would shut me up.

"I figured you for one of those women who doesn't fuss over their appearance, but can look completely beautiful all the same."

The heat rushed into my cheeks and burned my ears.

"Oh...ummm...thanks, but no really. I take ages in the bathroom. This does not happen easily," I laughed, completely embarrassed.

"I'm sorry, I didn't mean to embarrass you or overstep the mark. I just say it as I see it."

"Oh no, really, it's fine. It's not every day I get complimented by a good-looking man."

Shit, what did I say that for? Now he knows I think he's good-looking. And anyway, that was a complete lie. I got complimented every day by Riley, and he was even better looking than Ed Helms.

"I haven't ordered anything yet? Would you like a coffee or something cold to drink?"

"Actually, I'll have my usual—a tall dark mocha Frappuccino."

"Okay, I'll be right back." He stood and I watched his hips sway slightly as he walked.

"Oh my God!" the woman next to me said. "You lucky woman!" she continued smiling at me.

"What?" I asked, confused.

"He's gorgeous! Geez, I wish I had a boyfriend who looked like that."

"I wish I had a boyfriend who looked at *me* like that," said her friend.

"What do you mean?" I asked. "What are you talking about?"

"He's the hottest man I've ever seen."

"Well yes, but what did you mean by the way he looked at me?"

"He looked at you like he wanted to eat you," giggled the friend.

"Yeah, I'd be getting a room fast."

"Oh no, it's not like that. He's not my boyfriend or anything. This is just business," I explained. Why I was explaining myself to perfect strangers though had me beat.

Just then Ed walked back towards us. I heard the women sigh and turn away, but now I was uncomfortable. What did they mean by 'he looked like he wanted to eat me'? He was just being polite. Sure, I got embarrassed by the compliment, but that was all it was, wasn't it? And why did I have to over-think everything?

"Tom says to say hello."

"Thank you, Officer."

"Lizzie, I've asked you to call me Ed. Will you, please?"

"Sorry."

"It's okay, you don't have to be sorry. I've known you for a while now and think it would be easier if you called me by my name."

"I guess so...Ed," I added with a small smile.

"Now, do you want to fill me in on what you've heard about this missing person?"

I quickly brought him up to date with what we'd been told. He sat and listened patiently and only spoke once I'd finished.

"Well, this is a really old case but I did do some digging into it. The man you're referring to was Ronald Smithson, and he was indeed a butcher. The police at the time had him on record for a few misdemeanors but no prison time was given. He went missing on the night of August twenty-eighth, 1949. His girl-friend at the time reported him missing. She was worried because he owed her money and she thought he had run off with another woman."

I swallowed the lump in my throat, thinking of Riley and who he was with at the moment.

"Anyway, he never turned up. The file was closed as the police thought she was probably right."

Ed stopped talking as our drinks were delivered to our table. I smiled at Tom the barista and thanked him. He gave me a quizzical look, but continued on with what he was doing.

"Anyway, the coroner has verified through dental records that the bones in your garden did indeed belong to Ronald Smithson, and he died from a stab wound to the throat. I won't go into detail, but his death wouldn't have been a pleasant one."

I shivered at the thought of being stabbed in the throat and wondered what he'd done to deserve it.

"Was there anything in the records about someone disliking him intensely?" I asked.

Ed smiled. "No. Nothing concrete anyway. He'd been arrested and spent the night in lock-up for being involved in a few pub brawls, and the police at the time suspected him of chopping off people's appendages." I shivered.

"So what happens now?"

"It's out of my hands. The coroner has given his report, and the case has been referred up the chain, but because of the age of it, they won't waste too many man hours on it."

"So someone got away with murder?"

"It happens. Our rate of arrest is much higher today, but that's got a lot to do with technology and improved methods. We're talking sixty-five years ago and this town was a lot smaller then."

That was true, this town was a lot smaller then, so maybe someone from back then would remember Ronald Smithson. I made a note to ask Grandma Mabel about it.

"What happens with you now, Lizzie?" asked Ed, changing the subject back to one slightly more personal.

"What do you mean?"

"The house. Are you going to continue living there?"

"No. As soon as it's finished I'm selling it. Riley's right...it's already caused too many nightmares."

"That's not the house's fault though. You just got unlucky. By the way, did you hear that Joe Woods is up for parole?"

At the sound of Joe Woods' name, my head snapped up. "What?"

"I heard yesterday. He has some friends in high places and they seemed to have pulled in a few favors. His case goes in front of the parole board next month."

My head spun at his words and the thought that my stalker and attempted murderer could be back out on the streets soon.

"But don't worry, Lizzie, I'm sure it will be denied."

"God, I hope so." I didn't even want to think about what would happen if it wasn't.

"And if it isn't, we'll protect you." Ed placed his hand on my arm in a protective gesture, but jerked it away suddenly when my phone vibrated on the table next to me.

I distractedly looked at it and saw a photo of Riley's gorgeous face smile back at me. It was a photo I had snapped one day when he was getting into his truck. He looked happy and relaxed and was one of my favorite photos of him. I picked it up and swiped to answer it.

"Hi," I said quietly.

"I've finished with Allison and I thought maybe we could go and get a coffee down at the river. What do you think? You're not busy, are you?"

"No, I'm actually here now. You could meet me here if you like?"

I waited a beat for Riley to answer. "Okay. I'm not far away. I'll be there shortly." With that he hung up.

"Riley's going to join us. Hope that's okay?" I said, smiling at Ed.

"You know, I really need to get going, but you enjoy your drink." Ed stood abruptly.

"I'm sorry," I said, standing next to him.

"There's nothing to be sorry about, Lizzie. I really do have to go."

"Oh, okay. Well thanks for meeting with me and for the information."

"No problem, and if there's anything else you need, anything at all, ring me."

"Sure, I will."

"Promise?"

"I promise."

Ed extended his hand to me, and as I took it he squeezed and held on for a second longer than necessary. "Keep me informed with what you find out," he said, smiling.

"I will." I smiled up at him as he let go, turned his back and walked away. I heard the women next to me sigh as I sat back down. A minute later, Riley walked up.

"You were quick," I said just before he kissed me. His kiss was deep and involved tongue which I thought was a bit inappropriate considering we were in public, but I wasn't complaining.

Pulling up for air, Riley licked his lips and smiled. "You taste like a chocolate Frappuccino," he said.

I smiled up at him. "Guilty as charged."

"Do you want another one?"

"No thanks, but if you're getting yourself a drink, could I have a bottle of water please?"

"I'll be right back."

I watched his sexy backside as he walked towards the café, his jeans molding it to perfection. The woman at the next table turned to me, her mouth hanging open incredulously.

"Are you kidding me?" she asked. "Do you have some kind of super power or something?"

I smiled at her comment.

"They are the two hottest men I have *ever* seen, and both of them looked at you liked they wanted to eat you. Please, tell me your secret."

I shrugged. "I'm just lucky I guess."

"Geez, why can't I be lucky like that?"

Just then Riley walked back towards me. He noticed the woman staring at him and gave her his mega-watt smile. I saw her swoon and grab the table for support.

"Don't worry," I said to her. "It still has the same effect on me."

CHAPTER 11

"On the way home I have to stop at Mum's," I said to Riley as we walked back towards our cars. "Do you want to stop in?"

"What do you have to do at your mum's?"

"She called me earlier and summonsed me. Apparently she's having a clear-out for a garage sale and she wants me to come and get whatever I want before she sells it."

Riley smiled and moved in close for a kiss. "Sorry. You're on your own with this one. I'm going to head back and get a start on pulling that kitchen wall out so the plumber can do his thing on Monday."

"Really? Grandma would love to see you."

"Give her my love," he said, then kissed me lightly on the lips and headed to his car. I sighed. Looks like I'll be dealing with them on my own.

I got into my car and pointed it in the direction of Mum's. I loved my mum—I really did—but some days she could be just as intolerable as Grandma.

As I parked in her driveway, I noticed Molly was already there. Great, not only would I be able to find out how her date went, I would also have some extra help in diffusing the ticking bomb aka, my mother. I had this sinking feeling that Mum was going to ask me to have Grandma for a while so that she could have a break. Under normal circumstances, I'd be happy to oblige, but I had enough stress in my life and I didn't really need a houseguest as well.

"Hello," I called entering the house through the kitchen door. "Where is everyone?"

"We're in here," called back Molly, the sound of her voice coming from Mum's bedroom.

I dropped my bag on the kitchen bench and walked through the house. Stopping at the bedroom door, my mouth dropped open because there in the middle of the room was Grandma, dressed up in Mum's old wedding dress.

"What do you think? She asked, doing a twirl and nearly falling over.

Honestly, I couldn't form words let alone tell her what I thought. "Wh...wh...why?" I stammered.

"Mum pulled it out and gave it to me," said Molly.

I noticed her shudder as she said the words. I'd seen Mum's dress before and it was no more attractive this time. It had a high neck, long sleeves and big skirt with not one, but two hoops underneath it and made of lace. Now, I don't mean pretty, delicate lace, I mean stiff tulle covered with the largest, ugliest flowers I'd ever seen. Not for the first time, I was grateful for being the middle child.

"Oh look, here's the headdress and veil," said Grandma excitedly.

She pulled the blue tissue paper from the box and retrieved a veil that was several meters long, edged with the same ugly flowers on the dress. "Oh, your mother looked beautiful in this," said Grandma fondly.

"Has it always been that color?" I asked, noting the distinctive dark cream color to the dress.

"Yep, well she couldn't wear white, could she?" responded Grandma. "I mean, it's alright nowadays but back then it was kind of frowned upon. God knows why though, what with all the hippies getting up to goodness knows what."

"What do you mean 'she couldn't wear white'?" asked Molly.

"Well she was pregnant, wasn't she?"

"Pregnant?" Molly and I said in unison.

Grandma looked at us both as if we'd grown a second head. "Of course she was. How do you think you got here, Molly?"

"She always told us I was a honeymoon baby!"

"Your mother honeymooned at the caravan park up the road and she threw up every single day of it. You were not kind to her, let me tell you that," she said frowning at Molly. Just at that moment, Mum chose to enter the room.

"Molly do you wan...," she stopped mid-sentence, looking at Grandma. "What on Earth?"

"It might not fit you no more Nell, but it fits me great." Grandma smiled and attempted another twirl. I looked at the dress sagging as it hung on Grandma's spindly bones. "Can I have it? Molly doesn't want it anyway."

"What do you want it for?" asked Mum incredulously.

"Well, in case I get married again."

I heard Mum's sigh and watched her shoulders droop, as she shook her head.

"Yeah, that's a great idea," added Molly. "I'm not getting married for a very long time anyway."

"What?" cried Mum.

"How did your date with Matt go?" I asked.

Molly glared at me. Obviously she didn't want to talk about it in front of Mum and Grandma.

"You should invite him around for dinner tomorrow night," added Mum excitedly.

"That's great. I could invite my man too," said Grandma. We all turned to look at her. "It'd be like a double date."

"Your man?" asked Molly, grateful for the distraction.

"George."

I remembered Grandma had had a date on Thursday night with George Burnett, the old man from Bradley's tour.

"I guess your date was successful then?" I asked, smiling.

"Yep, I know it's early days, but I think he might be The Two."

"The Two?"

"Yeah, well your Grandfather, God rest his soul, was The One, so this guy must be The Two."

Made sense, I guess.

"There'll never be another man like my father," said Mum. "He was one of a kind. He'll be sitting up there with the Saints, looking down on you and thinking 'stupid old woman'."

"The Saints?" asked Molly.

"Of course he's with the Saints. Any man who put up with her for all those years would have to have been made a saint."

"Hey!" cried Grandma. "That's just plain rude. Your father, God rest his soul, was a good man, but I can tell you he was no saint."

The tension in the air built and I knew now was the time to divert and deflect. "Anyway, what stuff did you want us to look at?" I asked Mum, quickly changing the subject before World War Three broke out and Grandma came to live with me.

Mum glared at Grandma for a second longer, turned on her heel and left the room, muttering under her breath as she went. I couldn't hear exactly what she said, but it kind of sounded like 'crazy old woman'. I quickly followed her back down the hall and out to the garage.

"Where's Dad today?" I asked.

"He's gone to golf," huffed Mum.

Guess that was another subject I wanted to stay away from. Mum's back was stiff as a board, her shoulders rigid. I knew Grandma frustrated her, but she just needed to relax a bit and stop worrying about everything.

Seriously, if Mum didn't have something to worry about, she'd make something up. Not consciously of course, but she'd find something to worry about. I'm sure Grandma and George would fizzle out, and Grandma would not actually need Mum's wedding dress. And if she did, so what? What harm could come of two elderly people finding comfort in each other's company? I should have brought Riley, I thought. One smile from him and all her worries would be forgotten.

"Your stuff is over there," said Mum as we entered the garage, pointing to a pile of five large boxes. I looked around at the mum's piles of boxes and furniture, and wondered where it had all come from.

"Oh, okay, what's in them?" I asked.

"Have a look!"

"Alright, don't get your knickers in a knot."

"Lizzie, that's no way to speak to your mother. Have more respect, will you?" chastised Mum.

"Sorry, Mum. I just heard the way you spoke to Grandma so I thought it must be what we do now."

"What are you talking about?" she asked, even more frustrated than before.

"You did just call her a stupid old woman," I reminded her.

"Well she is! She's eighty-two years old. She should be knitting baby jumpers or crocheting doilies, not running around looking for a new man."

"If she marries George she might move out and leave you alone for a while." Mum stopped and looked back at me. That was something she hadn't thought of.

"Yes, well...we'll see, won't we? Now come over here and give me a hand. Between the two of us we should get this all in your car."

I looked at the size of the boxes she wanted me to take.

"I drive a Mini. There's no way all that will fit. I'll have to get Riley to come over with his truck."

Mum sighed. "Okay, but what's still here next Saturday gets sold."

"Where did all this stuff come from?" I asked.

"The attic space. There was another whole house of belongings up there. Your father's getting annoyed by it and told me I was to get rid of anything I hadn't used in the last two years. I can use the money to buy myself something nice." Mum smiled for the first time today. "I have my eye on a nice ring at Hogan's Jewelers."

❧

ON THE WAY home from Mum's, I decided to make a quick stop at the library. I wanted to do a quick search on Ronald Smithson to see what I could find. Westport was a lot smaller back then and I was sure *The Chronicle* would have mentioned his disappearance within its pages.

The Westport library was housed in a very old, small, two-storey municipal building that was extremely bland and boring. For such a small library though, it was surprisingly busy and it was always hard to find a carpark. I took deep breaths, only swore once and eventually parked my Mini. I walked in and headed to the counter with the big *Information* sign hanging above it. Now, two women usually worked this counter—one was Miss Nice Lady and one was Miss Cranky Pants. Of course, today Miss Cranky Pants was on duty, wasn't she? I should have just gone home and brought Riley back with me. She never scowled at him.

"Hi," I said, giving her my biggest smile. "Could you please tell me where I'd find the copies of the *Westport Chronicle* from 1949?" My smile didn't seem to make any difference, as I didn't have Riley's magic powers.

"The computers upstairs," she snapped, pointing to the staircase that ran the back of the room. "Knock yourself out."

I don't think she meant that literally, but I could be wrong. I thanked her and made my way to the back of the room and up the stairs. I found the row of computers easily and sat down at the nearest one.

It didn't take long for me to find what I was looking for. Some wonderful people of Westport had joined the twenty first century and had digitized all copies of the newspaper right back to 1903. *And* they had a search button. I typed in Ronald Smithson's name and *bingo*! Up popped every article his name was mentioned in...and there were quite a few.

Mr. Smithson appeared to have been popular in this area, but not always for the right reasons. Apparently he was a popular butcher, was an excellent shot at the gun club, had been tossed out of the local pub on more than one occasion and was once arrested, but not charged with urinating in a public place. But the story I was looking for didn't tell me much more than I already knew.

Ronald Smithson was twenty-nine years old when he went missing, and was on probation for assault. The police suspected he'd used his butchering skills to cut off someone's hand, but they could never find any evidence and the victim hadn't confessed to the truth. I guess that could explain why he had an extra hand in his pocket. His girlfriend at the time reported him missing as he owed her money and she thought he'd run off with another woman. I also found out that you could buy thirty-six acres of frost-free land with a house, two horses, a cow and four hundred chickens all for the bargain price of fifteen hundred pounds. Wow! That was cheap. Also the local ladies bowls was doing exceptionally well winning against Ackwood, and Betty Grable was starring in *When My Baby Smiles At Me* in Technicolor. So I guess, all in all it wasn't a total waste of my time. I just didn't know how this new information would help me.

I printed out the pages I wanted and closed the search engine I was using. Grabbing the paper off the printer, I pushed it all into my bag and headed home before Riley sent out a search party looking for me.

*

LATER THAT AFTERNOON, Dad dropped all the boxes to my house. I stood and looked at the pile in the middle of the lounge room and wondered what the hell I would do with it all.

"What's in them?" asked Riley, frowning.

"Who knows?"

"Are you going to open them?"

"No. They're probably full of things from my childhood and if I look, I won't want to throw anything out."

"Well, where are we going to put them?"

"Your house?" I asked hopefully.

"There's no room at my house."

I sighed. "Maybe we can put them in the old garage and deal with them later."

I sighed again. I hated the garage. To be honest it scared the shit out of me. It was all dark and creepy and full of spiders. Plus I worried that the roof may actually fall on my head.

"Why don't we just take it all to the dump?" asked Riley as he lifted one box that was particularly heavy. Lord knows what was in it.

"I can't do that!" I replied, indignantly.

"Why not?"

"Because."

"You need a better reason than that," said Riley, carrying the box and moving through the doorway, heading for the backyard. Obviously we were doing this now.

To be honest, I didn't have a better reason and I had had the same thought. I hadn't seen this stuff in years and I'd never once gone looking for it, so I obviously didn't need it.

"I promise I will go through it and throw away whatever I don't need," I said, dragging a box.

Riley looked back at me and grinned. He knew they'd sit out there forever without me going through them.

I followed him through the house and listened as my box clanged and crashed as I dragged it down the three steps to the grass.

"If you wait a second I'll pick it up for you," said Riley, grimacing as something inside my box smashed.

"I'm sure it was nothing important," I shrugged. "Anyway, why don't you go ahead of me and open the garage door," I added before he could complain that if whatever I had just smashed wasn't important, then maybe I should just throw it away.

He shook his head but picked up his pace, looking at the storm clouds brewing overhead. By the time I dragged my box up to the door, he had it open and had moved inside.

It had been a few months since I was in here. Watching as two mice scurried into a hidey-hole, I knew it would be a few more before I came back again.

The garage was made of the same timber cladding to match the house and the outside had been painted grey at some point in history. The inside had been left raw and over time, the timber had started to rot. Looking around me properly, I realized it had probably never been built to house a car as the floor was also timber and wouldn't have supported the weight. Right now I wondered if it would support *my* weight.

"Is it safe to be in here?" I asked, as Cat wound his way between my legs. He spotted the mice and hightailed back outside. Maybe I was feeding him too well.

Riley pushed his box against a wall and looked around.

"It should be," he answered. I heard the timber crack under his weight as he stepped towards me. "Maybe I should take a closer look at the foundations." He smiled.

"Okay. You do that and I'll get another box."

I followed Riley outside. As I moved to the house, Riley moved to the side of the shed and started to crawl through the dirt. "Bring a torch back with you please," he called after me.

Luckily I knew where Riley kept his torch, so I grabbed it and walked back outside. Handing it to Riley, I stood back and watched as his jeans rode low and his T-shirt rode high, as he crawled into the space under the floor. I gave a blissful sigh.

Whilst he was under the shed, I moved back inside the house and retrieved another box. By the time I got back, Riley had made it out of the floor space and was walking around the corner of the shed, covered in dirt. He brushed his jeans and took the box from me.

"What did you find?" I asked. "Is it safe?"

"Yeah, the timber foundations look okay, but there's a section towards the back that's closed in. It looks like a room but I can't see any doors leading into it."

"That's odd."

"Maybe there's trapdoor in the floor."

I followed him inside and waited as he pushed the box up against the other two we'd already moved. He moved to the back of the shed and looked at the floor. The floor was made of boards similar to what was inside the house but unlike those, these had never been treated with any sort of protectant. Now they just looked grey, scarred and brittle.

"I can't see any obvious trapdoor," said Riley, running his fingers through his hair, "but I think we're standing directly over the area."

"Why do we need to find it?" I asked, thinking of *The Amityville Horror* with the hidden red room.

Riley shrugged. "Just curious." He got on his hands and knees and felt around the edge of the boards. After a moment he stood and moved towards the door. I followed him, thinking we were giving up and just going to get another box. I sighed when I realized he was just going to get his pry bar.

I grabbed another box and followed him back to the shed, where he immediately started to lift floorboards. Once he had a section lifted of approximately three-foot square, he grabbed his torch and shone it down the hole. I squealed as three spiders ran from the darkness towards me.

Lying on his stomach, Riley looked deeper into the hole. "There's a box down there," he said, lifting himself back up.

"What sort of box?" I asked, curiosity now creeping in and wondering what other secrets this house held.

"I'm not really sure, but it looks wooden. I need to get a few more boards up and I'll be able to get to it." He pried at more boards and a few minutes later, he had cleared a hole big enough for him to drop into.

It was actually a lot deeper than I had imagined, and as Riley's feet hit the ground, his head disappeared from view.

"Watch out for snakes," I called, feeling for my phone in my pocket, ready to dial emergency services.

My heart rate increased as I heard Riley cry out. "Arghh!"

"What? What happened? What is it?"

"Nothing, I just banged my head." His head popped back out of the hole and I saw a gash on his forehead. By the time he had lifted a timber box out to me, blood had started to trickle.

"Oh my God, are you okay? I'll get you some ice," I said, ready to run into the house and grab a bag of frozen peas. Riley lifted himself out of the hole.

"Lizzie, it's fine. I just grazed it, no big deal." He used his sleeve and wiped the blood away. I looked at the dirt on his sleeve and shivered, making a note to get some antibiotic cream from the doctor next time I was there. The last thing I needed was for Riley to get sick.

He moved his attention to the box. It was approximately two-foot square and three-foot high and made of timber, the lid sealed down with nails.

"Is this all that was down there?" I asked.

"Yeah."

Riley used his pry bar to open the lid. I held my breath as dust rose into the air.

Excitement caused my stomach to flutter as I peered over the edge into the box. Then I felt the adrenalin spike as I screamed. "Arghhhhh! Arghhhhh!"

Looking back at me was a cat. A cat that resembled the one trying to trip me up. The one that had disappeared as soon as the mice turned up.

Riley grabbed my arm. "Lizzie! Stop screaming!"

"But...but...what the *hell* is that?"

"It's stuffed," explained Riley lifting it from the box. He examined it closely, and then shoved it towards me. "Meow," he said, laughing.

"It's not funny. That's gross," I huffed, my heart rate slowing dramatically. Riley dropped the cat on the floor and moved back into the box. He pulled out three leather bound books. That was much better. Flicking through the first one, he handed the other two to me. I did the same and realized they were diaries.

Riley finished flipping through the diary, put it on the floor and then proceeded to pull out four more. All were leather bound, all were red and all were dusty and making me sneeze.

"Why the hell would someone put all this in a box and then hide it under the shed?" Riley asked.

"Why would someone keep a diary?"

"So that they could look back on it one day and remember."

"Yeah, but the point is anyone can read them. It's hard to keep snooping siblings out of things like that."

Riley laughed. "I'm guessing you never kept a diary then?"

"No way, I did not need to write down all my deepest, darkest thoughts for Danny to find!"

I shuddered at the thought. It was bad enough that Riley could read my mind at times. If he knew the actual X-rated thoughts I had about him, I think even he would blush. I felt the heat creep up my neck at the thought of it.

"Well these obviously meant enough to someone for them to hide them like they did," said Riley.

I looked at the dates written on the inside cover, along with the name Avis Miller.

Avis was the lady who had previously owned the house. She had lived her life a spinster after she couldn't commit to her one true love, a woman named Wilhelmina.

"Maybe we should read them." I opened the front cover and as I started to read, thunder rumbled and shook the shed walls. I jumped as rain tapped on the tin roof.

"Maybe we should take them inside," suggested Riley.

"Sounds like a good idea," I commented, turning to head for the door.

CHAPTER 12

$\mathcal{A}$s we ran into the kitchen, the door slamming behind us, I wiped the rain from my face. I moved towards the lounge, ready to find a comfy spot on the couch, when something on the hallway wall came into view.

In an area about a foot square, was blood.

My stomach jumped as I sucked my breath in. Riley slammed into the back of me.

"What the..." he stuttered. Seeing what I was looking at, he stopped. Moving past me, he put the diaries on the floor and knelt for a closer look.

"Where's it coming from?" I asked, my voice trembling slightly.

"I honestly have no idea. I didn't see it when we were in here earlier."

"Me either."

"Maybe we just missed it."

"Riley, we walked past here three times. We would have seen it if it was there."

Riley ran his fingers through his hair and I heard his deep sigh.

"I think it's time we called the police."

Relief washed over me. Finally we were doing something about it.

"I'll call Ed," I said, reaching into my jeans pocket and retrieving my phone, before Riley could change his mind. Ed answered on the second ring. I put him on speaker.

"Hi Lizzie. How are you?" he asked, his voice friendly. Riley scowled.

"Not too bad," I replied, ignoring Riley's dirty look. Riley picked up the diaries and moved to the lounge, leaving me alone with the blood. I shivered as the wind from the storm whistled through the cracks in the door and quickly followed him, bringing Ed up to date as I walked.

"Okay," said Ed, "don't touch it. I'm at the scene of an accident at the moment, but I'll be there as soon as I can get away."

I sat on the couch next to Riley. "Thanks Ed. I'll see you soon." I hung up the phone.

"He's on his way," I said, half smiling.

"You have him on speed dial do you?"

"Of course not. He's in my caller list."

Riley's eyebrow rose. "Come on," I said, before Riley could question me as to why Ed was in my caller list. "Let's read these diaries while we wait."

AVIS'S DIARIES were old and musty, mould causing the edges of the paper to discolor. My fingers felt dirty as I turned the pages.

The first diary was dated January 1945 and told us a lot about Avis and her relationship with her mother. It appeared it was only the two women in the house as her father had died the year before. Her mother seemed to have a hard time with his death and relied on Avis a lot. At the age of fifteen, that must have been hard for her.

The second diary was more about Avis' feelings for a girl who lived across the road and how her mother had punished her when she found out about it. People weren't as understanding back then, I suppose.

The third diary was much more interesting though.

It started with Avis explaining how she had made a new friend named Ronald. She'd been heartbroken when her cat died, so a neighbor suggested she took him to Ronald, as he was a very good taxidermist. Even though Mister had passed, having him stuffed meant it would feel like he was still there. She struck up a friendship with Ronald (who, after that, she only referred to as RS). Whenever RS visited, they would hide out in the shed where her mother couldn't hear them. It was out there that she confided in him her darkest thoughts and feelings.

About midway through the diary Avis introduces someone named Leo—LGB.

It appeared that RS didn't like LGB very much and Avis felt he was just jealous of the friendship. Reading some of the entries about LGB, I thought RS was probably right. He didn't sound like a very nice person.

The entry dated May 19, 1949 was particularly hard to read.

LGB CAME TO VISIT TONIGHT. RS usually liked to be here whenever he was around, but tonight he couldn't be here. I wish he had have been.

LGB was intoxicated when he arrived, so I took him out to the shed and away from Mother. Even though I had given Mother her tablets and they made her sleep, LGB was being very loud and I didn't want him to disturb her. As soon as we entered the shed, I knew I'd made a mistake.

He immediately turned on me and attempted to kiss me. I pushed him away and slapped him and told him to behave. I would make him some coffee and sober him up. He slapped me back and told me it wasn't coffee he wanted. It was me.

I protested and tried to leave, but he pulled me to the ground and hit me. He said he would show me what a man could do. When he ripped my shirt open and raped me, I knew I never wanted a man again.

Afterwards, he left me curled on the floor crying and told me if I ever told anyone what had happened, he would tell everyone my secret— how I was really in love with Valerie.

"OH MY GOD, Riley. This is awful," I said, turning to him, tears in my eyes. I thought about what LGB had done to Avis and looked at Riley, with his beautiful eyes and caring soul, and I knew he would never hurt me.

"You should read this entry," he replied, his face grim. I took the diary from him and read.

The entry was dated June 10, 1949.

IT'S BEEN three weeks since that awful night and I think the worst has happened. I think I'm pregnant. I'm a week past my monthly date and I feel different. My breasts are sore, I cry a lot and I feel sick every morning. I don't know what to do. I know I need to talk to Mother about it but I can't. I'm so ashamed. RS is coming around tonight, so I think I will talk to him and get his advice. I haven't spoken to him about that night yet. I know when I do, he's going to be very angry and I worry about his temper.

OH MY. I can't believe it happened. I told RS about the baby and asked him what to do. He became very agitated and angry, and told me that he was going looking for LGB. I'm so worried about what he will do.

JUNE 11, 1949

·   ·   ·

RS DIDN'T COME BACK to me last night. So this morning I went to his shop to find him. He told me he did indeed find LGB and they fought. I know there's more to it than that, but he won't tell me. I'll find out though. He can't keep a secret from me for long.

JUNE 13, 1949

I FOUND out what happened the night RS fought with LGB. Now I wish I hadn't. He broke down and told me last night. He said LGB started to get quite violent. RS defended himself and in the process LGB had his hand cut off. I did ask what RS was doing carrying around his butcher's knives but he refused to answer me. I know the truth though. I'm beginning to think the rumors around town about him cutting people up are true.

Oh, how did all this happen?

I STOPPED for a breath and looked at Riley.

"Poor Avis," I sighed. "She sure knew how to pick her friends, didn't she?"

"Keep reading," said Riley grimly. I looked at the tight line of his mouth and braced myself for the rest of the story.

AUGUST 28, 1949

I DON'T KNOW what to do. How did this happen? I want to run far, far away! Maybe I should. But no—I have Mother to care for.

I KNOW I should go to the police, but I'm guilty in this now.

Tonight RS came over and we sat in the shed talking. This pregnancy is beginning to get difficult to hide from Mother. I know shortly I will have to tell her, but after tonight I just don't know. Maybe I should confess it all. RS had spoken to me about marriage and telling Mother that the baby was his. I guess that was better than the alternative.

After we had been sitting there a while, LGB turned up and demanded to know if the rumors were true. Was I pregnant? If so, he wanted the baby. I got to see for the first time that LGB indeed was missing his left hand. He still had large bandages covering his wound, but it appeared to be a clean cut at the wrist. I looked at RS and felt my stomach roll. How could he do that to a person?

Then I looked at LGB and remembered what he had done to me and I wondered if RS had been justified in his actions. But then RS opened his jacket pocket and showed us the hand he had since mummified. I turned my back, my sensitive stomach not being able to handle what I was looking at. A fight broke out and even though LGB was disabled, he pulled a knife from his pocket and lunged at RS. That was all it took. A flash of clothing, a scream, and RS fell, blood gushing from his neck. I couldn't handle it, the world turned black and I passed out.

I woke with LGB slapping my face and demanding I help him. It took a while, but then the memories came flooding back. The fight, the blood and RS falling to the ground. Dead.

I didn't want to help LGB. I wanted to call the police, but he threatened that if I didn't help him bury the body, he would tell the town I was pregnant with an illegitimate child and that I was in love with a woman. He would also tell them it was me who killed RS after finding out I was pregnant with his baby. LGB's girlfriend would give him an alibi for the time of death, so even if I did tell them who it really was, they wouldn't believe me. I looked down at myself and realized I had a lot of RS's blood on me. So I ashamedly helped him. We buried RS in my garden, where I could at least be close to my friend.

I want to take my own life, but I feel the life inside me growing and I know that it is an innocent. It deserves the right to live. I just don't know how I'll live with the guilt.

. . .

I SAT BACK in the chair, too shocked to talk.

❧

IT TOOK Ed another hour to arrive and in that time, Riley and I decided to call it quits on renovating for the day. Riley'd just gone for a shower when Ed's car pulled up in my driveway. I smoothed my hair and adjusted my skirt as he walked to the door.

"Hi," I said, opening the door and smiling.

"Hi, Lizzie, it's lovely to see you again." Ed was in his uniform this time and looked very official, his gun belt making him look a little bit sexier than ever. Not that I noticed of course.

"Come in," I said, stepping aside and allowing him to enter. As he passed me, I got the distinct smell of his aftershave. He smelled good too. "Would you like a coffee? I just made a fresh pot."

"Yeah, that would be great, thanks." He walked into what was left of my kitchen and sat down on one of the chairs. I moved to the one bench we'd left propped against a wall, and poured three cups of coffee.

"Three cups?" he asked.

"Yes. Riley's just in the shower, but he'll be down in a minute."

I saw the disappointment flash in Ed's eyes.

"Of course. Thanks," he said, accepting the cup I offered him. "He seems to be getting along with the renovation," he commented, looking around.

"I can't wait for it to be finished." I sighed.

"Not everything about the house is bad news."

"Really? Wait until I show you what we found today," I said, thinking about the diaries.

"Yeah. Where is this blood you called about?"

"Oh, that's near the front door, but that's not all I need to show you."

Ed gave me a quizzical look but stood and followed me back into the hall. He knelt down and examined the wall. After swiping at the blood with a swab, he sealed it inside a vial and stood.

"Do you mind if I take a look around?" he asked.

"No. I don't mind. Do whatever you need to do."

I silently followed him as he wandered around, checking the windows and doors on the downstairs part of the house. "Nothing else has been disturbed?" he asked.

"No. Only the second time I found the blood I thought I heard someone on the stairs. Turned out it was my imagination."

"Was this door locked on either occasion?" asked Ed, nodding towards the front door that we were walking past.

"No. I don't think so. Riley and I were getting ready to go out at the time. It wouldn't have been locked today either."

"You need to keep it locked at all times," he said, concern flashing in his eyes.

I nodded. "Where do you think it's coming from?"

"I don't really know. We'll get it tested and that at least will tell us if it's animal or human, or if it really is blood."

Shock ripped through me at his last words.

"What? What do you mean?"

"Just because it looks like blood doesn't mean it is. It could just be someone trying to scare you."

My mind reeled with Ed's words and immediately jumped to Allison.

"What else did you have to show me?"

"Hmm?" I could see Allison doing something like that. She could have easily slipped in the door when no one was around and sprayed the walls with fake blood. She already knew that I was scared in this house so why not amp up the fear a little bit more?

"You said there was something else you needed to show me," continued Ed.

"Oh yeah," I said, snapping out of my daydream. "We found some diaries. I think you'll be really interested in what's inside them."

We moved into the kitchen and Ed sat down at the makeshift table.

"This house certainly has a lot of secrets," he commented, looking around.

"Yeah. Sometimes I wish I'd never bought it." I sighed and sat down heavily on the chair opposite Ed.

"If you hadn't bought this house, we never would have met." Ed gave me a look that could have scorched the floor. I felt my face flame as Riley walked in the room. I saw his jaw flex, but he extended his hand to Ed.

"Hello again," he said, with a forced smile.

"Hi, Riley, it's a pleasure to see you."

I had the distinct impression it was anything but a pleasure. I was really unsure what was happening, so I busied myself getting up and making Riley his coffee. As I stepped into his zone, the air filled with the smell of a fresh shower. I smiled.

"So, where are the diaries," asked Ed, switching to official mode.

"Oh...um..." My brain muddled at the smell of Riley, and mentally I shook myself.

"I left them in the lounge. Would you mind grabbing them Lizzie," asked Riley, smiling at me.

"Sure." I had the impression Riley didn't want to leave me in the room alone with Ed for too long. I quietly walked past him and moved through the door to the hallway. The air in here was much cooler and I felt relief wash over me. I hadn't realized the kitchen had become so hot. Picking up the diaries, I walked back to the kitchen. I attempted to hand them to Ed when the pile slipped and they fell forwards. I went to grab at them, lost my balance and crash landed into Ed's face, breasts first. And as I had a scooped neckline on my T-shirt, Ed seemed to have a face full of my cleavage.

I think Riley will be wishing that he'd got the diaries himself, now.

"Oh my God! I'm so, so sorry," I spluttered, attempting to stand upright.

I felt Riley's hands around my waist as he pulled me back to standing. My face flamed and I wondered if a person could actually die from embarrassment. Ed didn't seem to mind though. He had a big grin on his face...until he saw the thundercloud on Riley's. He coughed, and bent to pick up the diaries.

"It's okay, Lizzie. No harm done."

"No. I'm really, really sorry."

"It's okay. Honestly, don't be embarrassed. Things like this happen to me all the time."

I had a moment of wondering if women threw their breasts in his face accidently or if it were more purposeful than that.

"Anyway," said Riley, unimpressed, "if you turn to the last diary and read the entries for the last couple of months, you'll see why we thought you should see them."

Thankfully, Ed turned his attention to the diaries and flicked through them, skim-reading as he went. When he came to the entry date August 28, he stopped and read more intently.

"Well, that explains what happened I guess," he said, looking up from the pages. "Now we just need to find out who LGB is. The coroner did lift prints off of clothing on the body, but we haven't been able to match them to anybody at the moment. He's probably dead by now, anyway." Ed sighed and stood up as his radio crackled. "That's for me," he said, adjusting the volume so he could hear it better. "Thanks for handing this over to me, Lizzie. I'll stay in touch and keep you informed of anything we find out about the blood. If it happens again, call me straight away."

Ed adjusted his gun belt and I followed him to the door. As he moved into the rain, I waved him goodbye.

THE FOLLOWING Sunday it was dinner as usual at Mums house. It was always a noisy affair, and today the only difference to any other Sunday was that Grandma had invited her boyfriend George, and Molly had been forced to invite Matt.

As soon as we arrived, I could tell Molly was on edge. Not that I blamed her. Personally, I would have introduced Matt on another night—like during the winter of 2040—but maybe it won't be such a bad thing. With Grandma and George, Matt may just sneak in under Mum's radar without too much inter-rogation.

"Hi Mum," I said, kissing her cheek as I walked past. "It's a full house tonight."

Mum gave me a tight smile, her cheeks flushed and her hair standing slightly on end. Maybe she was rethinking her idea of introducing Matt to the family tonight too.

"Lizzie, I can't do everything. You need to help me."

"Sure, Mum. What do you need doing?"

"Well, you can lay the table for me. Use the good cutlery, please."

Geez, Mum only got the good cutlery out on special occa-sions. Tonight must be pretty important to her. I wondered who she wanted to impress the most—Matt so he'd marry Molly; or George so he would take Grandma off her hands.

"Also," she added, "your grandmother is your responsibility tonight. If she plays up, it's your fault."

"Oh puh-lease," I said, rolling my eyes. "As if I can control her."

"Well, try...and don't roll your eyes at me, young lady."

I moved to the cupboard where Mum kept the good china and

cutlery, and pulled out what we needed. Taking it all to the dining room, I laid the table as best I could—considering we were squashing ten people around a six-seater table.

Re-entering the lounge, I found Grandma holding center stage with George sitting alongside her, looking love struck. Dad had his head buried in the paper. I guess he was unimpressed with her storytelling.

"Hi, George, we meet again." I smiled.

Riley moved over and extended his hand to George. "How are ya, George?" George took his hand and shook it. As he did, I noticed the white cotton gloves he wore and wondered about it. George must have followed my gaze, as he coughed and gave me a coy smile.

"Sorry about the gloves," he said. "I have a skin condition."

"Oh, that's okay. No need to explain," I said, slightly embarrassed I'd been caught staring.

Grandma seemed undeterred by my rudeness though, and continued on with her story about Westport 'back in the day'. I remembered what the old guy at the pub had told Danny.

"Hey Grandma, how good is your memory?" I asked.

"Sharp as a tack," she replied.

"Do you remember a story about an illegitimate child being born at my house?"

"How long ago?"

"About sixty years or so."

"Hmmm, let me think...there was a bit of a scandal back in the late forties, but I don't know whether the girl had the baby or not. I don't remember where she lived. I just remember a story going around about a girl who was raped and got pregnant from it."

"That's terrible," said Molly. "What happened to her?"

"Don't know. Do you remember that, George?" Grandma asked, turning to him. Up until now he'd been pretty quiet. "You would have lived here back then."

"No, no sorry, Mabel. I didn't live around here then," he explained, his toe tapping. He was obviously nervous about meeting us all.

"What about Ronald Smithson? Have you ever heard of him?" I asked.

"Yeah, I remember him," said Grandma, her face animated. "He was a butcher—liked to cut up more than cows, if the rumors were true. I remember him because he used to stuff things. Your grandfather, God rest his soul, wanted to take our dog Spot to him to get him stuffed. Once he'd died, of course. Spot probably wouldn't have liked it much if he'd been alive." She swished her false teeth around, remembering. "Anyways, I didn't go for it much. I think once you're dead you should be buried, not left on the mantle-piece for everyone to pat. 'How would you like it if I did that to you?' I said to Grandad."

"What was his reply?" asked Danny.

"He just told me we'd need a bigger mantle-piece."

"Why do you want to know about Ronald Smithson?" asked Riley, frowning at me.

"Oh...um...Ed told me that's who the bones belonged to."

"Ed?"

"Yeah."

"So he's Ed now, is he?"

"He told me to call him that." I shrugged, like it was no big deal.

Riley looked back at me, his thoughts unreadable. "You are staying out of this, aren't you Lizzie?" There was an undertone of warning to Riley's voice, one I probably shouldn't have ignored.

"Yep," piped in George. "It's best to leave the past in the past. That's what I say."

"I couldn't agree more, George," replied Riley.

I wondered if he was referring to the story of the bones or Allison.

"Dinner's ready!" called Mum, not a moment too soon. With

the look Riley was giving me, things were starting to get hot in here.

We all moved to the dining room and found our seats. I will say it was very squashed, but somehow we managed to fill our plates.

"George, why don't you tell us about yourself," said Mum.

"Not much to tell really," he replied.

"Rubbish," said Grandma, her potato falling off her fork. "You're just being modest. Why don't you tell everyone how you were a single dad before it became fashionable?"

"Now, Mabel. Nobody wants to hear about my boring life."

"Of course we do," said Grandma, enthusiastically. I looked around the table and thought George was probably right.

"I had a daughter, but she passed away during childbirth. I took the child and raised it as my own." George shrugged.

"That's so sad," said Mum.

"It all worked out okay. My granddaughter and I are very close."

Mum glared at the three of us. "I'm sure *one* day I'll know what that feels like," she mumbled.

"What happened to your wife?" asked Matt, speaking up for the first time. Actually to be fair to him, I had seen him trying to add to the conversation, but every time that he went to say something, someone else beat him to it.

"My wife?" asked George.

"Yes. The mother of your daughter."

"Oh...um...yes...um...she died as well. Giving birth also." George shifted uncomfortably in his seat. I wondered about it.

"You poor man. You never remarried?" asked Mum, horrified.

"No, never met the right woman after that. Anyway enough about me. Pass the potatoes will you please, Mabel."

"How old is your granddaughter?" asked Mum. She was a sucker for a sad story.

"What? Oh, she's thirty-two."

"Does she live locally? Lizzie might know her. They might have gone to school together." Mum smiled at the thought that the world was really much smaller than we gave it credit for.

"No, no, she doesn't live here. She lives somewhere else. Mabel, please pass the bloody potatoes, will you," he added sharply, dropping his fork to take the bowl she was holding.

Geez, obviously he really liked potatoes.

"Have you found anything else out about the bones in your garden, Lizzie?" asked Matt, looking at me.

"Kind of. Riley found a hidden room under my shed. He lifted the floor and found a box full of diaries and a cat."

"What kind of cat?" asked Danny.

"What kind of room?" asked Matt.

"Who put it all there?" asked Molly.

What was this—twenty questions?

"It was a stuffed cat, a secret room and I'm guessing Avis," I answered.

"What did the diaries say?" asked Danny. "Were they filled with secret affairs?"

"Did they tell you who put the body in the garden?" asked Andrew.

"Yes, as a matter of fact, they did." I smiled.

I heard the appropriate gasp go around the table.

"Well, who did it?" asked Danny, impatiently.

"Someone with the initials LGB."

"Who's LGB?" asked Danny.

"We don't know. It just said LGB. Apparently he raped Avis, got her pregnant and when Ronald Smithson—owner of the bones—confronted him, there was a fight and Ronald Smithson cut off his hand. LGB returned at a later date and killed him."

I watched as George moved and squirmed in his seat. Maybe my story was making him uncomfortable.

"So all we have to do is find out who LGB is and we'll have the case solved," said Danny, curiously.

"We don't have to do anything. It's all been handed to the police, so let them do their job," said Riley, glaring at me.

Danny looked at me, raised his eyebrows and mouthed *we'll find him* across the table.

"You know Mabel, I'm not feeling very well," said George. "I might head off." Maybe it was all the talk of severed body parts.

"What? You don't have to go," she said to George. She turned to me. "Lizzie, stop telling horrible stories. See George, she'll stop now."

"No really, I think I should go. I'll call you later tonight."

With that he excused himself from the table and left, Grandma hot on his heels.

Mum turned to me and stared. It was her *shut up and behave* stare. She was probably worried I'd chase Matt off as well. No need to worry though. Matt was grinning from ear to ear and probably mentally writing his next story.

CHAPTER 13

*M*onday morning I was woken by Riley's phone ringing. He rolled out of bed and answered it. I rolled over, grabbed his pillow and snuggled in. When he came back, he moved to the wardrobe and pulled out his work clothes.

"Who was on the phone?" I asked.

"Allison." My stomach flipped at her name leaving his lips.

"Oh?"

"The contract on her house goes through this morning and she needs some work done urgently," he said, dropping his boxers to pull on his boy leg underpants.

"So you just change your plans to suit her?"

"She's giving me cash." Yeah, I bet that's not all she wants to give you, I thought looking at his naked body.

"It's only six-thirty. Why are you rushing now?"

"The contract is supposed to go through as soon as the bank opens and she wants a meeting beforehand, so we can get started as soon as she has the keys." It all sounded plausible as Riley said it, yet I couldn't help but think she had an ulterior motive.

"Oh, I thought we were getting on with the kitchen today," I sulked.

"We will...this afternoon. Why don't you phone Danny and go shopping with him. You still need to make a decision on what bench top you want."

I sighed.

"Lizzie, you were supposed to make that decision a week ago."

"I know, I just thought you were going to come with me and help."

"Sorry, but I have to go," he said as he moved to the bed and kissed me. I put my arms around his neck and held on tight. His kiss deepened and it didn't take long for him to pull the sheets back and jump into bed, his boy leg underpants left on the floor behind him.

At least he would have something to remember when he was looking at Allison this morning.

I FOLLOWED him downstairs and watched as he hunted for his wallet. I moved to make a pot of coffee.

"Want one?" I asked.

"No thanks, I'm running late." He smiled.

I shrugged. "Just tell Allison that you were making mad, passionate love to me."

Riley found his wallet behind the kettle and put it in his back pocket. "Very funny," he said, smiling again.

"It's the truth."

"Yes, but I don't go around telling everybody about my sex life, thank you very much."

"I'm not telling you to tell everyone. Just her."

Riley planted a hard and fast kiss on my lips. "Love you."

"Love you too," I said to his retreating back. As I heard the door slam shut and then waited as his truck motor turned over, I sighed and looked at the clock. It was twenty past seven. Well, I managed to hold him up that long.

After I completed the morning routine of shower, teeth cleaning, make-up, hair, clothing (geez, no wonder it took me so long to get out the door in the morning), I made the bed, tidied the house and washed our breakfast dishes. I looked at the clock again and realized it was just after eight o'clock. Time to phone Danny.

Danny and Andrew closed the salon on Mondays, and today Danny was more than happy to meet me in town and have an excuse to get away from Andrew's mother.

I stopped by Danny's and picked him up. I watched as he closed the door behind him and ran down the steps towards my car. He was dressed differently today, in three quarter cut-off jeans and a red T-shirt advertising custom cars.

"Nice shirt," I said as he climbed into the car.

"Thanks. Andrew bought it for me. I told him I'd rather have the car but I don't think he loves me that much." Danny smiled. Looking at the car on the shirt and figuring it to be worth quite a bit of money, I thought Danny was probably right.

By the time we reached the kitchen shop, my blood pressure was reaching dangerous levels, compliments of the traffic and Danny's monologue about his mother in-law. Now, it wasn't Danny who was frustrating me, it was the way she was treating him. Sure, I knew my brother could be hard to live with, but he did not deserve to be treated like that and Andrew really needed to defend him a little more.

"I found a text she sent him," said Danny quietly. "She said she thinks I'm ruining Andrew's life."

"What?" I yelled.

"She said I spend too much money and that Andrew would be better off without me." I heard the emotion in Danny's voice.

"Don't listen to her. She doesn't know what she's talking about. You work hard in that salon and you earn the money you spend. You're hardly a freeloader!"

"She also said I need to help out more at home, but Andrew

has always loved doing the cooking. And you know me, I could burn water!" Danny pouted. "And I *do* my share of the housework, but she just thinks I'm hard to live with."

"You should send Grandma Mabel over to live with her for a week. She'd soon realize you're a saint."

"That's the other thing. She thinks our family isn't good enough. She found out about what happened to you with the stalker and how the Pastor was behind it all, and she thinks you're the reason the church closed."

I felt my stomach flip and a sickness creep in at the memory.

"I'm sorry, Danny," I said quietly.

"What are you sorry for? You didn't do anything wrong."

"Sometimes I wish I'd never bought that house."

"Rubbish, it could have happened to anyone."

"Yes, but look what's happening now."

"Nothing's happening now."

"Have you ever bought a house that came with as many secrets as mine?"

"Well no, but I've only ever bought one house and that's the one we're in now. Anyway, it's been four weeks since Harper dug up those bones and what have you found out?"

"Quite a bit, but none of it helps much."

"Have you been talking to that really cute officer?"

"Yes, but he doesn't know any more than I do."

"Next time you talk to him, invite me over."

"Why? Do you have information for him?"

"No. I just want to look at him, that's all." Danny smirked.

"Remember Andrew? God, how does he put up with you?"

"Of course I remember Andrew, but remember, Lizzie— there's no harm in looking. It's not like I'd do anything about it."

"Not with Ed Helms anyway." I smiled. "He's as straight as an arrow."

Danny sighed wistfully.

I pulled my Mini into a park on the rooftop of the shop, got out and waited for Danny. I smoothed my three-quarter cut-off jeans into place, straightened my red T-shirt and realized Danny and I were dressed like twins. Only he looked much more stylish and 'together' than I did.

"Lizzie, look out," cried Danny, looking at me over the roof of the car. I stared at him startled, as a flock of seagulls flew over, one of them skimming the top of my head as it went. I let out a small scream as Danny burst out laughing.

"What are you laughing at?" I asked. "That scared the hell out of me."

"Look at your shirt." He laughed again. I did, and realized that one of the seagulls had left his breakfast down the front of my shirt.

"Crap," I muttered.

"Yep, you got that right!"

I glared at Danny. "Well don't just stand there!" I cried indignantly. "Pass me a tissue or something."

"I don't have a tissue."

I sighed and opened my handbag, feeling the moisture seep through the flimsy fabric of my shirt. I shuddered and hunted faster. I sighed again.

"I don't have one either. What am I going to do?"

I looked down at my T-shirt. My choices were limited.

"Well I'm not walking anywhere with you like that," said Danny, finally controlling his laughter. "That's disgusting."

I sighed again. "I'm going home," I said opening my car door back up and climbing in to the driver's seat. I pulled my seatbelt over my shoulder and stopped. Danny climbed in next to me.

"Don't even think about it," he said, reading my mind.

"Danny, what choice do I have? If I don't take my shirt off, this bird crap is going to go all over my seatbelt. It'll be ruined."

Now it was Danny's turn to sigh.

"I'm sorry," I said, carefully lifting my shirt over my head.

"At least you're wearing a nice bra." Thank God, I thought. If

Riley hadn't gotten lucky this morning, leaving me feeling sexy, I would have been wearing my old comfy one.

"Sorry."

"Stop saying sorry!"

"Sorry." Shit

"You've said it forty-five times today already."

"Is that a lot?"

"I haven't said it at all."

Yeah, but that didn't mean much. I put the car in gear and thanked the universe my windows were tinted with the darkest tint I could get.

When I stopped at the traffic lights, I did notice one guy look twice at me. Obviously my windows weren't dark enough. Thankfully the light changed to green and I quickly accelerated away. The guy in the car next to me must have been in a little bit of shock as he was nowhere near as fast as I was off the mark. Turns out it was his lucky day.

As I sped up through the intersection, I noticed a silver Mercedes on my right speeding towards me, completely ignoring the red light it would have had. I didn't have time to do anything before it smashed into my little car, sending it sliding sideways across the bitumen. I heard the smashing of glass, the scraping of metal and the screeching of tires as Danny screamed in my ear and the airbag in my seat deployed. I was too shocked to react and allowed momentum to take my car wherever it wanted to go. Everything seemed to slow as the world around me disappeared into background noise and my airbag deflated.

I was vaguely aware of Danny moving in the seat next to me as my driver's door was wrenched open and voices came into focus. It was only when I heard the sound of sirens in the distance that I felt the tears well in my eyes and the shaking start.

UNBELIEVABLY, it was Allison's voice I heard as I was helped from my car. My legs worked, my arms worked and I'm sure my voice would work as soon as I could get thoughts together properly, so it appeared I was okay.

"Lizzie!" she cried. "Lizzie!" I looked up as a passerby restrained her.

"Miss, you need to stay back," he said to her.

"No, I know this woman," she replied.

"But you're hurt," he said.

I blinked as I looked up at her and noticed a small trickle of blood run down her temple. Confusion swirled in my muddled brain.

"Where's Danny?" I asked quietly, ignoring her completely.

"I'm here," I heard him say. I turned to see him being helped from the car. He moved to the footpath and sat down heavily as a particularly attractive paramedic ran to help him. If he wasn't fine, he soon would be. An older-looking paramedic pushed his way through the crowd that had gathered, and made his way towards me. It was Paramedic Jim.

I allowed him to help me to the curb and sat as he tended my wounds. Thankfully my little Mini had saved me from any serious damage, but I felt the tears fall freely as I looked at it sitting in the road, bent and broken.

"Lizzie?" I heard a deep familiar voice say. Standing in front of me, silhouetted by the sun, was Ed Helms. He moved to kneel, his face coming into focus.

"Ed?"

"Christ, I thought that was your car," he said, taking my hand. He was dressed in his uniform, so I guessed his visit here was an official one. "Are you okay?"

"Hi Ed," said the paramedic.

"Jim," nodded Ed. "What happened here?"

"W...well..." I stuttered. Feeling the security of Ed's large hands holding mine, the focus I had been regaining, started to slip away from me again. "Umm...I was...umm..."

"Just take your time, Lizzie." His grip on my hand tightened.

I took a deep breath and tried to control my breathing, as Paramedic Jim attached me to a monitor. I really hoped it wasn't monitoring my heart rate.

"My light turned green and I moved into the intersection when a car on my right hit me, but I know that I had a green light," I added with conviction.

"I'm sure you did."

"Lizzie," interrupted Paramedic Jim, "the lady that was in the car that hit you wants to see you. She says she knows you. Is it okay if she comes over?" he asked looking more to Ed than to me.

"I guess so," I said quietly, as Ed looked at me with concern.

Jim stood and moved to his partner, nodding to let the woman through. As the crowd parted, Allison moved into view.

"Oh, Lizzie!" she cried. I quickly pulled my hand away from Ed's before she noticed, but I wasn't quick enough. I saw the look pass through her eyes as she moved to stand in front of me. "I'm so sorry. I just didn't see the red light." The tears welled up in her eyes and I may be a bitch, but I'm sure they were fake and put on for show. "Are you hurt?"

"You know each other?" asked Ed, standing.

"Yes. I'm Lizzie's therapist," she said loudly, holding out her hand to Ed. Ed's jaw flexed as he took her hand and shook it.

"And you're the driver of the car that hit Lizzie?"

"Yes. I am," she added quietly.

"Well, I'll need to get an official statement from you shortly, but I'll leave you two alone for a few minutes whilst I speak to my partner and look over the vehicles. Will you be okay, Lizzie?" he asked kindly.

I nodded and watched as he moved into the road, stopping in front of my car. A lump formed in my throat as the tears fell again.

"He's cute," said Allison, following my gaze, as red and blue lights from the emergency vehicles flashed across her face.

"I need to call Riley," I said quietly, wiping my tears with the back of my hand.

"Oh, no need. I've already called him. He's on his way."

By the time Riley reached us, Paramedic Jim had thankfully covered my semi-naked torso with a blanket, and was strapping me to a gurney. He was pushing me into the ambulance as Riley rushed towards me, torture in his beautiful eyes. As I reached out to him and held on tight, I felt his heart beating fast against his ribs. Pulling me close, he kissed the top of my head and his heart rate decreased.

"Look at my poor little Mini," I cried, glancing at it as it was pulled on to the back of a tow truck.

"We can always get you another one," he said, his deep voice betraying his emotion.

"Surely they can fix it?"

We both looked up at her. Her bonnet was smashed, the side doors were smashed, the headlights were gone, the windows were broken, and I'm no expert on cars, but I didn't think wheels were supposed to be on the angle that they were at present.

"Maybe," said Riley, grimacing.

"Sorry, love," said Paramedic Jim, walking towards me, "but we need to get you to the hospital."

Fear danced in Riley's eyes.

"We just want a doctor to check the knock you've got on your head. That's quite an egg you've got growing there."

I reached up and felt my forehead and indeed, Jim was right. It felt like someone had put a tennis ball under my skin. In fact, now that the adrenalin had stopped pumping, I actually felt like I'd gone ten rounds in a boxing ring.

"Alright," said Riley, kissing me gently. "I'll follow you there."

"Where's Danny?" I asked, looking at Jim.

"He's in another ambulance. We'll meet him at the hospital."

"Is he okay?" Uneasiness snaked through my stomach.

"He's fine. We just want to get an x-ray of his arm," explained Jim as I settled back against the gurney, relieved. I quickly sat back up as Allison's voice rang through the air.

"Riley!" she called, touching his arm as she moved close to him. "I'm so sorry, Riley," she said, tears welling, as her eyes got wide. "I just didn't see the red light." As she spoke, I noticed she started to shake and the tears spilled over her lashes and down her cheeks. As she looked at Riley, her crying turned up a notch. She leaned forward and fell into his arms.

Jim chose that moment to push my gurney into the back of the ambulance. The last thing I saw was Allison burying her head into Riley's chest, as he put his arm around her shoulders and held her tight.

CHAPTER 14

A few days had passed since my run in with Allison but my body still felt sore from the impact. I will sadly report that little Mini could not be fixed, but the girl at the insurance company assured me that the money would be in my account in the next few days. Then I could go shopping for a new car. Somehow, I just didn't share her enthusiasm.

What's that saying? TGIF? That's all I could chant as I closed my computer on the accounting file I was working on, and headed down the stairs. I'd actually lost track of time, and I was now running late for Friday night get together. Bugger.

Work had slowed on my renovation due to Riley spending quite a bit of time at Allison's, apparently making her house habitable and safe from any intruders.

I was actually quite proud of the way I'd been behaving about it. I'd been very mature (If I say so myself) and only swore and punched the furniture when Riley wasn't around. It hadn't stopped us arguing a few times about it, though.

Sure, I understood he needed the money and apparently she was paying him a very good rate. I just wished she was an ugly hag and that Riley hated her.

I tried to distract myself from that thought as I packed Cat into his box. I opened the front door, about to step out when I remembered I should check the lock on the back door. I put Cat down, and went to the kitchen, flicking the light switch on as I went. I was about to make a quick dash across the room when I froze.

The blood was back. And this time it was double the amount we usually saw.

I felt the scream strangle in my throat as the wind blew the back door open, slamming the front one shut.

Time stood still as it whistled through the old house, and the hairs on my neck stood to attention, my breath stuck in my lungs. Cat howled from his box.

I spun around, grabbed the keys to my loan car and Cat, and got the hell out of there as fast as I could, dialing Ed as I ran.

THE SIGHT of the blood had freaked me out and my heart rate skipped outside the normal range, but Ed's words played on my mind. Was the blood real? I practiced some deep breathing and calmed myself with the knowledge that Ed was going to find out.

I pulled into Riley's drive and maneuvered past all the cars, realizing everyone had beaten me here.

"Hello," I called as I walked in, throwing my bag on a nearby chair. "Sorry, I'm late." I put Cat on the floor and opened his box. He immediately high-tailed it to the stairs and straight for Riley's bed. "You'll never guess what happened as I was leaving, though."

"What happened?" asked Riley, greeting me with a quick kiss. He moved past me to the refrigerator, opening it and retrieving two beers. I watched him as he moved back and handed one to Matt. Riley finally had another beer drinker to share a beer with. Molly moved to me and handed me a glass of wine.

I took the wine and drained the glass in one go, in the hope that the alcohol would settle my anxiety. Everyone was looking at me, waiting for an explanation.

By the time I had recalled the scene in the kitchen, everyone was draining *their* glasses and demanding a refill.

"I called Ed about it. He's on his way over there now."

"You didn't wait for him?" asked Danny.

"No. He didn't want me there alone, so he told me to leave. He's going to do his thing and lock the doors behind him." I shrugged. In the car listening as Ed told me to get away from the house I'd felt more freaked out than ever before. But sitting here with Riley and my family, I felt safe. Riley's house played a part in that feeling. Now I'm not an overly religious person. I do believe in God, but I'm more of a casual participant. However, I did wonder how I would feel living in an old church. Sure, I knew it was previously a house of God and surely he didn't stop protecting it once he'd upgraded to something bigger, but I did think of how many funerals would have been held here in the day. Funny though, all I felt when I was here was safe and secure.

"You should have a security system fitted," said Danny, rubbing the goosebumps off his arms.

"CCTV camera's would be better," said Matt. "You'll see exactly how it's getting there."

Riley nodded. "Yeah. That's a good idea. A friend of mine fits those. I'll give him a call."

"Don't stay in that house alone Lizzie," said Molly, looking at me, her eyes huge with fear.

"There's no need to worry about that," I said.

"There has to be a logical explanation," said Andrew.

Riley nodded. "Yeah, beats me what it is though."

"I don't care what it is. It creeps the hell out of me. The sooner I sell that house the better."

THANKFULLY THE CONVERSATION lightened with the more alcohol everyone consumed, and once we'd all eaten it felt like everything was back to normal. We were just cleaning up when Ed rang.

"How are you feeling?" he asked, his voice soft in my ear.

"Freaked out," I answered honestly.

"I can see why. I'm just locking up now."

"Really? It took that long?" I asked, checking my watch. It had been nearly two hours since I'd called him.

"No, not really. We took all the swabs we needed and I'm going to hurry the lab up with the results. Hopefully I'll have the results of the first swabs by tomorrow morning." Ed's voice sounded weary. "Most of the time was spent cleaning." I felt my breath catch.

"You cleaned?"

"Yeah. I didn't want you to have to clean it tomorrow." I didn't know how to respond. I was sure cleaning did not come into his official police duties.

"Oh thank you," I said lamely. "Umm...what time does your shift finish tonight?" I asked, my mind spinning.

"It finished five hours ago."

"What? That's a lot of overtime."

Ed chuckled. "I wish it was. No, I was at home when you rang."

I felt horrified and guilty at his words. "I'm so sorry. I didn't think," I said. "I saw the blood and panicked. I didn't even think that you wouldn't be at work."

"It's okay. I want to help you." For a moment Ed's voice felt intimate. "Lizzie, there's something I want to tell you, but I can't..." My heart missed a beat as a different kind of panic took hold. I was standing in the kitchen, looking at Riley as he smiled at me over his beer bottle. With Ed's voice in my ear, I felt like I was betraying him.

"Ed I really should go."

"Oh...umm...okay." He seemed taken aback with my abruptness.

"Thank you so much for your help tonight. I mean it Ed. I appreciate everything you've done." I wanted him to understand that I really was grateful but at the same time I didn't want to give him the wrong idea about my feelings for him. I heard his sigh.

"All part of the service Lizzie."

After he hung up, I moved to the wine bottle and poured myself another glass.

❧

TONIGHT WE WERE PLAYING RUMMIKUB. It was a game Andrew introduced us to, and it involved two to four players. Tonight there were actually six of us, so we decided to play in teams. Andrew and Danny, Molly and Matt, and Riley and I. I wasn't the best at the game, but thankfully Riley was. We played best of five. When we played single player, I always wanted to play best of twenty-seven. That way I may actually have a chance to win one! By our fifth game, we were in the lead. We were up two games thanks to Riley, Molly and Matt had one, and Danny and Andrew had one. If we won this game, we would win the match. If anybody else won, it would go to a tiebreaker.

Molly laid her tiles and called that she only had one tile left. I looked at our hand and excitement surged. I had it! I knew what I had to do to win.

I pushed my chair back and stood, leaning across the table to rearrange tiles into a winning combination.

"Oh here we go!" yelled Danny. "She's standing! Lizzie's about to win." Everyone laughed good-naturedly.

"You don't know that," I commented, trying to hide my smile.

"Everyone knows that," said Riley, rubbing my backside affectionately.

I looked around our group. All eyes were on me and they were all smiling.

"You stand up when you're about to win," said Molly, laughing.

"Lizzie has no poker face," said Danny.

Humph. "Yes I do! You don't know what tiles I've got."

"Go on then. Finish your go," challenged Danny.

I looked at the tiles in my hand. He was right of course, I was about to win, but now I had a dilemma. Did I want to win and let him know he was right, or should I sit back down and pretend he was wrong? I sighed and put the tiles on the table, declaring we had won. Everyone laughed as I sat back down.

"Told you so. Never play poker for real money." Danny thought he was hilarious.

"Don't worry about it," said Riley, kissing me above my ear. "It's one of the things I love about you."

I gave a contented sigh and leaned into him, happiness filling me with a warm glow. Then again, that could have been the wine.

"Do you want another beer, Matt?" he asked, standing and walking towards the fridge. Matt nodded.

I watched as Riley moved, thinking how sexy he looked tonight in his new jeans, his black T-shirt molding his body to perfection. As he reached into the fridge ready to retrieve two beers, his phone rang. He stopped what he was doing and pulled it from his pocket.

As he looked at the screen, he opened the back door and stepped outside. I heard him say, "Hi, Allison."

I looked to Molly. The atmosphere in the room changed as everyone looked to me.

"You're handling this a lot better than I thought you would," she said.

"What choice do I have?" I shrugged, clearing the plastic tiles off the table.

"Have you told him it bothers you?"

"Yes, but that always ends in an argument. I've only shut up about it because I don't want to drive him into her arms."

"Maybe that's her plan," said Molly.

"Ed says there's a possibility that the blood's fake. He said it could just be someone trying to scare me. I thought of her."

"Personally I think she's trying to *kill* you," said Danny.

I looked at him expecting to see a glint in his eye. Instead I saw he was perfectly serious. Riley chose that moment to walk back into our conversation. He looked stunned at Danny's words.

"Lizzie, Allison is not trying to kill you!" said Riley, picking up his beer bottle.

I didn't respond. Instead I looked at Danny, the events of the last few weeks racing through my mind. Everyone went quiet.

"Danny may have a point," I finally said, breaking the silence.

Riley scoffed. "Are you serious?" he asked, staring at me. "Christ! You are, aren't you?"

"Think about it," I said quietly.

"You know, if you gave her a chance, you might realize she's quite a nice person," said Riley, pulling the label off the bottle in his hand. "All she does is ask about you."

Humph.

"You actually have a lot in common," he continued. "She loves that stupid TV show you like, she wears the same perfume you do, and she's always asking about your house."

"She wears the same perfume?" asked Molly. "It's time to change perfume, Lizzie," she whispered, as Riley turned his back.

"Which perfume?" I asked, making a note to throw it out.

"The one I bought you for Christmas. What was it? Umm, A Dior one."

"What does she ask about the house for?"

"She really likes the choices you made and was hoping to do something similar to her place. She especially likes the wallpaper."

"How does she know what wallpaper I used?" I asked incredulously.

"She saw it last week when she dropped by."

"What? Where was I?"

"You were at your mum's."

"Why did she drop around?" My skin crawled with suspicion.

"To make sure that you were okay after the whole allergy thing."

"Sure."

Riley sighed.

"I just think she's trying to get me out of your life," I added.

"It is funny how she always seems to be around whenever your life is in danger," added Danny quietly.

"I know!"

Riley scoffed. "Really, Lizzie. You're being a bit dramatic, don't you think?"

"I've nearly died twice in the last month and who was there on both occasions?" I looked at Riley. Emotion danced in his eyes. "Hmmm?"

"It was a coincidence."

"Bullshit!"

"Why would she try to kill you?"

"Because she's still in love with you and she wants you back!" Ha. There, I'd said it.

"Lizzie, there's a flaw in that theory."

There was?

"Let's assume for a second that you're right and Allison wants to get back with me, then why hasn't she said anything to me?"

I sighed dramatically.

"Riley, you are such a man! She has been telling you."

"Thank you for realizing the obvious. And yes I am a man, as you put it, but I clearly do not recall Allison saying she loves me...at least, not in the last few years."

My stomach churned at his words, but I lifted my chin and carried on.

"She flirts with you. That's her way of saying it."

"Rubbish. If it were me, I would just walk over to her, tell her how I felt and kiss her."

"Women aren't like men though, are they?"

"Seriously, Lizzie. You're wrong. She's a completely sane, rational person, and sane, rational people do not go around killing other people. Plus she has absolutely no *reason* to kill you."

The room filled with silence, everyone afraid to move. Personally, I was so caught up in my theory I'd forgotten they were all there.

"Lizzie has a good point though, Riley," said Matt, the first to be brave and speak.

Riley turned to him, his expression quizzical.

Matt shifted uncomfortably. "I don't believe in coincidence. Years of reporting has proven that. I can guarantee you that whenever I have reported on a crime, the guilty party is the one who is there at the time."

"Well, of course they were there at the time of the crime," scoffed Danny. "How could they have done it if they weren't there?"

Molly looked to Danny and glared.

"Maybe you're looking at this from the wrong angle," Matt continued, undeterred by Danny mocking him.

"What do you mean?" I asked.

"Well, let's say you're right that Allison is trying to kill you. What other reason would she have?"

I sunk into a nearby chair and considered what Matt had said.

"She doesn't have any reason," said Riley heatedly. "Until Lizzie walked into her clinic, they'd never even met."

Riley was right about that.

"Okay. What's happened since then?"

"Nothing," I said reluctantly.

"Harper found the bones in your garden," said Molly.

"No, that was before I met her."

We all sat in silence considering the events that had happened since I'd met Allison.

Eventually Danny looked up and said, "Maybe she's not trying to kill you. Maybe she's just in the wrong place at the wrong time."

"Maybe she's in the right place at the right time," snapped Riley. "What would have happened if she hadn't been there the day you had the anaphylactic shock?"

"I wouldn't have been in that café, and I wouldn't have eaten the peanut oil," I pointed out. "And, by the way, it was Allison who ordered that food. Did she really tell them about my allergy?"

Riley looked at me, his expression stony. "It's a coincidence and you need to stop accusing people of something so horrible," he said, his tone suggesting this was the end of it. He turned and walked from the room, slamming the door behind him.

We all sat in silence.

"Well, if I was you Lizzie, I'd be careful around her," said Matt. "Like I said, there's no such thing as a coincidence."

Riley's car door slammed and the motor turned over.

I felt the tears sting my eyes and emotion clog my throat.

Why didn't I just shut up?

Molly came to me and pulled me in for a hug. "He's just gone to let off some steam."

"What if I've pushed him into her arms?"

"Riley loves you. Have faith in that."

"Yeah well, I thought Scott loved me and remember what he did to me?"

I'll never forget the night I walked into my then boyfriend's bedroom and found him doing the nasty with his secretary.

"Riley's not Scott. He wouldn't do that to you."

"I hope not," I whispered, as Molly pulled me in tighter.

Conversation slowed after that and by the time the clock struck midnight, I woke Danny and Andrew up from the lounge and sent them home. Matt had left about an hour before after he'd got a call from his cameraman Sam, saying there was a big accident on the Highway and they needed to be there for coverage.

"Molly, go home please. I'll be fine," I said, exhausted.

"I don't want to leave you alone," she said, yawning.

"Honestly. I'm fine," I lied. Riley still hadn't come home. He'd sent me a message about an hour ago saying he'd gone to visit Jared and would spend the night there. "Please, Molly. I just want to be alone." What I really wanted was to sit in the shower and sob, but I didn't want Molly to know that.

Molly debated what to do. "Okay, but ring me if you need me. It doesn't matter what time it is. I'll be straight over. And if Riley comes back, slap him senseless for me."

I smiled in spite of myself. "I will. Right after I've slapped him for Danny, which will be right after I've slapped him for myself."

"Good. Maybe that will make him see sense."

I locked the door behind her and made my way upstairs. I was too tired for the shower, so I splashed my face with water and climbed into bed.

It felt cold and lonely without Riley. Only after I'd emptied the box of tissues drying my eyes, did I manage to fall into an exhausted sleep.

I woke as a weight shifted on the mattress. I knew it was Riley. I could smell his delicious aftershave that still held even after all these hours.

The sheet pulled back and he slid in behind me. As his arm came around my waist and pulled me close, he whispered in my ear.

"I'm sorry, Lizzie."

I felt goosebumps break out where his breath touched my skin and instantly forgave him.

"Me too," I said, snuggling my bottom closer to him, enjoying his warmth. The world was safe once again.

CHAPTER 15

Saturday night was Mal's birthday, and the family was having dinner to celebrate. With Allison in my life so much lately, I felt I needed a wardrobe revamp in order to make myself feel a little more confident, and Molly was just the person to help me.

Westport isn't the largest town on the east coast. The last census said it had a population of thirty thousand. It had one large hospital, one cemetery and one shopping centre. Pretty much all everyone needed.

Molly and I were, at present, in the ladies section of the one and only department store, and I was trying on a grey dress Molly had picked out for me. Molly stood outside the fitting room door, bringing me up to date on Matt, and judging by her dreamy tone, I figured things were going better than planned. I will admit he seemed to fit with us pretty well, and he'd stayed strong throughout last Sunday's family dinner, not once looking for the exits—which is more than I could say for myself. I usually looked for the exits at least twice during dinner.

"How's things with Riley?" she asked, as I lifted the dress over my head.

I pulled it down and reached backwards to pull up the zip. "Yeah, okay," I said, cursing quietly as the zip caught in my hair. "He came home last night and we had a good talk. I just need to keep my opinion about Allison to myself from now on. Molly, I'm stuck," I cried.

"Well, open the door and I'll help you."

I turned to the door, my head on a weird angle leaning backwards, and opened the lock.

Molly laughed and stepped inside to help me. "Seriously, Lizzie. How do you get out of the house in the morning?"

I sighed. "Just help me, will you."

"Turn around."

I did as asked and felt my hair being pulled from the follicle as Molly pulled the zipper back down. Pushing my hair over my shoulder, she pulled the zip up effortlessly.

Smoothing the dress into place, I stood back and looked in the mirror, Molly's reflection beaming back at me.

"It's gorgeous!" she trilled.

Really? The dress was made of a dark material I think Mum had once used to cover her couch. It had an unflattering round neckline, fell straight and fitted to my waist, and then puffed out with a very large skirt, complete with tulle underskirt.

"Umm...it's not really me, is it?" I screwed up my nose.

"The problem with you, Lizzie is you have no taste. This dress is a designer brand and believe me—it's gorgeous."

I looked back at myself in the mirror. "Maybe it needs shoes?" I said, unenthusiastically.

"Here," said Molly slipping out of hers. She kicked them towards me. I bent to straighten them and as I did the back of the skirt flipped up, showing Molly my underwear. I jumped up and pulled it back down.

"Hmmm, maybe this one isn't such a good idea," said Molly frowning. "You've already got a talent for embarrassing yourself. You definitely don't need any assistance."

Thank you, God.

I hurriedly removed the ugly dress and pulled the next one off the hook.

It was aqua blue colored silk, straight-fitting to the knee with navy blue band around my waist. As I slipped it on, my waistline suddenly lost three inches and my height grew. At least the dress gave the illusion that it had.

"Okay," said Molly resignedly. "This one suits you a lot better."

"It kind of reminds me of something Allison would wear," I said, smoothing the skirt into place.

"Hmmm," said Molly, eyeing me critically. "No, I don't think so. She wouldn't wear anything like it."

"How would you know? You've never met her."

"I googled her. This dress isn't slutty enough."

I laughed. "Allison doesn't really look slutty," I said resentfully. "Every time I've seen her, she's always looked nice." I felt the words choke in my throat.

"Well in this dress, you look nicer."

I looked at Molly and smiled. "Let's hope that Riley thinks so."

"I may not know Allison, but I know people like her. She's a skank, and no matter what anybody says, I think she's deliberately trying to hurt you."

I rubbed the fabric through my fingers, considering what Molly had said, swallowing the lump in my throat.

Molly put her arms around me and pulled me tight. After the best big sister hug, she let go and held me by the shoulders.

"You know what we should do? We should buy one of those little voodoo dolls they sell at the markets and on Friday night we'll stick pins in it."

"I don't think it's that easy."

"Then we'll Google exactly how to do it and voila! Her hair will start to fall out and she'll get ugly."

I laughed at Molly's enthusiasm. "Sounds like a good plan. We'll just have to keep Riley out of the room when we do it."

"And don't go getting all self-righteous about it," added Molly. "Allison is a bitch if ever I saw one. She deserves everything she gets."

I just hoped that she didn't get Riley.

"Now, take this dress off and meet me downstairs. I think I need a sugar hit and that chocolate shop is just the place that will do it."

Molly opened the fitting room door and stepped out. I watched her retreating back and was just closing my door when the one next to me opened. And out stepped Allison.

I sucked in my breath and hid behind the door, hoping she hadn't seen us or heard us.

Shit!

❧

I PAID for the dress and met Molly downstairs in the chocolate shop. This was one of my favorite shops for lunch, as just about everything you ordered contained chocolate. We decided to skip real food and ordered an Italian thick hot chocolate with chocolate crepes for me, and a cappuccino and chocolate banana pizza for Molly. Insulin dependency, here we come.

Over lunch Molly asked me about Bradley.

"I haven't seen him this week, Molly."

"Maybe he's moved his tours to someone else's back garden."

"Yeah, I kind of miss him though."

"Are you serious?"

I nodded. "He's sort of cute in an annoying kind of way, and the crowd he brings with him can be very entertaining."

"I watched his video diary last night," said Molly, spooning the froth off her cappuccino and eating the chocolate. "He said he knew who killed that body in your garden."

I sat up straighter in my chair at Molly's words.

"What?"

"You haven't seen it then?"

"No. Did he say who did it?"

Molly shook her head. "He just said to tune back in tomorrow and all will be revealed."

"Maybe we should tune in then," I said, pulling my phone from my bag. I swiped it opened and pressed the appropriate app. I searched Bradley and waited for the list of his videos' to appear. The last one was dated two days ago.

"That's the one I saw," said Molly, peering over the top of the phone.

"He hasn't uploaded a new one yet," I said, disappointed. I clicked on the last video and made a mental note to speak to Bradley if he turned up today.

Molly and I sat in silence as Bradley appeared on the screen. The video was a short one, only lasting thirty seconds, and it appeared to be filmed in the same location as all his others. A garage. I realized I didn't really know too much about him. I knew he was only in his early twenties, a few months ago he had moved out of home to live with his girlfriend, but she dumped him after the first week. He was stuck paying rent on his own. I had no idea where that was though.

I watched his boyish grin spread, his facial hair a day past needing a shave. He looked animated as he spoke, saying he had found a clue to who had killed Ronald Smithson, and that he would reveal all after he had spoken to the police. He felt it was his duty to inform them first. He then left us a teaser about logging back on tomorrow and he would reveal who the murderer was.

I looked at Molly, my curiosity piqued.

"Ed hasn't phoned me with any news. I would have thought Bradley would have spoken to him."

"Ed?" Molly looked at me, eyebrows somewhere around her hairline.

"The policeman helping me with information."

"Is this the really good-looking one with the dark skin?"

I nodded.

"Hmmm..."

"I know what you're thinking, and it's not like that. He's just a friend."

"If you say so."

I stuck my tongue out at Molly and made a note to call him later to see if he had any news.

❦

DON'T ASK me how it happened, but Riley had dobbed me in to bake Mal's birthday cake. *Surely it couldn't be that hard?*

After the initial panic subsided, I watched *The Great Bake Off*, and decided that of course I could make a cake. After the third attempt, four emergency calls to Mum, and a quick dash to the supermarket to buy a packet mix, I even managed to produce something that looked and smelled like a cake. And I'm sure the icing would cover the top so no one would even notice the burnt bits.

I put all the dirty dishes in the dishwasher and headed to my house to see how Riley was progressing.

When I got there, my driveway was blocked with Allison's car. I parked on the road and beeped my car locked. Memories of last night stuck in my mind like a red-hot poker along with the memory of the last time I saw her. The snapshot I had was of how she looked at the site of the accident being held by Riley, and the look of familiarity in his eyes. It broke my heart.

After Riley had climbed into bed last night, we'd had a heart to heart, and I had managed to pluck up the courage and ask him how long the two of them had been together. He told me that they had been together for nine months and she had been his first love, but in the end he realized they were not meant for each other and he ended it by joining the army. He now admitted he was running away. At the time, it had felt like the easier option.

We discussed our previous relationships. It appeared Riley had been a lot busier than I had been, totaling up four more partners than I'd had. Looking at his gorgeous blue eyes and rock hard abs, I could see why.

Nevertheless, I was apprehensive about Allison being parked in my driveway.

I quietly opened the front door and walked into the hallway. I heard Riley's deep, sexy laugh float towards me. My heart skipped a beat as I reminded myself how angry he'd got when I'd doubted his feelings for me.

I put my bag on the bottom stair, put a smile on my face and stepped into the kitchen.

"Hello," I said.

"Lizzie! Hi," said Allison, with a smile.

"Oh hi, Allison, I didn't expect you to be here."

"I came over to see how you were. I feel so guilty about what happened."

"Don't feel guilty. I'm fine," I replied.

"But every time I close my eyes, I see Riley's face and how hurt he would have been if anything had happened to you." Her eyes filled with the thoughts.

"Well, you don't need to worry about Riley being upset. I'm perfectly fine and I can assure you I'm not going anywhere!"

"Yes, I can see that," she replied.

I moved to Riley and kissed him hard on the lips. I felt him stiffen. As we pulled apart, he glared at me. *Shit.*

"Maybe you should see a counselor," I said, laughing. "Maybe they can help you with that." Not that one ever helped me, I thought.

"Oh ha ha ha," said Allison, with a tinkling laugh. "You're funny, Lizzie."

Riley didn't seem impressed with my humor at all.

"Well, I probably should go," said Allison, finishing a coffee in her hand and placing the cup on the bench next to Riley. As she moved to leave, she gently touched his arm. "See you tonight."

What?

"Yeah, and I promise I'll get started on that broken lock tomorrow."

After she left, I closed the door behind her and stepped back into the kitchen. "Broken lock?" I asked, referring to his comments to Allison.

"She has a broken lock on her bedroom door she wants fixed."

"She lives alone. Why does she need her bedroom door to lock?" I asked, hating the fact that Riley would be so close to her bed.

"Lizzie, do you remember the first job I ever did for you?"

I thought back eight months to the day Riley and I met.

"Yes, you pulled the carpet up from the attic room."

"No, that's what I came to do. What I actually did was fix the lock on your bedroom door."

Oh. That's right. I remember now.

"But that's because I kept locking it and in the morning it would be open."

"Exactly. You wanted a lock that worked. Allison feels the same."

"But my door was only open because I had Joe Woods sneaking in and watching me through the night. I'm sure Allison doesn't have a stalker," I sulked.

Riley's jaw flexed at the memory. "I hope not," he snapped.

"What are you more upset about, Riley? Joe attacking me or someone else attacking Allison?" Tears stung my eyes but I blinked them away before I lost control. As much as Riley and I had talked, we were yet to have a screaming row. Funny, because that's what I felt like I needed.

Riley sighed, releasing his anger. "I don't want anyone being attacked by anyone," he replied quietly. Turning his back, he picked up a hammer and moved through the door to the deck.

I gave an internal scream and made a mental effort to let go of my emotions and stop another argument before Riley defended her anymore. I took a deep breath and released it to the count of three.

"Did Bradley's tour stop by today?" I called after him.

"No. Why?"

"That's unusual. He's always here by lunchtime."

"Why do you want him?" Riley asked again.

"I just want to ask him about a video diary he has. He says that he knows who the killer is."

Riley popped his head back through the doorway, his eyebrow raised questioningly.

"There's no harm in staying informed," I said.

"Is that what Ed Helms is doing for you? Is he keeping you informed?" Riley asked, stepping back into the kitchen. I could see the anger flash in his eyes and wondered how the hell this turned on me so fast.

"What?"

"Lizzie, Allison told me what happened at the crash site the other day and how Ed Helms was there to help you. Did you call him? Because you never called me."

"No, I didn't call him. And the only reason I didn't call you was because Allison stopped me, saying she'd already called you!" I yelled.

"Well he got there awfully fast, and from what I hear he was paying particular attention to you."

I scoffed, but the memory of the way Ed held my hand came rushing back.

"Did he help Danny the way he helped you?"

"He didn't help me. He was just concerned if I was okay." I shrugged my shoulders nonchalantly.

"Yeah, I know. He was so concerned he visited you personally in the hospital to make sure."

"Is that jealousy I hear?" I asked.

Riley sighed deeply and ran his fingers through his hair. "No, it's not jealousy. No more than what you feel for Allison is jealousy."

"Riley, it's hardly the same thing. Allison has had sex with you! Ed has *never* touched me." I felt the air between us crackle with electricity, and the atmosphere turned thick and dangerous. As Riley looked deep into my eyes, his thoughts unreadable, I gulped, the picture of Allison's legs wrapped around his body making my throat close.

He shook his head, threw his hammer on the ground and stormed out the door. As the front door slammed shut, I felt the tears skim my lashes as they escaped. *Shit.* Why didn't I keep my mouth shut?

❦

RILEY and I stayed out of each other's way for the rest of the afternoon. The renovation of my little house was nearly complete, the only jobs left being fitting the new kitchen and the painting of the back deck. Once that was done all we had to do was sand and stain the flooring and level the backyard.

I decided to get a head start on the painting. I tried to keep my mind off the argument and kept looking for Bradley and his tour to appear. By five o'clock he hadn't turned up and I started to worry. I know he could be an annoyance at times, but over the last month I'd grown to like him. I put my paintbrush down and pulled my phone from my pocket. I typed him a message.

Hi Bradley, I haven't seen you today. Hope you're okay I'm waiting to hear who the killer is!

Then I waited for a response. By five-thirty I still hadn't heard back and thought that if he hadn't replied by tomorrow, I'd follow it up. I honestly had no idea where Bradley lived so I made a mental note to call Ed and ask if he would find Bradley's address and check on him for me.

I moved inside to Riley. I found him with his head inside the wall, looking at some plumbing. Resting my back against the door jamb I waited a beat, just admiring the view. Today he was wearing his usual work clothes of jeans and an old T-shirt, but watching as it pulled tight across his back whenever he moved, I felt my hormones stir and butterflies awaken in my stomach.

He felt my stare and turned.

"Hey." He smiled, his eyes soft.

"Hey," I said back.

He stopped what he was doing, wiped his hands on his jeans and moved towards me. Stopping in front of me, he gently lifted his fingers to my nose and wiped off some stray paint from the tip of it. He chuckled.

"I think you have more paint on you than you put on the walls." He smiled the mega-watt smile and I knew all was forgiven.

"Would you like some?" I asked, nuzzling my nose into his neck.

He laughed and carefully took my face in both his hands. I felt my stomach flip as he lowered his head and gently kissed my lips. My spine dissolved as his soft lips moved over mine and the world became a good place once again. I gave a blissful sigh.

When he pulled up for air, he looked down at me. "I'm sorry about before."

"Me too," I replied. "I'm so afraid of losing you, Riley," I said quietly, voicing my deepest fear.

"I'm not going anywhere. This is my favorite place in the world."

I looked around what was once my kitchen.

"My kitchen?"

Riley chuckled. "No...right here...with you."

I gave another blissful sigh, stood on my tiptoes and kissed him deeply.

$\mathcal{B}$y the time we got back to Riley's house, the sun had set and we were running late. I'm not going into detail here as to why we were running late, but I had a memory of a conversation I'd had with Danny about how I never got any work done with Riley around. My renovation may be behind schedule, but damn, it was worth it.

Riley walked into his kitchen ahead of me and threw his wallet on the bench along with his car keys and phone.

"Ah, Lizzie...you might want to come here," he called.

I beeped the car locked and moved to him.

What I found was Cat sitting on the kitchen bench, gnawing on the birthday cake I had made for Riley's dad, Mal. Shit.

My heart stuttered in my chest as I ran at Cat shooing him away.

"*Oh my God!*" I cried, looking at what Cat had done.

"It's not so bad."

"Are you kidding me?"

We stood and surveyed the damage. My round cake was now not so round.

"What do I do?"

"Nothing."

"I can't take it like that!"

"Don't worry about taking it at all."

"But it's the birthday cake. Your dad can't have a birthday without a cake."

"Can you fix it?"

I picked up a knife and cut off the edge Cat had been nibbling on. I scraped the icing over it and stood back.

"If you cover it with sprinkles you'd never know," said Riley.

I sighed. "Bloody cat!"

❧

I RELUCTANTLY TOOK the cake to Riley's parents after he assured me it was fine and his dad would just appreciate the effort I'd gone to.

I carried it on my lap on the drive and more than once considered throwing it out the window. But then I remembered how I'd felt the year Mum had forgotten my birthday cake and knew that no matter what it looked like, I had to take it.

Riley pulled his truck into their driveway, and I followed him into the house.

"Hello sweetheart," said his mother Anna, kissing his cheek as he passed.

"Hi Anna," I said, smiling.

"Is that the cake?" she asked, kissing my cheek as she spoke. "Oh, I can't wait to see it."

Really? She was about to be very disappointed.

"It's not much," I said, inwardly cringing.

"Lizzie, you're too modest. I'm sure it's lovely."

I followed her through to the kitchen where I found Shelly, sitting at the table, cradling a sleeping Mia.

"Hello gorgeous," she said, her eyes twinkling as she spoke to me. See, that's why she was my second favorite Thomas.

"Hi Shelly."

"Lizzie has the cake," explained Anna, excitedly.

"Oooh, let me see," said Shelly, standing and moving closer to the bench where I put the cake down. Riley kissed her cheek as he walked alongside her.

At that moment Jared walked into the kitchen with Mal.

"You're just in time," said Anna, smiling at the boys. "Lizzie has your birthday cake."

"Hello Lizzie," said Mal kissing my cheek. Jared pushed him out of the way and gave me a hug.

"Let me just get a knife. I might not be able to wait for dessert," he said with a laugh.

I felt the dread in my stomach as I looked around their happy faces.

"Maybe we should wait for later," I said, hoping to stall.

"Don't be silly. Jared won't really eat it," laughed Shelly.

I'd make a bet he wouldn't.

Maybe the cake wasn't as bad as I remembered, I thought as I lifted the lid on the container. Everyone leaned forward for a look, Jared licking his lips as he did so. I stood back and felt my cheeks flame.

Time stood still as everyone stood frozen, all looking at the lopsided cake, the white icing filled with chocolate cake crumbs and sprinkles after my attempt at spreading it all over the missing piece.

"Oh! Well...it's...umm...lovely," said Anna.

Mal coughed to clear his throat. I heard the *unph* from Jared as Shelly elbowed him to stop him laughing.

"Thank you, Lizzie. It looks...delicious," said Mal.

"You should have used more sprinkles," said Riley in my ear.

Thankfully the doorbell rang and saved me from any more embarrassment. Everybody quickly hurried away from the disaster of my cake, and made themselves busy in the hope that it would miraculously disappear. Well, I guess I'd never be asked to make the cake again.

I placed the lid back on the container as Anna ran off to answer the door. Shelly passed Mia to Jared who then followed Riley and Mal into the lounge room. Shelly came and put her arms around my shoulders.

"It's okay," she said, sensing my unease. "You should have seen the first meal I ever cooked for Anna and Mal. I invited them over for a roast, but what I didn't realize was just how much the meat shrunk when it cooked. I think everyone had a piece of meat about the size of a fifty cent piece."

I smiled up at Shelly, grateful for her attempt at making me feel better. It was then I heard Anna's voice coming back through the kitchen door.

"That was such a lovely thought, Allison. But you really shouldn't have," I heard her say.

Wait a minute. Did she just say *Allison*? My heart missed a beat as I looked up to see Allison walking into the room, a large cake box in her hand.

"Well, I was just so thankful you invited me to dinner, and I remembered how much Mal loved the birthday cake I made him one year. I thought maybe he'd like another one as my way of saying thank you," she said. "Oh, hi Lizzie."

I stood and stared after her, as she moved to place her cake box on the bench.

"It was such a coincidence bumping into you like that," said Anna, smiling. "I've been thinking of you a lot lately."

"Ooh, I hope it was all good." Allison laughed.

"Of course it was all good." Anna laughed, then turned to Shelly and I.

Shelly's grip on my shoulder tightened.

"Allison, this is Jared's wife Shelly," said Anna, introducing the two women.

"It's a pleasure to meet you, Shelly. The last time I saw Jared he wasn't even dating." She laughed, lightly.

"Are you Allison as in Riley's *ex*-girlfriend Allison?" asked Shelly, having difficulty disguising the horror she was feeling.

Allison giggled again. "Yes, but we don't talk about that, do we Lizzie?"

I smiled awkwardly, unable to respond. My mind was only just registering her earlier comment to Riley about seeing him later.

"Allison was lovely enough to make Mal a birthday cake," said Anna, shifting uncomfortably.

"But Lizzie made the cake," said Shelly.

"Oh I'm so sorry, Lizzie. I didn't realize," said Allison.

"It's okay. Mal can have two cakes." Anna smiled.

"No, no don't be silly," said Allison. "Just throw mine in the bin. It'll be fine."

Anna opened the cake box Allison had put on the bench. I had a discreet peek. Sitting inside was the most exquisite cake I had ever seen. It was square, sat about five inches high, covered with blue and white icing that looked exactly like wrapping paper. On the top was a blue bow, all made from some sort of icing and a nametag that read *Happy Birthday Mal.*

"Oh my, I can't throw that in the bin!" cried Anna.

"Really, it's fine. Here let me do it," said Allison, moving to pick up the box.

"I'm sure Lizzie doesn't mind if we have both," said Anna, looking at me.

I'm sure she was really wishing I would throw mine in the bin so we could eat Allison's.

"It's not my best effort anyway," continued Allison. "I've only been decorating cakes for a short time and this one didn't turn out exactly how I wanted it. See here," she said, pointing to a small polka dot that was not as round as the rest. "No matter what I did, I just couldn't get every dot perfectly round."

"Well, yes it is lovely," said Shelly, finally finding her voice. "But I'm sure Lizzie's will taste better."

I remembered Cat sitting on the bench eating it, and thought at least one living creature may agree. Then again...Cat had never tasted Allison's, so maybe not.

"I'm sure it does and I bet it looks better too," said Allison sweetly. "Can I see it, Lizzie or do I have to wait until after dinner?"

I felt Anna and Shelly's eyes on me as my face flamed.

"After dinner, I think. Keep it as a surprise." It was going to be a surprise alright.

As we moved into the lounge to the boys, Shelly grabbed my arm and pulled me back. Only when Anna and Allison were out of earshot, did she turn to me.

"What the hell does she think she's doing?" she asked.

I shrugged. "I think she's trying to win Riley back."

"What?"

"She's been around a lot lately and she all but told me she's still in love with him." I felt the tears sting the back of my eyelids.

"Don't worry about it. He's never going to leave you for her. I mean just look at her. She's a stuck-up princess."

God, I loved Shelly.

"I don't know. We had a really big fight about her last night and then again this afternoon. It's alright now, but he gets really defensive when I talk to him about her. He thinks it's all in my mind."

Shelly crossed her arms over her chest. "Hmm, he came over really late last night. He was talking to Jared about something, but I went to bed and forgot to ask about it this morning. Let me talk to Jared. He'll know what's really going on in Riley's head."

"Thanks." I gulped.

It was a good idea to know what Riley was really thinking, but a part of me was worried I may not like what I heard.

ℰ

ANNA WAS AN EXCELLENT COOK, but in all honesty my appetite had upped and left me. I picked at the delicious beetroot and feta salad, and listened quietly to the conversation around me. I sat on Riley's right and Allison had managed to get herself seated on his left. She had Mal next to her at the head of the table with Anna next, alongside Jared. Shelly sat opposite me at the other end.

Anna seemed not to notice I wasn't enjoying dinner, her attention solely on Allison, talking about old times. When she offered to find the old photo albums and go through the photos, I felt Shelly kick me under the table. I looked up at her and could see what she was thinking. She hated this as much as I did. She elbowed Jared and tried to indicate that he should change the subject because I was uncomfortable.

Jared gave me a compassionate look.

"Hey Allison, I hear your driving's got no better with age."

I saw her blush

"Jared!" said Anna.

"It's okay, Anna. Jared's right. My driving is terrible. Poor Lizzie can pay testament to that."

All eyes turn to me. I half-smiled.

"Even though I really didn't think I deserved to be treated the way I was by the police. It was an accident and they could clearly see that."

"What do you mean?" asked Mal.

"Well one officer in particular was really rude. I'm sure he thought I deliberately did it. Which I didn't!" I felt Riley shift uncomfortably in his chair.

"Which officer was that?" he asked.

"Officer Ed Helms," replied Allison. "I won't forget that name." I noticed as she glanced my way, giving me a quick but mean-ingful look.

"You should report him," said Anna.

"Well, I thought about it, but by the way he was treating Lizzie, I thought he must be a friend, so I decided to drop it. I wouldn't want him getting into trouble."

Anna and Mal looked at me for an explanation.

"Well of course he'd defend Lizzie if he was her friend," said Shelly, thinking she was helping me. I'd already felt Riley's body tense, and would really like the conversation to move on to something else.

"No matter, if he was on duty he should have acted professionally and left personal feelings aside," said Mal.

"Jared, you should look into it," said Anna, turning to Jared.

"If Allison has a complaint, she should go to the station and talk to his superior," he answered reluctantly.

"Honestly, I just want to forget about it," said Allison. If she wanted to forget about it then why did she bring it up? "They're charging me with dangerous driving, and I really don't want to aggravate anybody. I'm hoping I can just pay a fine and it will all go away."

I heard Anna and Mal suck in their breath.

"Can Lizzie get the charges dropped?" asked Anna, turning to Jared once again. Honestly, you would think I wasn't even in the room.

Jared sighed. "She can talk to the prosecutor and see if he will drop it, but ultimately that's up to him."

All eyes turned to me. I felt the heat creep up my neck and smother me. I was the victim here and yes, I wanted her charged, whether she meant it or not. She could have killed me, or worse she could have killed Danny, but looking around the table, I felt a pressure build inside me.

I looked at Riley. He was pushing his salad around his plate, his appetite obviously no better than mine. I wanted him to defend me and tell everybody to back off. Allison deserved what she was getting. But he didn't. He just sat quietly.

"Umm...I'll see what I can do," I said, averting my eyes and looking at my plate.

"Don't stress, Lizzie," said Allison, sliding her chair back. "I'm sure it will all work out. Now, would you all excuse me please while I visit the little girls' room?"

All three Thomas boys stood as Allison walked away from the table.

I felt my shoulders drop as she stepped out of the room. Mal sat back down and conversation turned to some football game that was on TV last night. Anna stood and moved to clear the dirty plates from the table. I went to help.

"No Lizzie, you sit. I'll get the dessert ready. Shelly would you mind helping me?" Anna's posture was rigid, and I got the distinct impression she was a bit miffed with me. I guessed Allison must have been her favorite of Riley's girlfriends.

Shelly gave me a compassionate look as she moved to help Anna, and I was left alone sitting at a table with the three men, all of whom were pretty much ignoring me. I fiddled with my napkin as Riley's hand moved under the table and came to rest on my leg. His reassuring touch filled me with happiness.

I was about to put my hand on his, when his phone beeped in his pocket, signaling a message. He moved his hand to retrieve it.

Pulling his phone from his pocket, he swiped at the screen. He blushed, quickly turning the phone off and shoving it back in his pocket.

I looked at him quizzically.

He gave me a tight smile and turned back to the conversation with his dad and brother, his body language rigid and unnatural.

I wanted to ask him about the message when Allison walked back into the room, sat down next to Mal and joined in on their conversation.

I couldn't have joined in even if I had wanted to. I didn't know one end of a football from the other.

✿

BY THE TIME dinner was over I was exhausted, my shoulders were tense and I had a headache. And I still hadn't heard back from Bradley.

I stepped out into the cool fresh air, looked up and saw my first star for the night. I thought of my mum, and something she used to say to me when I was a kid popped into my mind.

"Star light, star bright, first star I see tonight. I wish I may, I wish I might, have this wish, I wish tonight." I closed my eyes and made my wish. Now I know I shouldn't tell you my wish because it won't come true, so let's just say it involved Riley. And Allison was not a part of the picture at all.

I opened my eyes as Riley brushed past me and moved to the car. I followed him and got into the passenger seat. He'd been pretty quiet throughout dinner, and more so when his mum served Allison's cake for dessert, saying it would be rude not too as she was the guest. At the time, Mal had winked at me, saying he would eat mine for lunch tomorrow. Personally, I was secretly pleased Allison didn't get to see my cake.

I could usually figure what Riley was thinking, but not this time. I watched his face as the streetlights flashed by, and thought back to the conversation earlier about me getting the charges against Allison dropped.

"Riley, do you think I should talk to the prosecutor about dropping the charges?" I asked quietly. My heart pounded loudly as I waited for his response.

"I think you should do what you feel is right," he answered, still keeping his eyes straight ahead.

"I will do what I think is right, but I'm asking for your opinion."

Riley stopped at a traffic light and looked at me seriously.

"No, I don't think you should have the charges dropped. She

was driving dangerously and she could have killed you." He reached out and took my hand.

Relief spread through me as a smile played on my lips for the first time since Allison had walked into the kitchen.

"However," he said smiling, removing his hand and accelerating as the light changed to green. "I think from now on you should buy all our cakes from the bakery."

I swatted his arm playfully as we laughed. Maybe my wish would come true after all.

CHAPTER 17

The following morning dawned sunny and hot once again, and I decided I should get on with the painting. Riley had gone to the hardware store to get something important. No idea what that was, but it didn't really matter, did it? I pulled out my phone to send him a message asking him to bring back something yummy from the bakery, when I saw the message I'd sent Bradley the day before. He still hadn't replied to it. I'd actually missed his cheeky grin the last few days, and really hoped everything in his world was okay. I decided to call him to see.

I listened to the dial tone ringing, but after what felt like an eternity it went to his message bank. I left a message for him to call me, then dialed Ed Helms. He answered almost immediately.

"Lizzie, it's good to hear from you. I've been meaning to call you actually."

"Oh really? Is everything okay?"

"Yeah but there's been a delay on the lab results. There was a big murder in the city and forensics have put everything on hold until the lab has processed their work first."

"So we don't know if it's real blood or not yet?"

"No, sorry. But I'll keep chasing it up. You haven't had any more appear?"

"No. Not as yet. Hopefully it never will."

"Fingers crossed," said Ed, his voice oozing compassion. "Is this a social call?" he asked.

"Umm...not really, I was hoping to ask for a favor actually."

"Of course, whatever I can do, I will."

"Well, you know Bradley, the guy that runs the Westport Tours?"

"Yes, I questioned him recently about the rumors he'd heard involving the body found in your garden."

"The thing is, he hasn't been around for a couple of days now, and I'm worried about him."

"Have you tried to call him?"

"Yes, but he's not answering his calls, his messages or Facebook. I also checked his Twitter, Instagram, Google Plus, LinkedIn, YouTube and Blog, and he hasn't uploaded anything since Monday." I honestly didn't understand how Bradley had the time to stay that connected.

"Hmmm...okay. I'll look into it. I'm sure he's fine, just taking some time out, but if it'll put your mind at ease, I'll pay him a visit."

I smiled with relief that someone would check on him. "Thanks. Did you see his video diary about knowing who the killer was?"

"No. Sounds like I should have though."

"So he didn't call you?"

"No. I haven't heard from him at all, but I'll definitely follow it up." I heard Ed's breathing, deep over the phone. "How are you otherwise?"

"Yeah, I'm good thanks." I thought about Anna's advice to Allison, and felt guilt run through me. "Umm, actually there was one thing," I said. "Allison turned up at Riley's parents' house for dinner last night, and I think she's going to report you for being rude to her the other day."

Ed contemplated what I'd said.

"Do you think I was rude to her?"

"No, but I don't like her very much."

He laughed.

"I just wanted to give you a heads up. She may not go ahead with it, but I thought you should know."

"It's okay, Lizzie. My boss is pretty cool."

I sighed. "So you won't get into any trouble?"

"None that I can't handle." He laughed. "But Lizzie, be careful around her."

I heard the warning in his words and felt the prickle run up my spine.

"Is there a reason I need to be?" I asked.

Ed's sigh was loud in my ear. "Just be careful. Please."

RILEY RETURNED HOME about an hour later. I'd finished painting the back wall, cleaned my brushes and was sitting down having a coffee when he walked in. He looked particularly happy about something.

"You were gone a long time," I commented.

"I ran a few errands while I was out," he said, moving to me, and kissing the top of my head. He sat in the chair opposite.

"The coffee has just brewed if you want a cup," I said.

"No thanks. Actually, I want you to go and pack."

"Pack?"

"Yes. Pack. You've been under a lot of pressure lately. I think you deserve this," said Riley, handing me an envelope. I carefully took it from him and opened it. Inside was a piece of white A4 paper with a printed reservation for the Hilton Hotel in the city. It was for two nights, starting tomorrow.

"Oh my God! Really?" I asked, looking up at him. I'd always wanted to stay at the Hilton, but had never been able to justify spending the money.

"I know we're not going very far, but I thought a break would be nice. Time for you and me." Riley took my hand and pulled me into his lap. I looked up and saw the sparkle in his eyes.

"Just the two of us. No interruptions or family dramas?"

"Nope. Just us. For two days. To do whatever we want."

I sighed blissfully as Riley kissed me softly on the lips. The tension in my shoulders relaxed as I gave in to his kiss and put my arms around his neck.

As the floor scorched under my toes, I pulled up for air, my hormones racing. "Maybe we should get a little bit of practice in. You know, just to make sure we're good at this," I said.

Riley smiled and gathered me up in his arms. Taking the stairs two at a time, he pushed the bedroom door open with his hip, and dropped me on the bed.

"I think we should practice a lot," he said, jumping next to me. "We don't want to waste our time at the Hilton not knowing what we're doing."

I giggled and rolled on top of him, pushing his shoulders back to the bed as I did so. My hormones were racing at approximately three times the speed of light as I placed my hands on his flat stomach and lifted his shirt. Lowering my head, I nibbled his neck, his breathing ragged in my ear. I heard the moan escape his lips as he lifted my shirt over my head, very deftly unhooked my bra and threw it across the room.

Now this is the part where I would normally ask you to please close your eyes, but as with everything in my life, we got very rudely interrupted by the phone.

"Ignore it," said Riley, his fingers working magic as he spoke.

"Okay. Sorry."

Riley put his arms around me and rolled me over to my back

where he continued on his plan, kissing his way down my neck. The doorbell rang. *Shit.*

Riley lifted his head and looked at me. "Ignore it." As he moved his head an inch lower, I moaned and thought I'd have no trouble ignoring the door.

It rang again.

"Lizzie, I know you're in there!" It was Danny.

"Stay quiet and he'll think we're not home," mumbled Riley, his mouth full of my flesh. *Oh boy!* He sure knew what he was doing!

The doorbell rang again. And again.

"Open up," yelled Danny. "I need to talk to you."

Now, I really was enjoying what Riley was doing, but all I could hear was the constant ring of the doorbell and Danny's voice. Hardly an aphrodisiac.

I sighed. "I'm sorry. As much as I want to, I can't ignore him."

"That's okay. His voice kind of killed it for me too." Riley rolled over onto the bed and ran his fingers through his hair, a habit he had when he was frustrated. Well, he wasn't the only one.

"Can you go and let him in while I find my bra? You know, if you're presentable and all." I looked at Riley's excitement and thought it would probably give Danny a heart attack.

Riley sighed and stood up, pulling his shirt back into place. "Don't worry, after hearing that voice, it'll hide for hours now."

I giggled as I watched Riley's glorious back walk out of the room. I climbed off the bed, retrieved my bra and T-shirt and spent a couple of minutes in the bathroom splashing cold water on my face before going down stairs.

I found Danny in the kitchen crying, with Riley standing next to him. When I'd first met Riley, Danny's crying had kind of freaked him out a bit, but now he knows it's just another day in the Fuller family.

"What's wrong?" I asked Danny, picking up the tissue box and handing it to him.

"Andrew, that's what," he replied, snatching a tissue as he spoke. "We're supposed to be going away tomorrow and he says he wants to cancel it! I've been looking forward to this time away without his mother. It's the only thing that's got me through the last few weeks."

"Well why does he want to cancel?" I asked. Riley had slunk out the back door the second I had walked into the kitchen. Lucky bugger.

"He says no one will look after her. There's nothing bloody wrong with her, Lizzie!"

"But Andrew must have a reason to think that there is," I said soothingly.

"She's just a manipulating cow," said Danny, blowing his nose.

"Danny! You can't say that."

"Why? It's the truth."

I was about to ask Danny for more details when my phone rang. I picked it up and saw the caller was Andrew.

I showed Danny the phone. "Why's he calling me?"

Danny shrugged as I swiped the screen and answered the call. "Hi Andrew."

"Lizzie, is Danny with you at all?" I heard the anxiety in Andrew's voice as he spoke.

"Yeah, he's here."

"I've been trying to call his phone but it must be playing up as it's not even ringing. Could I speak to him please?"

I handed the phone to Danny. "Apparently your phone's playing up," I said.

Danny shook his head and mouthed, "I switched it off. I don't want to talk to him."

"Man up, Danny and talk to him. You'll never sort it out otherwise."

Danny glared. I didn't care. Tomorrow I was going to the city for a couple of nights away from them all and the drama that went with them.

"Your shirt's inside out," snarled Danny as he snatched the phone from my hand.

I looked down at my shirt and realized he was right. My face flushed. Of course everybody knew what Riley and I got up to in the dark, and sometimes even in broad daylight, but it was still embarrassing to get caught in the act. I turned on my heel and walked outside to where Riley was sitting on the deck. Danny could sort his own bloody problems out.

THE NEXT MORNING I woke excited about the few days ahead. I'd lived and worked in the city for about ten years before buying this house, so I knew it pretty well, but in all honesty it wasn't the city that was making me excited. Or the hotel, even though it was pretty spectacular. It was spending time alone with Riley with no interruptions. Last night we had both agreed to only answer our phones if we thought it could be an emergency. In my case that was only after Mum had rung about seven times and left a voice message. Then I'd call her back. We couldn't check in until after two pm, and it was only seven am now, but our bags were packed, Cat had been left with the run of the house and a bowl full of biscuits.

Molly had agreed to come over every day to make sure he was okay. She had my phone number so if anything went wrong with Cat, she could leave me a message and I would call her back. I was determined my family was not going to interrupt my sanctuary. Riley was right. I was pretty wound up and anxious. That was partly because I couldn't go a day in my family without a drama, partly because I was still trying to figure out why those bones were in my garden, but mostly because of Riley's working relationship with Allison.

Yes, I knew that was one of the reasons why he was taking me away. He wanted to show me I was the only woman he was interested in, but I still felt threatened by the time he spent with her. Since the purchase of her house had gone through, he seemed to be spending more time with her than me lately, and may I remind you that Riley and I got together *after* he had helped me with the renovations he'd been doing here?

I was sitting in my kitchen waiting for him to return from his dad's, when I looked out the window and saw Ed's police car pull into the driveway.

I walked to the door and opened it before he rang the bell.

As he stepped into my personal space, I got a nose full of his woody aftershave and had to shake myself to clear my senses. Looking closer at him, I could see the line of his mouth was drawn tight, and I felt anxiety swirl.

"Is everything okay?"

"Maybe we should go inside," he said, stepping up close so he was almost touching me.

"Ed, what's wrong. Is everything okay?" I asked as panic rushed at me.

"Lizzie, let's just go inside."

"Is it Riley?"

"No. As far as I know, Riley is perfectly fine."

"Then what is it?"

He sighed. "I followed up on Bradley." My stomach flipped.

"And?"

"Can we go inside?"

"Tell me please. What's wrong with Bradley?" Anxiety already had a hold on me.

Ed let out a long breath. "I'm sorry, Lizzie. He's dead."

"Dead?" I couldn't have heard him right.

"Yes. I found him this morning. He'd been shot. It looked like it happened a few days ago."

I felt the world sway and the room turn black, as my stomach rolled. Ed reached out to me as I stumbled and fell forwards. His strong arms came around me and lifted me inside. As he gently placed me on the couch, Riley walked in the door.

"What's going on?" he asked. Seeing my white face, his expression turned to concern as he rushed forward to me. "What happened?"

"Bradley's dead," I whispered. "He's dead."

Riley looked at Ed for an explanation.

"We're not sure, but we think it may be connected with a video diary he's got."

"The one about the body in my garden?" I asked, my stomach diving south.

"We need to look deeper into it. Nothing's certain at this stage, but Bradley had no prior convictions or any associations with crime whatsoever. The last video diary he made on Monday stated he knew who killed Ronald Smithson and to watch tomorrow when all was to be revealed."

"That means whoever killed Ronald Smithson is still alive and living in Westport," I said.

"Like I said, we don't know anything for sure. It could just be a coincidence." I thought of Matt's advice about coincidences.

"Is Lizzie in danger?" asked Riley, concern creasing his brow.

Ed looked uncertain. "I don't think so. Unless you know who the killer is?"

I shook my head. "No. Bradley never confided that to me."

"I'll have a patrol car drive past here every hour keeping an eye out for anything suspicious. Just don't stay alone until this is over, Lizzie."

"We're going away today."

"How long are you going for?"

"Two days," answered Riley.

"Good. Let me know when you get back and we'll decide what action we need to take then. If any," added Ed.

BRADLEY WAS on my mind throughout the trip into the city and even though I knew we were going away to relax, I wondered if I could possibly forget him long enough to do that. But upon reaching the hotel, it felt like we'd escaped to another planet away from our normal lives.

The hotel was amazing, with one tower for permanent residents and the other for guests. I stood and looked up at the sun reflecting off the glass windows as I waited for Riley to give the valet his keys. I sighed contentedly.

Entering the grand reception made of glass and stone, we did the check-in thing. We were informed our room wasn't quite ready, but we were very welcome to use the hotel facilities and they would call as soon as we could have the room key. Turning to head to the restaurant, we came face to face with Mum and Dad. *WTF?*

"Mum! Dad! What are you doing here?" I asked, my voice sounding very much like Alvin the Chipmunk.

"Oh, love!" laughed Mum. "We didn't know you were going to be here too."

Too? Who else was here?

"Are you meeting someone else?" asked Riley, who seemed just as shocked as I was.

"Well we're not exactly meeting them, but they are here." Mum smiled. Dad just looked uncomfortable.

"Who's here, Mum?" I asked, my heart rate increasing.

"Danny and Andrew, of course. They said they were going away last week remember?"

Yes, but I had no idea it was to this hotel. "But...but...they had an argument. They cancelled..." I stuttered.

"Oh, they kissed and made up. Andrew relented and got a carer in for his mother. I don't believe for a second she's really that sick," tut-tutted Mum. I shook my head, trying to clear it and make sense of what I was hearing.

"Why are *you* here?" I asked.

"Well, when they told us about this place it sounded really nice so your father and I decided to use the money we raised from the garage sale and treat ourselves."

"But...but...what about the ring?" I asked, distinctly remembering Mum telling me she was going to buy a ring with that money.

"Well when I went to Hogan's Jewelers somebody had already bought it," explained Mum.

At the mention of the ring Dad shifted uncomfortably next to her. I looked to him and wondered what he was up to.

"So Danny and Andrew are here too?" asked Riley, verifying he'd heard correctly.

"Yes, I think they've already checked in. Hang on let me see. Danny sent me a message when we were in the car." She lifted her phone from her handbag and scrolled through the menu until she found what she was looking for. "Here it is. Yes, they're in room 815. What room are you in, love?"

I looked at Riley. He looked at the paperwork in his hand.

"Oh, we don't have our key yet," he explained, looking at me shiftily. "They're going to call us when our room's ready."

"Oh, okay." Mum turned to Dad. "Go and check us in, Bill. See what room we're in. Wouldn't it be funny if we were all on the same floor next to each other?" Mum laughed, but I didn't think it was funny at all. Riley had just discreetly shown me the paperwork in his hand and it did indeed show our room number—816 —right next door to Danny.

No! This can't be happening!

I think Riley saw the panic in my eyes as he put his arm around my shoulders.

"We'll go and get a drink in the bar," he explained to Mum. "Let us know when you're checked in." He gave her the megawatt smile and steered me towards the bar. As soon as we were out of earshot, he turned to me and said. "Don't worry, once your parents are in their room, I'll go back to reception and explain the situation. I'll see if we can move."

"Maybe we should change hotels." I sulked.

Riley smiled and ordered me a drink. I know it was only midday, but I needed an alcoholic drink to soothe my nerves. It had been a stressful morning. Mum and Dad joined us a few minutes later.

"Our room's not ready yet," she explained, "but they gave us our room number. We're in 1005. Not next to Danny and Andrew, but maybe we'll be next to you." She smiled. "Are you sure they didn't tell you your room number?" she asked, looking at Riley. "They told us ours."

"I'll go and chase it up," said Riley, winking at me, and then walking back to the reception.

"Isn't this exciting?" asked Mum. Dad had gone to the bar to order them a drink too.

"Yes. Very," I replied. I know, I know, I was thinking exactly the opposite, but Mum just looked so excited I didn't want to disappoint her.

"I just messaged Danny and they're at the pool. Maybe once we've all settled into our rooms, we could have afternoon tea together?"

Dad approached the table and put a fruity-looking drink in front of Mum. I heard his sigh as he sat down. I had a feeling he wasn't all that excited about seeing us all here. We sat and sipped our drinks—well, to be completely honest, I'd skulled mine—and waited for Riley to return.

"I'm sorry, Lizzie," said Riley, sitting down next to me, "but our room is on the fifteenth floor. We're nowhere near your family." He frowned, making me want to giggle. God love him. Who knows what he'd had to do to get our room changed.

"Ohhh...that's disappointing," cried Mum.

"No, let the kids have some time alone. They don't want to spend it with us," said Dad.

I looked at him and saw him wink. I don't know who was having the dirty weekend here—us or them. I shuddered, thinking I needed to forget that's what they were doing or there would definitely be none of that happening in our room. Of course, I know Mum and Dad still had a sex life, but it was something I never *ever* wanted to think about.

"Our room's ready now if you want to head up, Lizzie," said Riley.

"Oh okay, we may as well get settled in."

Riley had his arm around my waist as we walked to the elevator. We stood in silence as the doors opened. A few people moved aside to allow us in, and we stepped inside.

"Lizzie?" I heard a female voice behind me and turned. It was my post lady, Chloe. Dear God. Did this place have a special on or something?

"Oh hi!" I said, my voice sounding like Alvin again. "Fancy seeing you here!"

"I know. Of all the hotels in the city and we run into someone we know. What are the chances?"

Yeah, that was my question. What were the bloody chances?

"Oh this is Brody—my boyfriend."

The man standing next to her put his hand up and waved. "Hi," he said.

He was pretty cute actually, with his dark hair and deep brown eyes. If I'd been single, I would definitely have checked him out.

"Lizzie and Riley live on my post run," Chloe explained to him. "They're the ones doing up the old house I told you about."

Brody nodded. "Sounds like you're doing a nice job of it," he commented to Riley.

"Thanks. It keeps me busy." Riley smiled as the elevator pinged and the doors opened.

"This is our stop," said Chloe. "Enjoy your stay." She smiled as we stepped aside and let them exit. Once the doors were closed I turned to Riley.

"We plan one dirty trip away and not only does half my bloody family turn up, so does my bloody post lady!"

The elderly gentleman standing beside me smiled.

"Relax, they're all here for the same reason we are," said Riley as the elevator stopped at our floor.

That was not a comforting thought. I sulked all the way to room 1505.

My sulking didn't last long. Once we were inside the room, my mood changed dramatically, helped by the luxurious king-sized bed placed in the center of the room with a view out over the city. At night that view would be spectacular.

"Riley, this room must have cost a fortune," I said, feeling guilty because I knew money was a bit tight at the moment.

"Actually, this room is an upgrade. I explained the situation we were in to the lady at reception, and she felt so bad for you she upgraded us for free." Riley gave me the mega-watt smile. I knew his methods. She'd been so dazzled by his smile, she would have given him anything he'd asked for.

I laughed and threw myself down on the bed, spread-eagle style, all thoughts from this morning long forgotten.

Riley took one look at me, assumed it was an invitation and jumped on top. Now I could have chastised him and told him it was in fact *not* an invitation, but in all honesty, I didn't want to.

"Hang on a minute," I said, pushing him aside and reaching for my handbag. "I have to turn my phone off."

CHAPTER 18

*A*fterwards, Riley went to the bathroom for a quick shower. I'd told him to go first as I would take ages, but the truth was, I didn't want to leave the bed. It was large, luxurious and comfortable. I felt like I had been transported to another planet that consisted of only Riley and me. Once I got ready and stepped outside this room, the real world would come crashing back around me. I stretched and sighed blissfully. I could hear the shower running and Riley humming a tune that played on the radio a lot. I closed my eyes and allowed myself to drift to sleep.

I was woken by the beeping of a phone. I knew it wasn't mine as I'd switched mine off, and I hadn't been in a hurry to switch it back on again. Now the annoying thing about Riley's phone is that it will continue to signal a message until you actually open the message. I always tell him to change the setting, but he liked it that way. He knows he gets too involved with work and forgets it ever beeped in the first place. This way, he has to answer it.

Unfortunately, he was in the shower and hadn't heard it. I sighed and rolled out of bed. Reaching the dresser, I picked up his phone and swiped at the screen. It was a message from Jared asking him about a fishing trip they were planning. I left it for Riley to reply to, reminding myself to tell him about it later. I was about to put the phone back down when my fingers—all on their own I promise—hit the back button, taking me back a page to the list of all his prior messages. I knew it was wrong and I should have stopped there, but I couldn't. Not after I saw the name *Allison* sitting proudly at the top of the list, with the words *Thinking of you xo*, underneath.

My heart stuttered as I looked at the closed bathroom door, Riley still humming the song he had stuck in his head.

He'd never have to know if I read them would he? I mean, how would he know? I'd just have a quick look and then put the messages back exactly how I'd found them.

My fingers clumsily touched the screen and I held my breath as I waited the millisecond for the stream of messages to appear.

They were of course in backward order, the last of which read exactly *thinking of you xo*. Above it was a photo. The image was small and it took me a second to figure out what I was looking at, but once I opened the photo and saw the larger image, I had absolutely no problem making out the naked side boob complete with nipple standing to attention.

My hands fumbled as nausea rolled in my stomach.

The incriminating photo arrived on Thursday night. Right in the middle of dinner with his parents. Now that I think about it, I do remember him receiving a message and appearing to be embarrassed about it.

THURSDAY 27TH 7.32pm

I'm having a hard time concentrating on what your parents are saying. I can feel the heat off your body as I try to sit still next to you. It made me think of the time you and I sent messages to each other during that boring dinner party. I thought this might be fun Allison xoxo

. . .

211

I ONCE AGAIN HAD TO LOOK AT the photo, my stomach clenching as I did so.

THINKING of you xo

THE BLOOD POUNDED in my ears as sweat broke out on my forehead. I looked for Riley's response to her, but there wasn't one. What did that mean? Did he just meet her in the bathroom and have a show-and-tell in person?

I tried to think about what happened later that night at dinner, and whether or not they were both out of the room at the same time, but I couldn't remember. The nausea causing the convulsions in my stomach made rational thinking difficult. My knees buckled at the thought of my world being destroyed and I sunk to the floor.

I was so consumed with what I was looking at and the repercussions of it, that I hadn't heard the shower turn off and Riley re-enter the room.

I looked up at him standing directly in front of me, his face pale, and his eyes huge.

"Lizzie. Please listen to what I have to say. Please."

I gulped, memories of how I felt only half an hour ago floating in my mind.

"I...I'm not sure if I want to throw up," I managed to say.

I took a few deep breaths and desperately tried to control the convulsions. Riley ran back to the bathroom, returning with a wet towel. I took it from him and wiped my clammy face, welcoming the coolness. Riley sat down next to me.

"It's not what you think," he said, his face full of concern.

"What am I thinking?" I croaked, tears stinging the back of my eyes.

"You're thinking Allison and I are having an affair."

Well, it appeared he really could read my mind.

"We're not. She sent this to me during dinner at my parents' the other night. I was too shocked to even ask her about it. Then I thought about everything you'd said to me about her and how we argued about it. I thought you were just being silly and jealous, but you weren't. You were right about her."

"Why didn't you delete the message then?"

"Because I wanted to talk to you. I wanted to show you the photo and tell you everything, just not like this though."

"Is this why we're here?" I asked.

"Yes. No." Riley ran his hands through his wet hair. "The night I got the message, I couldn't stop thinking about you and all the things I'd said to you. How I'd defended her. I felt really bad and I wanted to make it up to you. Plus here, it would be harder for you to run away and not hear me out."

"Huh. I would not run away!" I said indignantly.

Riley looked at me and smiled. It wasn't the earth-shattering mega-watt smile. It was his small, intimate smile—the one only the two of us shared.

"Okay maybe I would have, but how should I react to finding a nude photo of another woman on my boyfriend's phone? What do you expect?"

"I'm not asking for anything more than for you to believe me. I have never encouraged her. In fact, if you read through all the messages, you'll see that."

I realized I was still holding the phone, almost as if my life depended on it. And to be honest, my life *did* depend on it.

"Read them all please, Lizzie." Riley's eyes pleaded with me.

I opened the phone and scrolled back through the messages, reading them in reverse order. My mind jumbled, but the closer to the beginning I got the clearer it all became.

Prior to the naked photo, Allison was the last to send a message.

· · ·

HI RILEY. I have some changes I want made to the bedroom. Can you pop over and take a look for me please?

I'M a bit busy atm but I can pop over this afternoon. Is it urgent? I can organize a mate to help if it is.

OH NO. It's you that I want

OK. I'LL MESSAGE you later and let you know what time.

I'LL BE WAITING.

SERIOUSLY, how could he have not got the meaning in that?

I continued to read backwards and admitted that they were mostly about the work he was doing at her house. I stopped and read the first message she'd sent. It had been the evening of the first time I had met her at her office, back when I thought my only problem was having nightmares.

HI RILEY. It was so good to see you today. Couldn't believe my eyes Allison x

HI ALLISON. Yeah it was unexpected that's for sure. btw how did you get my number?

. . .

OH YOUR MUM gave it to me. Luckily she hasn't changed the home number

LUCKY

SO HOW LONG HAVE YOU and Lizzie been together??

EIGHT MONTHS

COOL. Do you love her?

YES. Why do you ask? Is it important to her treatment?

NO SILLY. Just curious.

SO HE'D TOLD her he loved me.

I turned away from the screen and looked into his eyes. Riley had the most expressive eyes. If you looked closely you could see his emotions dancing right inside them. Right now, they told me he was hurting. He needed me to believe he wasn't having an affair. He needed me in his life as much as I needed him.

"Please don't let her destroy us," he whispered.

I nodded slowly, the fear from a few moments ago disappearing. "I'm sorry," I said quietly. "I'm sorry I doubted you."

Riley grabbed me and pulled me into him, his heart beating loudly in his chest. He held me tight...tighter than he'd ever held me before, and I felt like I had so much love for him my heart would explode. What did I ever do so right in this world that I managed to find a man like Riley?

Whatever it was, I was eternally grateful.

WE'D RELENTED and agreed to meet everyone at the pool for afternoon tea, but I put my foot down for dinner. Riley had promised me a romantic candlelit dinner for two and by crikey, I was going to get one. So at seven o'clock, I stepped out of the bathroom in my favorite white dress. I'd done the smokey-eye thing and had used as much product as I dared to tame the curls. I hoped I'd done enough to impress him.

"Maybe we could have a candlelit dinner in our room," he said, smiling at me.

"So you like the dress?"

"I'd like you better out of the dress, but seeing how we're going to the dining room for dinner, this is probably more appropriate."

I swatted him and followed him to the door.

We made our way to the restaurant in the hotel and waited to be shown to our table. It was all very beautiful, if a little daunting. Sure I'd been to many beautiful, high-end restaurants before, but every single one of them made me nervous. I tended to be clumsy at the best of times. Add nerves to that and the results could be disastrous, but Riley was so relaxed that after a few minutes, I relaxed too.

I looked at him as we sat at our table and almost had to pinch myself. He was wearing a blue shirt, open at the collar, with his black trousers. It was rare for me to see him so formally dressed and it was actually a bit of a treat. He looked sexier than ever with the five o'clock shadow, and as he smiled back at me, those gorgeous sexy crinkles appeared around his bluer-than-ever eyes. He reached out and took my hand, and the butterflies darted around in my stomach. Even after all these months, he still had the ability to make those butterflies dance.

I held eye contact with him and felt an intimacy I'd never known before him, and I prayed to God—*please don't take him away from me.*

When I had first met Riley, I remember thinking how I would like to crawl into his skin and stay there forever. That still hadn't changed. When I was with him the world was a safer place and all my worries and anxieties disappeared.

I was enjoying the moment when I heard a female voice from behind me.

"Oh my goodness, Lizzie. We need to stop meeting like this."

I looked up to see my post lady, Chloe smiling at me. Tonight she looked better than I had ever seen her look. Usually she wore the brightest high-visibility shirt I had ever seen, her hair color changing weekly. Tonight she wore a really pretty, pink floaty dress, her hair now with lots of blonde highlights, her blue eyes sparkling. Next to her stood Brody, who judging by the look she was giving him, was the reason her smile was so bright.

"Chloe. Hi." I smiled back. "You look lovely," I added.

"I feel so uncomfortable," she said, smoothing her dress. "I'm not used to this sort of dining. I'm more of a pizza kind of girl."

"Yeah, I know what you mean. That's usually my kind of a night out too, but this is pretty nice," I said, gesturing around the room.

"I know. I had to try it. Another thing to cross off the Bucket List!" She grinned as the waiter coughed discreetly, suggesting she should move on. "Oh, time to go by the sounds of things. Enjoy your dinner."

"You too."

She took a few steps and the waiter held out a chair for her. Looks like they were at the table right behind me. I sighed. So much for a night away where nobody knew who we were.

I will admit that even though fancy dining wasn't my thing, I did enjoy myself and I only embarrassed myself once. That was when I bumped the waiter's elbow causing him to spill the wine all over the floor, but he told me it was really no problem and busied himself cleaning it up. Ooops.

I'd ordered a coffee with my dessert—tiramisu and it tasted as good as it looked—and was sitting back in my chair, people-watching. Riley had excused himself to use the little boys' room, so I used the time to have a good look around. It didn't take long and the conversation between Chloe and Brody drifted my way.

"Oh my goodness, Brody! I was so embarrassed at work yesterday," I heard Chloe say.

I felt her pain. Maybe she could add to my book on 101 ways to embarrass myself.

"I had to make a delivery to Mr. Jefferies but he can't get to the door because he only has one leg, so I leave it with his pain-in-the-ass neighbor."

I understood pain-in-the-ass neighbors too.

"Anyway, yesterday I delivered Mr. Jefferies his new leg."

"How did you know what it was?" asked Brody.

"Because it looked like a leg wrapped in brown paper. Anyway, when I opened the back of the van to give it to the painful neighbor, I found Theo sitting on top of it, paper ripped open and gnawing on the toes. Seriously, I nearly fainted!"

I laughed as I visualized this. Theo was Chloe's little Chihuahua. I'd met him a couple of times as he often rode in the van with Chloe as she worked. He was a cute little thing and would seriously fit in my handbag.

Brody laughed. "He probably thought it was the biggest bone he'd ever had."

"Yeah, not very tasty though," added Chloe.

"You deliver some really weird things," said Brody.

"Yeah, I've delivered ashes, legs and hands among other things. The worst was probably the meat I delivered to the local supermarket. Of course it was packed in gel packs to keep it cold, but I don't think I'll ever buy meat from there again."

Me either after hearing that story.

"Did you just say you delivered a hand?"

"Yeah, an old guy who lives over the back of the retirement village lost his so they posted him another one. Actually you know the guy. You've done some work for him."

"Really? Who?"

"Leo. Leo Burnett. You know, he looks like *Droopy Dog*."

"Isn't his name George?"

"That's what he goes by, but he has to show ID to take the possession of the parcel and I promise you his name is Leo. Leo George Burnett." *LGB!* The hair on my arms stood up.

"So is that why he always wears those cotton gloves?" asked Brody.

"Yeah, he tells people he has a skin condition and maybe he does, but personally I think he doesn't like people to see the fake hand. Goodness knows why. Loads of people have fake limbs these days."

Brody said something in response, but I didn't hear it over the blood pounding in my ears. LGB. Leo George Burnett. George Burnett. Could this be the same man Grandma was dating? I mean that would be a pretty big coincidence, wouldn't it? Or would it? Just then Riley returned to the table.

"Riley, I think we need to go home."

"Why?" he asked, stunned.

"I think Grandma may be in trouble."

CHAPTER 19

*R*iley convinced me that maybe I should ring Molly instead. Running home when we didn't even know if Grandma was with George seemed just plain stupid. Fair enough, I guess.

Only Molly's phone was either switched off or not in a service area. At least that's what the recording on the phone told me. *Damn.*

I tried to call Mum's house to see if Grandma was home, but no one answered. She also didn't answer her own mobile phone.

"Why don't you try that *Find My Phone* app?" suggested Riley. "That'll tell you where she is."

I pulled my iPad from my bag and typed in the web address. After putting in Grandma's user name and password, it told me exactly where she was—401/27 Pickett Street. George's house.

Riley made good time getting us home. We'd left all our belongings at the hotel, with the intention of going back there after we'd made sure Grandma wasn't with George. Thankfully Westport was only a half hour drive from the city and at this time of night, the trip was even faster.

I was about to pick up my phone and give Ed a call when

Riley's phone rang instead. I looked at the caller. It was his mum.

He pressed the answer button on his hands-free.

"Hey Mum. What's up?"

I heard Anna's tears before I heard her voice. My stomach flipped again.

"Oh Riley, I'm sorry to bother you. I know you've gone away, but it's your dad."

"What's wrong with him?" asked Riley, panic tainting his voice.

"He's having chest pains so we called the ambulance. They think it may be his heart."

Could this night possibly get any worse?

WE DECIDED I would drop Riley off at the hospital, and call Ed to ask him to meet me at George's house. We didn't know if Grandma was in danger, but I didn't want her there even if she wasn't. As soon as she was safe, I'd race back to be with Riley, and Ed could do the whole arresting thing with George, if indeed George and LGB were the same person.

The Westport General Hospital was positioned on my side of town, taking up the entire block with Main Road to the North, Nelson Road to the South, Wood Street on the West, and Bell Road on the East. The ER was accessed from Wood Street. Riley parked the car opposite the Ambulance entrance and killed the engine.

I quickly kissed him and gave him a hug, wishing with all my heart I could stay, just to be with him. I saw the worry in his eyes as I waved him goodbye and he ran into ER.

I said a silent prayer that Mal would be okay, and got behind the wheel of Riley's truck. I'd tried Ed's number a couple of times, but it kept ringing out. This time was no different. *Why was no one available when you needed them?*

I sat back and thought my next move through, and decided I would drive to Pickett Street and do a bit of surveillance to see if Grandma was okay. Putting the truck in gear, I turned it around and headed in the right direction, redialing Ed as I went. After my fourth attempt, I gave up and left a message for him to call me as soon as possible—it was urgent. But I was sure he'd figure that out from the ten missed calls he had from me.

The night had turned out to be a wet one, the drizzle causing the headlights of on-coming cars to have a halo effect. At that moment I felt cold, lonely and sad. I thought of Riley sitting in ER with his family, and I thought of Mal. If only I could see a star tonight. My wish would be that he was okay.

Reaching Pickett Street, I turned the truck into the Grange Retirement Village and made my way to 401. I was surprised to see that it was a six-storey unit block with a roof top garden.

I pulled the truck to a stop in a park that was partially covered by an overhanging tree, and killed the engine. I got out and crept towards the building, checking for unit numbers. It appeared George's was the unit on the ground floor.

I looked towards it, but couldn't see if Grandma was there as the front curtains were closed. I chewed my thumbnail as I checked my phone for messages. Nothing. As the rain fell, I moved back to the truck.

I didn't know what to do. I couldn't exactly go knocking on his door and demand to know if Grandma was there, yet if she was in danger then sitting here was just silly. But why would she be in danger? She didn't know who LGB was.

I sat there for about half an hour debating whether I should have a walk around, when a car pulled into the driveway. I ducked down in my seat a little bit as the female driver got out and beeped the doors locked. As she passed under the light from the porch, I noticed the woman was Allison.

Not for the first time today I thought *What the f...?*

What was she doing here?

She inserted a key in the front door of the building and let herself in.

Okay, I had to find out what was going on. Opening the truck door, I got out, pocketing my phone as I did so. I moved silently using the bushes to shield me, and ducked under the window. Even though it was a rainy night, the window was open an inch. An inch I strained to listen at, hoping to hear anything that might indicate Grandma was there.

I heard George's laugh.

"Hi Grandpa," I heard Allison say.

Grandpa?

"Hello, girly, you're just in time."

"Why have you got Mabel Phillips tied up?"

"Well we were on a date, and she started asking questions about my hand and how I lost it. She's a bit smarter than I gave her credit for—which is a bit of a shock as I hadn't given her any credit for being smart at all."

I heard Grandma protest.

"Shut up," said Allison, as I heard the slap. "I've wanted to do that to your stupid granddaughter for weeks, but instead I had to contain myself. If I'd known it felt that good, I would have bloody done it."

"Allison, don't get distracted. This isn't about your love life. We need to sort this mess first."

"Grandpa, there's nothing to sort."

"Of course there is. They know the truth. I'm eighty-seven. I can't go to jail now."

"Relax, you're not going to jail. They may not know anything."

"They know everything! Avis's diary tells the whole damn story."

"They don't know it's you," said Allison patiently.

George thought about this for a second.

"But what about that video thing on the Internet? The one that named me."

"I handled that."

"What did you do?"

"I made the kid remove it from the Internet and then I killed him."

I suddenly realized I didn't need to worry about Riley leaving me for Allison. This woman was certifiably insane.

"We will need to get rid of Mabel though. Maybe we should just kill Lizzie too. It would solve more than one problem. She'd no longer be in my way to get Riley back."

I knew she was after him.

"I've tried to get rid of her a few times, but she doesn't want to die."

I dropped to my knees and hid below the windowsill as my phone started to ring in my pocket. My hand shook as I hurriedly swiped to answer it.

"Hi Lizzie, its Ed." I could hear the smile in his voice. He obviously thought this was a social call.

"I need help," I quickly said. "I know who the killer is and he has Grandma."

"Where are you?" His voice instantly changed to police mode.

I gave him the address and a quick rundown on what was happening.

"Okay. Stay where you are. Do not enter the premises. I'll be there with back up as soon as possible."

I hung up the phone and tried to slow my heart rate as a shadow passed between myself and the streetlight.

"I knew I heard a vermin out here," said Allison, standing over me. She grabbed my hair and pulled me to my feet. I looked at her and wondered if I could take her down. I mean, I had anger, contempt and jealousy on my side so I could take a pretty mean swing at her, but on closer inspection she *was* the one with the gun. I decided to play nice and do what she said.

She grabbed my arm and pushed me towards the door, looking around her as she went.

"Are you alone?" she asked.

"Y...y...yes." I said, my voice betraying my fear.

She slammed the door behind us and pushed me forwards into the room where Grandma was tied up.

"I thought this country had anti-gun laws?" said Grandma, as Allison pushed me to the floor.

"You really need to shut the hell up, Mabel," snarled Allison.

"Don't talk to her like that," I said.

"Lizzie, Lizzie, Lizzie," said Allison, walking close to me. "Please don't give me a reason to kill you sooner than I want to."

"Allison!" said George. "Stop. We don't want any more dead bodies. We have enough already."

"Grandpa, I have to kill her anyway," she said, kicking me in the stomach with the pointy toe of her Louboutin. "First of all, she knows too much and second of all, I really, really want to. I just don't want to rush it." She pouted like a child.

George laughed. "Yeah, I guess I can see your point."

Allison turned to me, her gun shiny under the overhead fluorescent bulb. "Have I mentioned how much I hate you, Lizzie?"

I whimpered as she kicked me again. Grandma yelled.

"Hey Bitch, leave her alone!"

Allison backhanded her with the gun. I looked up to see Grandma's eyes glaze and her head slump.

I moved myself into a sitting position. I'd been in a situation similar to this once before, and as it turned out it taught me a lot. First off, I could handle fear—at least this kind of fear. It apparently brought out the fighter in me.

"Go fuck yourself, Allison," I said.

"Ooh hoo hoo." She laughed. "Listen to you. If Riley could hear you now, what would he think of that potty mouth?" She grabbed my mouth with her free hand and scrunched my lips together. I swatted her away.

"I know it was you with the blood," I said, trying to keep her talking long enough for Ed to arrive and save the day.

"What? What are you talking about?"

Oh, so it wasn't Allison then. She stood, the hand holding the gun falling to her side.

"Just so you know, Lizzie. Once I've killed you, I'm going to take Riley back. Yes, he'll be upset at first, but he doesn't really love you. So it won't take long for him to forget you. Then I'll remind him of how great we were together and we'll get married and have lots of children." A dreamy look clouded her eyes. "Oh and lots and lots of sex. Yes. We won't be able to keep our hands off each other. I mean, I already have experience with him, so I know just what he likes." Her eyes glittered, giving me a glimpse of crazy.

George turned his back on us, covering his ears. "La la la," he hummed as he sat on the lounge chair opposite us. Allison stopped, her face only inches from mine.

"Yes, I know how much he loves to hear breathing in his ear. I know how much it arouses him."

I wanted to block my ears like George had done. I knew how much Riley liked that too.

Allison giggled. "Oh, I also know how much he loves..." She moved close to my ear and whispered.

I'm not going to tell you the details of what she said, but she was spot on with exactly what Riley liked best.

She laughed loudly, moving away from my ear. "Oh yes. I'm going to do that to him *a lot*!"

Hatred for her built inside me.

"But you only have yourself to blame, Lizzie. You see, if you never bought that house, none of this would have happened."

"How the hell do you figure that?" I spat.

"Well you see...you were right when you said you recognized me from the auction. I wanted to buy it that day, but my stupid bank couldn't get their shit together fast enough. If I had bought it, the bones would have stayed safely buried and you would never have met Riley. Your stalker, Joe Woods would never have been watching you, causing all those nightmares. You never would have walked into my office that day, and we would never have met."

As Allison spoke closely to my face, my phone vibrated in my hand. She shifted her gaze and snatched it away from my hand.

Scrolling through my call list she saw that my last call was to Ed.

"Shit! She's called the bloody police." She cursed as she stood, turning her back to me.

As she threw my phone across the room in temper, I took my opportunity and kicked her in the back of the knee.

She fell forwards as the gun discharged, the bullet lodging itself into George. I heard his scream as Allison fell to the floor. I didn't stop to see what had happened to him. Instead, I got to my feet and rushed at her from behind. I needed to get the gun out of her hand before she spun around and shot Grandma.

I underestimated her strength. She grabbed my clothing and pulled me over her shoulder, slamming me into the floor. She then held the gun on me.

"I should just kill you now," she yelled, her eyes crazy.

"Allison," I heard George croak.

She instantly turned her attention away from me. George lay in the chair, a pool of blood appearing on his chest, seeping through his shirt, his complexion pale. Allison hurriedly went to him, and fell to the floor.

"Grandpa, I'm sorry. I'm so sorry," she cried. "Don't move, I can help you."

"No..." I heard George reply.

My attention on Grandma. She hadn't regained consciousness after Allison hit her.

I crawled over to her and checked her pulse. Her eyes flickered, and I felt my heart rate decrease. I quickly untied her and dragged her to the floor behind the couch.

Allison's primeval scream rang through the night air, and I

turned just in time to see George take his final breath. I felt the tears sting my eyes as panic raced through me. I didn't know how to get out of here. I couldn't leave Grandma, yet I knew I couldn't get out with her. I only hoped I could prevent Allison from killing us both before Ed got here with back up.

I stood up, prepared to do whatever it took, when Allison turned to me.

Her eyes were wild, her usually perfect make-up running down her face. Her hair messed, making her look crazier than before.

"You!" she spat, her voice low and menacing.

My heart missed a couple of beats.

"This is all your fault!"

With that she ran at me, hatred replacing the crazy in her eyes. I felt her body pound into mine as we fell to the floor. She rolled off me and I took my chance, scrambled to my feet and ran for the door, hoping to get her away from Grandma. She was faster than I was though. Grabbing my hair, she stopped as the flash of blue and red lights shone through a gap in the curtains.

Help was here.

I saw the panic in her eyes as she quickly considered her options. She looked at me and pushed me forwards as she bent to retrieve the gun. I tried to duck from her grasp but stopped as she pointed the gun at my head. I knew without a shadow of a doubt she would pull the trigger.

"You're my ticket out of here," she said. "Get going." She moved behind me, forcing me out of the unit and towards the stairs at the back of the hall. I didn't know where she was taking me, but I decided until I had a better plan, I should just go with it.

We walked up six flights of stairs and came to a door. She pulled a key from her pocket and opened it. We walked out onto the rooftop garden. It looked like it would have been nice at some point in time. Right now, it just terrified me even more.

She pushed me to the edge of the safety rail and made me step over it. I was grateful the rain had stopped and the roof was not any more slippery than it was. Holding me by the arm, she followed and forced me towards the edge. Leaning precariously over it, I looked down at the scene below.

I could see the flash of lights of two police cars, as four officers moved towards the building.

"Stop!" called Allison.

"What are you doing, Allison?" yelled Ed, as all officers pointed their guns in our direction.

"What does it look like, Officer Rude."

She obviously hadn't gotten over how he'd been rude to her the day of the car accident. Great.

"It looks like you're not thinking clearly. Why don't you take a step away from the edge and let Lizzie go?"

"No!" I yelled, thinking she would probably love to do just that, allowing me to fall to my death.

Allison laughed. "Oh no, I'm taking Lizzie with me. She's the reason you're going to let me go. You wouldn't want her hurt now, would you?" She laughed.

Ed was six storeys below me, but the strobe lights from the cars gave me enough light that I could see his face clearly.

He gave the order for everyone to holster their guns. They did as asked. I noticed a shadow move close to the building and to the door, and prayed it was back up.

"What do you want us to do?" he called up to her.

"I'm not sure. I haven't thought this through. Give me a minute, will you?"

You could have sworn she was talking to the kid at the deli counter at the supermarket, while she tried to decide what meat she wanted. As she stood debating what she wanted to do, I heard the door behind us open. Allison turned as I fell forwards an extra inch, the roof tiles slipping under my feet.

My heart raced as I saw Ed's fear as he looked up at me.

"Let her go, Allison," I heard Riley say. I moved my head and saw his eyes huge and vulnerable.

Seeing him, Allison's grip on my arm loosened.

I felt the world slip a little bit more.

"Riley! What...what are you doing here?" she asked, her tone uncertain.

"I've come to get you," he said.

A sob escaped my throat.

"Get me?"

"Yes, isn't that what you want? Us to be back together?"

"Well yes. It is."

"Then put Lizzie down and come over here."

Riley smiled the mega-watt smile, and Allison swooned under his gaze. I wanted to use the distraction to push her away and run, but I still hung precariously close to the edge with Allison the only anchor point to safety. She also still had a gun.

"Do you really love me, Riley or are you just saying that so I'll let Lizzie go?"

He took a deep breath. "I really love you. I always have."

Okay, I know this was all for my benefit, but it still hurt to hear those words leave Riley's lips.

"But, how do we get out of this situation?"

"It's okay. I've got a plan. We give Lizzie to Ed, and he'll be so happy he won't even notice us slip out the back door."

Allison looked down at the scene below us, and I saw the crazy slip out of her eyes.

"You're trying to trick me," she said, tears welling behind her lashes.

"I'm not. I really love you," Riley said.

Time stood still as Allison looked between Riley and me, her grip on my arm tightening.

"You love her, don't you?" she whispered, looking at Riley.

Riley shook his head.

"Look at her and say you don't love her?"

Riley moved his gaze to me. As our eyes locked, the clouds parted and allowed the moonlight to shine through, and I saw him gulp. He couldn't say it.

"Say it!" she yelled.

He closed his eyes, and when he opened them, he looked at me and said, "I don't love you Lizzie." I saw the tears skim his lashes.

Allison screamed. "You're a liar! You do love her."

Her hold on my arm tightened as she took a step closer to me, and to the edge, and I felt the roof tiles slip. As my feet scraped, trying to get a grip, the old tiles gave way. I fell, pulling Allison along with me. As the world moved in slow motion, I saw everything clearly for the first time. I saw Ed below me screaming orders to his colleagues, leaving them and running to the building, I saw Allison as she fell past me, the night air consuming her, and I saw Riley running, his arms outstretched. I heard Allison's scream in my ear as she fell, her arms reaching for anything she could grab. But the only thing she could get was air. Momentum propelled her towards the ground and her screams stopped.

As gravity pulled at me, my arms flailed, but somehow I managed to grab at the guttering. The metal cut my fingers as my weight pulled me downwards. It was as Riley's hand came into view, that the sob escaped my lips.

I had never been so scared in my life. Riley pulled me towards him, his arm straining under the weight, the effort too much as I felt his hold on me slip. Allison's dead body sprawled on the ground below came into my view, and as I looked back at the fear in Riley's eyes, I knew I didn't want this to be it. I wanted more time with him.

I swung my other arm around to grab at something, anything, when another hand reached out and grabbed me. Together, they pulled me up and to safety, the force pulling me forwards and into the arms of Ed.

CHAPTER 20

*O*nce again I sat in the ER, Paramedic Jim standing at the
end of the gurney, shaking his head at me.

"You know, Lizzie they're going to give you your own room
here if you keep this up."

I knew he was joking. He knew me well enough now to know
that humor was the best way to distract me. And distraction was
the key to me coping. Well that and denial, but the *To Be Sorted*
bin in my head was overflowing so much, I was having a hard
time shutting the lid on it.

I laughed. The laugh soon turned into a cry, and before Jim
knew what was happening, I was sobbing.

Jim was quick with the tissues though. And he was kind
enough to hand me the oxygen when the sobbing got to the stage
where I could no longer breathe. At the moment, Jim was my
support buddy. Poor bugger. He must have done something seriously wrong in a previous life to have been landed with me.

Riley had been sent off for a scan on his shoulder, leaving me
alone with Jim. Apparently my weight had done some damage as
he tried to pull me up from the guttering. Humph.

Ed had been left at the scene of the crime, waiting for a team of experts to arrive and do their thing mopping Allison up from the cement. Thankfully he had also rescued Grandma Mabel. She'd been sent off in another ambulance, where I had since heard she was doing perfectly fine. She just needed a stitch where Allison had hit her with the gun.

Mum and Dad were on their way. I honestly hoped they would be so busy worrying about Grandma that they would forget about me all together.

A nurse walked closer to my gurney and spoke to Jim. I was moved into a cubicle and lifted off the gurney and into a bed.

"Looks like your duty is done," I said to Jim, blowing my nose on a tissue as I spoke.

"Oh that's okay," replied Jim. "I've got nowhere better to be."

"That's really sweet of you, but I'm sure there are other people in Westport who need saving."

"Maybe, but you're my best customer. Got to look after the regulars." Jim laughed.

I didn't think it was as funny as it sounded. Tears pooled again. Jim moved closer and put his hand on my shoulder.

"It's over now love. Things can only get better."

I liked his optimism, but just then I heard Danny's voice over the noise of the ER.

"Where is she?" I heard him cry. "Where's Lizzie?"

Jim looked at me sympathetically. "Ah, that would be Danny," he said, sighing. "The car accident didn't harm his voice then?"

The curtain was pulled back with a flourish and in marched Danny followed by Andrew.

"Oh my God, Lizzie. We were so worried when Mum called, we rushed straight here." He ran at me and grabbed me in a very enthusiastic Fuller hug.

"Danny," I squeaked.

"Umm...Danny, you might want to let her breathe," said Jim. "It's kind of important to her health."

Danny let go and stood upright. "Oh, well okay then. Has Mum been in to see you yet?"

"No. Is she here?"

"Her car was out the front."

I sighed. "She's probably with Grandma."

"Yeah, where is Grandma? I want to see for myself she's okay."

"I'll go and find out for you," said Jim, moving the curtain aside and stepping out.

"Mum's a bit pissed at you," said Danny, crinkling his nose.

"What?"

"Just thought you should know."

"Why's she pissed at me?"

"Because Grandma was with you when all this happened. And all our dirty little trips have been ruined because of it."

"Yes, but I didn't plan it. And I didn't tell Grandma to date some psycho, did I?"

I wondered at the logic of how this was all my fault. Thankfully though, Riley walked into the room. His smile made my night a whole lot better.

"How's your shoulder?" I asked.

"Yeah, it's okay. They think I've pulled a muscle or something."

"I'm sorry," I said, as he kissed the top of my head, smoothing my hair as he did so.

"It's not your fault. I should have been ready for the weight to drop and then I wouldn't have hurt it."

"I'll start a diet tomorrow."

"Lizzie, I lift far greater weight than you in my job every day."

I shrugged. "Yes, but it doesn't have gravity pulling it at great speeds, does it?"

Riley's eyes clouded at the memory and he pulled me in tight. Maybe he had his own *To Be Sorted* box happening.

A nurse opened our curtain and walked in. She pressed a few

buttons on a monitor she was hooking me up to and smiled at Riley. "Back again, Mr. Thomas?" she asked.

"Unfortunately," answered Riley. It took me a moment to catch on, but when I did, panic and guilt surged through me.

I turned to Riley. "Oh My God! I forgot to ask about your dad! I'm so sorry, Riley. How is he? What happened?"

"It's okay. Dad's okay. There's nothing wrong with his heart."

"But why did he have chest pains?"

"Apparently it was a bad case of indigestion. He'd been eating some cake that just didn't agree with him." Riley laughed as my cheeks flamed.

"Has Lizzie been baking again?" asked Danny.

I punched Danny in the arm. "How did you get to George's?" I asked Riley thinking of his evening for the first time.

"I used Mum's car. Jared offered to take her and Dad home, so I asked to borrow it. I messaged you, but you didn't answer, so I decided to stop by. I didn't expect what I found though." Riley's eyes clouded again.

"Did you have to go back and get your truck?" I asked, thinking how I never wanted to visit The Grange again. Riley sadly nodded his head.

The three of us sat in silence, all lost in our own thoughts, until Mum and Dad, Molly and Matt all arrived, and grilled me about what exactly had happened tonight. Matt seemed to be the only one who was excited about the story I told. I figured I'd be first report up on the six o'clock news tomorrow.

By the time we were all released and told to go home for a good night's sleep, the clock had struck 3 a.m.

Riley helped me into his truck and then climbed in the driver's side.

"I told Ed I was taking you back to the hotel. He's going to call tomorrow to get your statement," he explained.

"You're driving back to the city now?"

"Yeah, it's only a half hour away. At least we can wake up late in the morning and enjoy what's left of our holiday."

I sighed thinking how pissed Mum was going to be that my holiday, unlike hers, was not ruined...only interrupted.

"Hey, how come you never told me you knew George?" I asked, turning in my seat to face Riley.

"I didn't know George."

"But he was Allison's grandfather."

Riley shrugged. "She once told me her mother had died when she was young and that she was raised by her grandfather, but she never spoke about him, and I definitely never met him."

"How does that happen?" I asked incredulously. Riley knew everything about me, and I mean *everything*—even the location of a very inappropriately placed birthmark.

"It never came up. Honestly, I never really knew that much about her."

"What did you talk about then?"

Riley cringed. "We didn't really talk all that much. It wasn't that type of relationship."

I gave a disgusted sigh as I figured out what he meant.

Typical bloody man.

❧

IT TURNED out that Allison actually had a bit of history when it came to violence. Ed confessed that she had two restraining orders against her. One from her previous husband, and one from the previous husband's new wife. The charges against her were dropped after she went into a domestic violence rehab program. Apparently he found out about them when she was charged with dangerous driving, but he couldn't tell me because of privacy laws. That's what he meant when he told me to be careful around her.

We also found out where all the mysterious blood was coming

from. After Riley and I had finished our dirty little holiday, we came home to a house full of it.

It turned out it was animal blood and Cat was sneezing it. The sad part of that story is the vet said he had a nasal tumor. Cat has since been put on medication to slow its growth, and Mike the Vet is confident he will die of old age before the tumor gets him, which is great news. As cantankerous as he is, I'd kind of grown to love him.

Three weeks had passed since Allison had died. And in those three weeks, both Riley and myself had been on a mission to finish the house. What Allison had said to me that night had stuck in my mind. If I had never bought the house, none of this would have ever happened.

I knew I couldn't turn back the clock and buy a different house, and as I looked at Riley, ready to hammer the *For Sale* sign into the ground, I knew that even if I could, I wouldn't change a thing. Because for all the bad things that had happened, he was a shining beacon of happiness and joy that I wouldn't sacrifice for anything.

"Ready?" he asked, looking at me.

"Ready."

He picked up the hammer, and I smiled as he hit the timber post, knocking the sign into the ground. Once it was secure, Riley pulled me in close and we looked back at the house.

A little under a year ago this house had been sad and broken. Now it stood tall, the new paintwork gleaming, ready to start the next chapter in its existence. I felt a thrill, hoping that its future was a lot better than its past.

"We did it," said Riley, leaning down and kissing me.

We pulled up for air as we heard a car pull up behind us. I turned to see Ed Helms step out of a police car.

He hadn't been around very much since Allison had flipped out. My stomach clenched with apprehension and gratitude, the sight of him bringing back raw memories of that night.

He looked very official in his uniform, his sunglasses pulled down shielding his eyes.

"Riley," he said, nodding. "Lizzie," he said softly, smiling, his gaze falling to me.

"Hi Ed. I haven't seen you for a few weeks."

Riley shifted uncomfortably next to me. He still thought Ed had a crush on me. I did say, 'who cares? I only have eyes for you', which led to us fooling around a little bit, and after that Ed was forgotten. I guess, with him standing here in front of me smiling, I could see Riley's point.

"Is this an official visit?" asked Riley.

Ed lifted his sunglasses, his eyes locked on mine. "I'm afraid so," he replied, all humor missing from his voice.

I felt my stomach clench again.

"I'm sorry, Lizzie. I just received the news that Joe Woods made parole. He's on his way back to Westport as we speak."

EPILOGUE

J'll admit I'd gone into free-fall when Ed said those words. In fact, I'm a little bit embarrassed to admit that if Riley hadn't been there holding me up, my knees may have given out and I would have fallen to the ground. But Riley was there. And so was Ed. And that's what would make all the difference. This time I knew what was coming and I had the support to fight it. And who knows—maybe Joe Woods had found a new love, someone who may enjoy the kind of attention he was willing to give, and he wouldn't bother with me at all.

And if not, Riley had said we could move to another town. Bless him, even though I knew that wasn't an option. My life was here, and I loved Westport.

As I lay with my head resting on Riley's chest, the gentle rise and fall lulling me into a place of security, I knew everything would be okay.

It had to be.

Continue reading Lizzie's adventures –

. . .

Deathly Desire
Lizzie ~ Book 3

https://bit.ly/3KBWWHr

DEATHLY DESIRE

on't worry. *Do not worry.* It'll be okay. Well, that's what I was telling myself. The man standing two meters away, his gun pointing directly towards me, didn't look so confident.

"Please, please I can explain," I said, my voice trembling.

"Put your hands in the air where I can see them!" he commanded, his police radio crackling next to his ear.

I immediately did as asked, which was a bit difficult sitting on a window ledge with one leg in the house and one leg out. My head was bent as the opening wasn't all that large and it didn't allow for a lot of room to raise my hands. But I did my best.

"But...but you don't understand," I stuttered. "This is my house. I live here. Well, not here exactly. Not now. But I did. And technically it's still mine." I tried to explain the situation.

"What's your name?" he asked, adjusting his stance to better balance his weight.

"Lizzie. Lizzie Fuller."

The policeman lowered his gun, but he didn't put it away. "Really?" he asked cynically.

"Yes, *really.*"

"If you're Lizzie Fuller like you say you are, and this is your house, then why have I caught you breaking in the window?"

Okay, that was a bit embarrassing. "I can explain."

"Please do," he said, allowing his arm holding the gun to fall relaxed at his side. I guess I didn't look threatening in the position I was currently in.

"Well my boyfriend Riley is in Ackwood today. He owns his own building company and he was needed there to do a really important quote." I turned my head and grinned at the officer, hoping he believed my explanation. He should do. It was the truth. "Riley dropped me off here on his way to work."

"And? What does that have to do you breaking into this house?"

"Well I left my handbag in his car you see, and my keys are in it."

"You don't have a spare set?" he asked, his eyebrows somewhere around his hairline.

"Yes. But they're at Riley's."

"Then why didn't you just go back there and pick them up."

"Because my handbag with all my keys in it is inside his car. It was either walk back to his house and break in, or stay here and break in. It wasn't a hard choice. His has a fancy alarm system," I explained

"You couldn't call him to come back and give you your bag?"

"Well..." How did I explain that Riley was running extremely late for his meeting and I'd already cost him enough time this morning? "If the window hadn't been open I would have, but why bother him if I didn't need to? Can I climb out of this window?"

To be honest I was getting a cramp in a place I didn't want to explain to this man. I seemed to have embarrassed myself enough already.

He took a few steps backwards, his grip tightening once again around his gun before he nodded. "Move slowly and keep your hands up."

I let out a sigh and attempted to get out of the window. It wasn't that easy when I had to keep my hands in the air, but I managed it, only catching my foot on the window sill at the last minute. I tripped, falling forward, doing my best with my hands. I landed with a thud, face first on the timber decking that ran the length of the back on my house.

Bloody hell that hurt!

As I rolled onto my back I hoped to hell that I didn't have splinters in my nose.

"Are you okay?" the officer asked, attempting to hide his smile as he holstered his gun, and then lifted me by holding me under my armpits. He was pretty strong and had me back on my feet with one easy swoop.

"Yes," I mumbled, completely humiliated. I was writing a book on 101 ways to embarrass myself. I think I needed to change the title to 102. "What are you doing here anyway?" I asked, brushing some dust from my T-shirt.

"I have orders to drive past every hour and keep an eye on things. When I received the call that a break in was in progress at this address, I got here ASAP." Without even asking him, I knew who would have reported the break and enter. It would have been my nosy neighbor Hazel, and she would have done it to annoy me.

"Do you have any ID on you?" the officer asked.

"No. It's in my handbag.

The officer sighed as he considered me. I thought about what he'd just said and why he was watching my house. You see, a while back I had a stalker. Turns out he was a pyscho who had killed a few people, but he'd fallen in love with me. Senior Sergeant Ed Helms of the Westport Police Department had recently informed me that my stalker, aka Joe Woods, had gotten parole and was on his way back here.

"Ed!" I yelled, suddenly remembering he could verify who I was. "I mean Sergeant Helms. He knows me."

The officer jumped at my outburst but then nodded. "Don't move," he said, pulling a phone from a pocket on the very complicated bullet proof vest he was wearing. As sweat ran down the side of his face I figured that the vest was hot. As I eyed the Taser attached to his belt, I too started sweating, but for a completely different reason. I think it scared me more than the gun did.

I stood very still whilst Senior Sergeant Helms was contacted. Once the call was over the officer looked back at me and smiled. "He's in the area so he's going to stop by and see for himself."

I groaned. "We can wait inside if you like. I can put the air conditioning on." Judging by the stern look that I got back, I figured that we would be waiting right here.

The morning was already turning out to be humid, making my skin clammy and uncomfortable, and I yearned to be inside with the cold air blasting us. But the officer held his ground, glancing around the yard as we waited in awkward silence.

I used the time to assess him, taking in his broad shoulders, stocky frame and round face. I had no idea what ranking he held, but he had no stripes on his epaulet, and he didn't give me the air of a seasoned officer. No, he appeared to be much fresher from the academy.

Thankfully Ed didn't take too long. As soon as he walked around the back of the house and onto the deck, his face lit up and his super white smile took over. As he laughed, I scowled back at him.

"Lizzie, you never fail to disappoint. I was having a bad morning until I got the call about this." He rocked back on his heels and let out a deep chuckle, his toned biceps flexing as he removed his sunglasses, and his teeth dazzling white against the dark chocolate color of his skin.

I did my best to ignore his smile.

"It's okay, Jono," he said, turning to his colleague. "She's who she says she is."

"Sorry," Jono said, giving me a small smile. "You've gotta be careful, you know."

Yes, I did indeed know.

"I'll take it from here," said Ed, still smiling.

Jono nodded. "Sure. Do you still want me to drive past hourly to check on things?"

"Yep. Until further notice."

Jono seemed satisfied with that. "Righto. Nice to meet you Lizzie."

"Ummm, you too," I responded, as he tipped his cap and sauntered off around the corner towards the front of the house.

Once he was out of sight, I looked at Ed as he stood silhouetted against the sun. At close to six foot three, he cast a large shadow over my five foot two.

"I'll make sure I distribute your photo once I get back to the station. That way everyone'll know what you look like."

"Do you have my photo?" I asked, my breath hitching at the thought.

"No. I'll need to take one."

I hated having my photo taken, and knowing that it was going to be plastered all over the wall of the Westport Police Department wasn't encouraging.

"Ummm, would you like to come in for a coffee?" I asked, self-conscious under Ed's stare. Riley had a theory that Ed had a crush on me. Riley might be right.

"Sure. That would be lovely."

He followed me as I pushed on the back door, ready to hastily make my way inside. Only problem was, I'd forgotten the door was locked and I almost bounced off it as I hit it hard.

Ed caught me as I stumbled backwards.

"Sorry about that," I mumbled as my cheeks heated up and I remembered I was locked out. "I just need to break in first." I hastily stepped away from Ed and made a beeline for the window, and was about to lift my leg over the sill (thank goodness I'd worn shorts today, was all I could say) when Ed put his hand on my shoulder and stopped me.

"Lizzie, why is this window open?" His eyes were no longer smiling. Now they were sharp and in full police mode.

"Pardon?"

"The window. Why is it open? Did you leave it open yesterday?"

Did I? I didn't think I had.

"We're watching your house for your safety and you leave a window open?" he asked, incredulously.

"Well, I...ummm...maybe the real estate agent showed someone through and forgot to close it." The house was currently on the market and looking for a new owner as I now lived at Riley's. And besides, it held far too many secrets for me to deal with.

Ed let out an elongated breath. It was only eight in the morning and already I'd frustrated him. Ooops.

"Stay here. I'll go and check it out," he commanded. When in police mode, Ed could be very bossy, and I could see how he had made it to Senior Sergeant.

I sat heavily on a nearby chair and watched as he squeezed himself through the small open window leading to my lounge room. Once inside, his footsteps echoed on the timber flooring as he did a surveillance walk through the house. After what felt like an eternity, the kitchen door lock clicked, and Ed reappeared.

"It's clear," he said, as the lines around his mouth turned up with a smile. "You need to talk to your real estate agent, though. She cannot leave the house unlocked."

"I will. I'll call Natalie today. I promise." I clasped two fingers together and lifted them to my brow, giving him a scout's honor.

"Why isn't Riley doing a walk through in the morning?" I had a feeling that there was nothing more that Ed would like, than Riley screwing up.

"He usually does," I said, defending him. "But this morning he was running late and I told him to just drop me at the door." I didn't add why he was running late, but I'm sure the smile on my face gave it away.

The look in Ed's eye told me he noted it, but he didn't ask for details.

"Lizzie I don't want to scare you, but Joe Woods did his first signing in with his parole officer this morning."

I gulped. "So he's definitely here then?"

"Yes. He's definitely here. He has a restraining order stating that he's not allowed within two hundred meters of you, but that means nothing if he doesn't want it to."

I gulped again, the butterflies doing a fancy little dance in my belly.

"I just need you safe," continued Ed, his eyes softening. "Help me out, will you?"

I nodded, feeling a bit ashamed of myself. "Sure. From now on if any doors or windows are open, I'll call for help first."

Ed seemed happy with my response, as he nodded his lips turned up into a full smile.

"Can I come in now?" I asked, still standing at the door.

He moved aside, but didn't step out of the doorway, so as I entered the kitchen my body brushed up against his, and I heard a quiet groan escape his lips. My heart palpitation almost took my breath away.

Thankfully, once out of his personal space, the smell of fresh paint and building materials settled my heart rate.

My house was a small two bedroomed detached Victorian. When I had purchased it the best way to describe it was that it was a cross between a gingerbread house and a house of horrors. More on the side of the house of horrors. Especially after the day that my stalker Joe Woods had attacked, causing me to fight for my life.

I knew that Ed was right. I should be more careful. It wasn't something that I wanted to go through ever again.

"I'm sorry Ed. I promise from now on I'll be careful. And I will follow up with the agent making sure she locks up properly."

Ed nodded and his shoulders relaxed. "How's she working out?" he asked.

"She's alright. She's a bit stuck up but I don't really care as long as she sells the house." Our real estate agent Natalie had been recommended by Ed. She was tall, blond and gorgeous. I hated her, and not because she was gorgeous. She honestly thought she was better than me. But her job was to sell my house and as long as she did that, I could tolerate her.

"Have you had many people interested in buying?"

"A couple," I responded, moving to the coffee pot and filling it. I then took two cups from the overhead cupboard and found a packet of biscuits, while I waited for the pot to heat up. Did I know how to look after my guests or what?

"Any serious interest?" Ed asked.

"I did have one offer but it was way below market value. I want it sold, but not enough to make a loss on it."

"Fair enough."

An awkward silence filled the air between us, and I busied myself pouring milk into the cups, doing my best to ignore Ed's intense stare. Thankfully my phone rang giving me a distraction. It was my Grandma. Not quite the distraction I was hoping for.

"Sorry," I said to Ed. "It's Grandma Mabel. I'll call her back later," I explained, switching the phone to silent.

"How is your grandma?" Ed asked.

Grandma currently lived with my parents. After Grandpop relocated to somewhere beyond the Pearly Gates, she had lived alone. That was until she set the oven on fire. Thankfully the only thing of value she lost was her savings, as apparently the oven is the safest place to keep your money. Who knew? After the fire, mum had moved her into my brother Danny's old bedroom. It seemed like the safer option.

Ed and Grandma had met last month. I'd had the honor of

driving her to her weekly doctor visit and Ed had been in the carpark when I came out. Grandma hadn't stopped talking about him yet.

"She's great. Currently single." His brow creased as confusion flicked through his eyes. "In case you were in the market," I explained, giving him a full smile as I poured the hot coffee into the cups. "She wanted me to let you know."

As I picked up the cups and walked towards him, I noted the blush that had started at his collar.

"Ahhh. Well, tell her thanks," he said, accepting the cup that I offered him. I laughed at his grimace before taking a sip of my coffee.

Ed's eyes softened as his grimace turned into a small smile. "But she's not the Fuller that my heart belongs to."

The hot coffee burnt my tongue as I choked on his response, spitting half of my mouthful across the space between us.

Bugger that was hot!

Ed immediately jumped into action, moving to the sink and grabbing a tea towel to mop both himself and me. As he rushed back to me he awkwardly debated whether to mop up my cleavage or hand me the towel. I made the choice for him and snatched it out of his hands.

"I'm sorry," he said quietly, his eyes boring into mine. "I thought you knew." I'd had an inkling, but to hear him say it threw me for six. For once I was lost for words.

After a minute of awkward silence, he said, "You don't have to say anything." That was good, because I had nothing. "I know that you're with Riley, but if ever you feel that the fits not right, I'll be here. Waiting."

Okay, that took my breath away.

"Ummm," I nodded. "Thank you." I mean, what else could I say?

Eᴅ ᴛᴏᴏᴋ ᴀ ᴠᴇʀʏ unfortunate photo of me for the police station wall. I looked at it as he checked it, the smile not once leaving his face. I wasn't the world's most photogenic person, and I really hoped reality was better than that photo. My long dark hair was frizzier than normal, my brown eyes were wide with dismay, and my overly large chest was prominent. I sighed as I waved him goodbye, then trudged up the two flights of stairs to my office, ready to tackle some work. After all it was why I was even here today.

Half way up, I heard the knock on the door. It was probably Ed back for an even more humiliating photo.

Retracing my footsteps, I did the right thing and checked the peep hole before opening the door. However, all I could see was the porch, the two front steps and the flowers I had planted around it. Hmmm, that was strange. I didn't think I had misheard a knock, so I took a deep breath, double checked the chain was securely in place, and then opened the door.

On the mat that welcomed visitors to my house was a package all wrapped up in pretty paper, a pink ribbon tying a note to the top. The note was gently swaying in the breeze, and curiosity prickled as I looked around for who could have left it. I couldn't see Ed, not that he would have put it there. I couldn't see my parcel courier Chloe, so it hadn't come by mail. In fact, I couldn't see anyone, and by the time my eyes hurt from holding them so wide and scanning the street, I decided that all was clear. Closing the door, releasing the chain and then reopening it, I bent to retrieve the package.

Nerves mixed with excitement as I closed and locked the door and then tore at the wrapping, wondering who had left me a present. Sure I should have opened the note first, but that was something I never did.

My excitement quickly turned to dismay when I saw the gift was a large tub of crunchy peanut butter. Now, I'd never been a fan of peanuts, but since a recent lunch with my ex-psychologist turned bad, I had ended up in hospital with anaphylaxis, peanuts were now my enemy.

My stomach flipped as I placed the tub on the hall table and turned my attention to the note.

The envelope had my name printed in large font across the front of it, and after sliding my finger under the seal, I retrieved a small piece of paper with the word 'Enjoy' centered in bold type.

Was this a sick joke?

I ran into the kitchen and pulled back the blinds, wanting to have another look at the street from the safety of being inside. As I did a black sedan, just like the one driven by my stalker, drove past, a gloved hand waving from a half-opened window. My heart missed a whole series of beats, my knees buckled and I sat heavily on a nearby chair.

THE GIFT HAD MEANT that I received a second visit from Ed in one day. He wasn't a fan of crunchy peanut butter either, it seemed. Well, I was basing that on his grim expression when I handed it to him. Along with the note, it was placed in a plastic bag and had a police escort off the premises. Ed was going to have it checked for fingerprints, with the hope that Joe Woods would soon be back where he belonged. Even though, I did remember Joe being in jail when I had learned of my allergy to peanuts so I did wonder why he would have sent it. But I had my fingers crossed that he was the culprit.

After Ed once again waited while I tripled checked locks on the door, he left me to make my way up the stairs once more, this time making it all the way to the top and into my office.

I loved my office. It was my favorite part of the house, and in times of stress it was the room that calmed me. Which was great, considering at that moment, I really needed calming.

Twelve months ago when I had purchased the house, I knew I

wanted the bedroom in the attic to be my workspace. As a self-employed bookkeeper, I didn't need a lot, just a desk, a computer, and lots of room to sort piles and piles of fiddly little receipts. At the time the attic was just one big room with disgusting wallpaper and horrible carpet. But Riley had changed all of that. It was now painted a calming shade of white, the little dormer window looked out over the yard and down the street, and Riley had installed a small bathroom and storage room in the back. The slanted ceiling made the room feel cozy and safe, and when I was in it all the worries of the world disappeared. But this house was for sale. This room would no longer be my sanctuary.

Was I sad about that? In a way, yes. I'd miss the room, but I knew that Riley would build me another one somewhere. So why was I feeling so flat about it today? Why wasn't the room calming me?

I moved to the window seat and looked down on the yard, thinking about my mood, wanting to delay opening the many boxes of receipts I needed to sort. I aimlessly watched as our local parcel courier Chloe delivered a package to my neighbor Edward. I watched as Mrs Jessop from the end of the street took her dog Trixie for her routine morning walk, and I watched as a black sedan pulled up to the curb outside my house. My heart skipped, but when the car door opened and a middle-aged woman with bad taste in clothing and hair frizzier than mine stepped out and snapped a couple of pics of the For Sale sign in my front yard, my anxiety settled.

I then remembered that I needed to book an appointment with my mind trainer. I'd tried a few things to settle the nightmares I still encountered. At first I'd tried ignoring them, but they upset Riley, so I knew it was time to open the To Be Sorted box in my mind and try counselling. That didn't work out too well for me, as my psychologist turned out to be Riley's ex. She also turned out to be the psycho in psychologist, and after her I moved onto medication.

But I hated the medication as all it gave me was more nightmares. So now I was trying some mind training and hypnosis. I'd only been once and if last night's nightmare was anything to go by, I think I needed to at least go twice. Picking up my phone to book the appointment, I noticed the missed call from Grandma. Ooops.

My parents' number was on my speed dial list, and judging by the speed that my call was answered, I figured Grandma had been sitting next to the phone waiting for it to ring.

"Hey girlie," Grandma called loudly. The arrangement of Grandma living at my parents worked well for her, but I had noticed the large vein in the middle of mum's forehead now pulsed at an alarming rate.

"What's happening?" I asked.

"Not a lot."

"Oh. Okay. Well what can I do for you?"

"What are you talking about?" I could hear the click as her teeth swished around. A habit she had when she was thinking.

"You called me earlier. I'm just returning that call," I explained. At eighty five, Grandma's mind was usually sharp as a tack, but at times she had her moments. Hey, I'm not complaining. I was thirty-three last birthday, and I had my moments too.

"Oh, that's right. I need a lift. Your mother's gone out and I need to get to the bingo hall before lunch time. I got a date."

As far as I knew Grandma and Grandpop had had a long happy marriage. Since his passing, she seemed to be making up for all her missed opportunities.

"Cool. Sure. I can come and get you." Thankfully I had a spare set of keys hanging up downstairs. "Does mum know where you're going though?"

"I'm not a kid! I can go out without your mother's permission," Grandma snapped.

"Alright! Just checking. I'll pick you up at eleven."

"Don't be late."

After hanging up the call, I dialed Mum's mobile phone. You know, just to check that it was okay for Grandma to go out on a date. If Mum was cranky with any of us, she refused to make us our favorite dessert, and Sunday's family dinner sucked without dessert.

"Hey Mum. Whatcha doing?" I asked, going for the happy, easy going vibe.

"Why do you need to know?" she snapped. "Isn't it enough that the women in this family cause me enough stress? I can't even take half an hour for myself without everyone calling me?" Geez, it wasn't even nine yet and already the Fuller family was cranky.

"Well, I'm just checking that I can take Grandma to bingo at eleven. She has a date."

I heard the sigh down the phone line. Mum sighed so much I often wondered how she didn't pass out from lack of oxygen. Right now, I could imagine the crease between her eyes deepening, and her lips pursing with every exhalation of breath.

"Whatever." She snapped. "I don't have time for her antics."

"So I can take her?"

"Yes. Take her. But you're responsible for her," she added.

It was my turn to sigh. How did I get myself into these situations?

After ending the call, I sat and stared at the mountain of boxes calling for my attention. I even contemplated opening the first box, ready to start an hour of sorting receipts. I hated receipts. Hated them! And I hated sorting them even more. So why was I a bookkeeper then? I honestly had no idea anymore.

Maybe I should make myself a cup of coffee. That may give my motivation the boost it needed. And if not, what better way to procrastinate than with caffeine in your hand?

Feeling happier already, I ignored the six boxes that were screaming my name, and moved back down the stairs towards the kitchen. Cat was sitting on the bottom stair tread, his fur raised, hissing. I'd inherited Cat with the house, and this behavior wasn't uncommon for him, but he seemed more irritated than usual. Sidestepping him and hoping to avoid getting scratched in the process, I made my way to the kitchen. And screamed.

A man was standing in the open doorway, smiling at me.

Lizzie's adventure continues...

Available now

WHEN THE PAST comes back to haunt you.

. . .

I THOUGHT I was ready for a new adventure in my life, but really, what was I thinking? I should have been dreaming of a vacation with my super-hot boyfriend Riley, but instead another old house that is in desperate need of some love and attention, has charmed me. And guess what? This house has a secret too. Urgh!

Who is its owner? Why is he so hard to find? And why does he own nine other deserted homes in Westport?

If I can sell the first house of horrors I presently own, find the answer to these questions, and purchase this house before someone else does, then hopefully I can start a new chapter in my life. A much happier one.

Of course, my crazy family never make life easy, and Ed the super sexy policeman has just declared his undying love for me which definitely complicates the situation, but I'm determined to put the past behind me.

Only that becomes difficult when that past reappears and mixes with my future.

Now I need to solve a forty-year-old mystery, dodge a psychopath, placate an irate realtor, and learn if there's a copycat killer in Westport, all before the star of my nightmares catches up with me. Because if I don't everything I love will be at stake.

So far my next adventure isn't looking as much fun as I'd hoped.

DEATHLY DESIRE IS the third book in this light-hearted romantic mystery series. If you like crazy families, fun engaging reads, and a sweet romance, all tied together with a ribbon of danger then you'll love this instalment in The Westport Mysteries

Available now

FREE BOOK?

I'm offering a free e-book to everyone who signs up to my mailing list. I promise not to spam you and only send out a handful of newsletters a year!

www.bethprentice.com

Do you want to know where it all began?

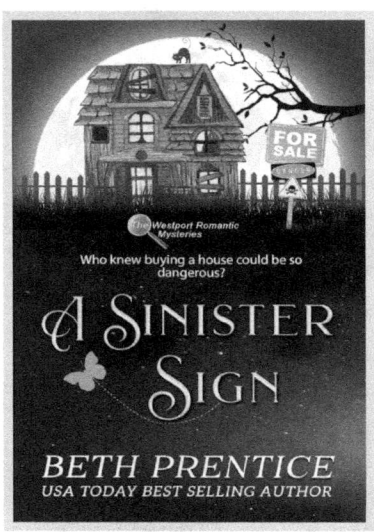

Who knew buying a house could be so dangerous?

I recently had the great idea that moving back home to Westport and being close to my family again would be good for my soul. But now that I am close to them, I've quickly realized that I need to find a home all of my own. I love them. I really do, but the idea of living with them is kind of low on my to do list. Especially now that grandma has moved into my childhood bedroom. Thankfully it hasn't taken me long to find the house of my dreams – or nightmares. It's really a question of perspective.

The lonely run-down old Victorian in need of major renovations has tugged on my heartstrings, and before I can stop myself, I've fallen head over heels in love with it. Unfortunately, I'm not the only one who wants it, and the other bidders aren't playing nice.

Deadly accidents, missing real estate agents and a chilling stranger, are all sinister signs that this is not the house for me.

Only I'm determined to rescue this fixer upper or die trying. Now all I need to do is to win the auction and stay alive.

If only it was that easy...

A Sinister Sign is the prequel to Lizzie's adventures in Westport. If you like crazy families, cozy reads, and a sweet romance, all tied together with a ribbon of danger, then you'll love The Westport Mysteries.

www.bethprentice.com

ABOUT THE AUTHOR

Beth Prentice is the USA Today Bestselling Author of the Westport Mysteries. Killer Unleashed, her GHP debut novel, received a bronze medal in the 2016 Readers Favorite International Book Awards. Her main wish is to write books you can sit back, relax with, and escape from your everyday life...and ones that you walk away from with a smile! When she's not writing you will usually find her at the beach with a coffee in hand, pursuing her favorite pastime—people watching!